C0001?6042

Published in Great Britain by
L.R. Price Publications Ltd., 2022.
27 Old Gloucester Street,
London,
WC1N 3AX
www.lrpricepublications.com

Cover artwork by L.R. Price Publications Ltd.
Used under exclusive and unlimited licence by L.R. Price
Publications Ltd.

ISBN-13: 9781915330093

Your Sin

Bruce Adam

Dedication

For my late wife, Lilla and our remarkable children, Rosalind, David and Suzanne.

"Be sure your sin will find you out."

Numbers 32.23

Prologue

It is as if every sense is heightened by your impending death. You hear the crunch of the frost on the grass under your trainers and the monotonous rattle of an early magpie. The lamps in the park are still lit, illuminating sections of the sparkling bushes that seem to huddle together against the cold and revealing scattered polystyrene take away containers and discarded beer and Buckfast bottles. There is the brown smell of decaying vegetation and the breeze carries the scent of dampened bonfires.

As you thought, no-one is about at this time in the morning.

Passed the statue of the town's historic benefactor, his frock coat carefully rendered in stone and decorated liberally with pigeon shit. Negotiate the slick slope to skirt the deserted children's play park. As the wind picks up, one swing creaks back and forward as if being pushed by a ghostly hand.

Off the path and into a clump of woods. The shadows are deeper here and the silence is

1

broken only by your footsteps brushing through the fallen leaves and the rustling of the plastic bag you are carrying containing the length of washing line.

You are suddenly shivering uncontrollably. The thin jacket and tee-shirt you are wearing provides little protection against the early morning cold. But it is the memories of your mum bringing you here when you were little and playing hide and seek amongst these same trees that really chill your blood.

What would she have felt if she was still around? And what about your girlfriend? Don't you have a responsibility to her? Surely it is better for her to know the truth, even though it will almost certainly kill any love she has for you, than to know you died like this? Then there's the poor bastard who eventually will find you here. When will that be and what kind of state will you be in? Perhaps it will be a dog walker whose pet has wandered off the path. What if it is a child? A discovery in the woods like that will give them nightmares for years. And then your next of kin will be asked to identify you. Can you put her through that?

But the alternative is the look of disgust on her face when she finds out your dirty little secret. She loves you and she will no doubt say she forgives you, but you will always be aware of the distance that will open between you - how she will have to hide her disappointment every time she looks at you. Your friends will shun you too. Your future will be tainted forever by one stupid, shameful act.

You reach the tree you have selected. It has an overhanging branch low enough for an easy climb; high enough to do the job. You take the washing line out of the bag and begin to create the noose.

You remember a book you found in the school library a few years ago when the class were doing debates and your topic was whether or not to bring back capital punishment. It was the autobiography of the last hangman in Britain called, 'Executioner – Pierrepoint'. It was fascinating.

3

Despite his profession - a family business by his account - he came over as humane, agonising over the unnecessary suffering of Nazi war criminals after the Nuremberg trials as they awaited execution, because from their cells they could hear the springing of the trap-door of the gallows, knowing it would soon be their turn. In the end, he had been proud of the speed and efficiency with which he had managed the grisly project. In many ways he had been an engineer, calculating the height and weight of the condemned and working out lengths and angles to ensure a quick end for them.

And you want that for yourself. You found the instructions for tying a noose online. It has to be as effective as Pierrepoint's nooses once were more than six decades ago. But what if it doesn't work and you are left to a horrible death by slow strangulation?

And then there are the other unpleasant consequences of hanging. Don't the victims shit themselves? You read somewhere that hanging gives you an erection. The thought makes you laugh suddenly. Is that seriously what you are worried about?

You realise you are on the edge of hysteria. With a kind of grim determination you form the knot. It looks authentic at least. You test it by putting your left arm into the loop and pulling the line sharply with your right. It tightens quickly around your arm, so much so that you struggle to undo it.

Putting the line around your shoulders to free your hands you begin the short climb up the tree, trainers digging into the rough bark, finding handholds in the thinner branches and deformed burrs on the trunk. It and the branches are still slippery with frost. You reach the low, overhanging branch. Hauling yourself to a point above it, you drop carefully onto it and begin to edge your way along it on your hands and knees.

You take the line from around your shoulders, loop it around the branch and tie it tightly so the noose dangles above the leaves on the ground beneath. Have you ever paid attention before now to their many colours – brown, red, green and yellow - as they lie dying there?

Despite the morning chill, you are sweating. Perspiration runs down your brow and stings your eyes and your white tee-shirt feels clammy. There are ochre stains on it from the tree trunk. They'll be a bugger to get out. She will kill you. The absurdity of the thought makes laughter bubble up once more but it quickly turns to gasping sobs.

Eyes blurring with tears, you pull up the noose, place it around your neck and tighten it. Your research revealed that the knot should be below the left angle of the jaw. If you launch yourself off the branch with sufficient force, your neck should break. It should be quick.

But surely you would have time to feel some pain. And what about afterwards? Darkness forever? Didn't Catholics believe you went to Hell if you committed suicide? You were never religious but what if at least some of it was true? Plenty of people believed it, after all. And plenty of people also believed this was a cowardly act.

You have had all of these thoughts in the days before, of course. Why are you having them now when you have made your decision? You sit there, feet dangling above the abyss as the sweat chills on your body and the light changes above the trees as dawn begins to break.

Now

Chapter One

Shona Patterson

Shona got to the yard that ran behind the High Street just as the forensic team were getting set up. She had been just about to leave the station after a twelve hour shift when the call had come in but decided to drive over to have a look at the crime scene while it was still fresh.

A woman's body lay sprawled face-down next to the bottle skips. Blood pooled out under her head looking black in the dim light. Short blonde hair. Her expensive-looking pencil skirt and designer raincoat were pulled up to her waist exposing floral patterned knickers under her tights. Shona wished someone would pull it down to at least give her a bit of dignity but she knew that wouldn't happen 'til they had finished photographing the scene and gathering evidence in situ. At least they had cordoned off the yard and would soon erect an incident tent around her.

An open handbag - again designer by the look of it - lay a few feet from the body, some of its contents strewn around it. Shona hunkered down trying to get a better look at them. She could see a leather wallet, a brush, a lipstick and a pack of tissues.

DS Cameron came over to her. He always looked as if he had stepped straight out of a menswear catalogue; an impression only slightly spoiled by the vinyl gloves he was wearing. She rose quickly. She was conscious that her trousers had ridden down as she squatted there and she didn't want him to have the unlovely view of her arse crack. She had to get back to the gym.

"Doc Lawrence doesn't think the body has been there long, Inspector. Obvious massive blow to the back of the head but he'll check for other injuries when they can move her." Shona looked over to where a slight figure was leaning over, examining the body. Even in a Tyvek suit his diminutive stature identified him as Lawrence.

"There was over two hundred pounds in cash in her wallet. Credit cards still there, too, in the name of Isabel Tyler. Strangely, no sign of her phone."

"Who was first on the scene? she asked.

"Patrol responded to a call from a young guy who works in the pub that backs on to the yard. He had come out to empty bottles into the skip and saw her lying there. That was around 10.40." He pointed over to the lock-ups at the end of the yard. Two uniformed PCs were hovering in front of them. "Right - this backs onto the Wallace Arms, a charity shop and a nail bar doesn't it?"

"Aye and Telford's Bakery." She walked over to the two officers, notebook in hand. Christ, they say you feel old when the police start looking younger but the male PC looked as if he hadn't started shaving yet and the female officer wouldn't have looked out of place running round a school playing field with a hockey stick.

"Inspector Patterson. Don't think we've met." The woman constable replied,

"I'm PC Dunk and this is Constable Sillars."

"What's the story?" Dunk again responded. Her partner continued to stare up the yard. He looked as if he was trying to focus on not throwing up.

"We were on the drunks beat patrolling along the High Street when we got the call so we got here in minutes. The guy who found her was standing by the skips waiting for us to arrive and we saw her lying there."

"Did you touch anything?"

"I went and leaned over her. I could see the blood and the gash on the back of her head so I felt her neck for a pulse. I couldn't feel one so I asked Chris - Constable Sillars - to radio it in."

"So when you found her she was face down."

"Yes."

"And her handbag was like that when you found her?"

"Yeah. Looks like Gucci unless it's a knock-off."

"You didn't move her?" Dunk shook her head. "Anything to add, Constable Sillars?" He cleared his throat, before saying,

"Her - clothes - looked - disarranged. Do you think she had been ..." He left his comment hanging in the air as he blushed furiously, making him look even more like a schoolboy in fancy dress. This kid was going to have to seriously toughen up unless he only wanted a short police career, Shona thought.

"At this stage we don't want to speculate, Sillars. You can go for now but get your reports in ASAP." They walked off, skirting the yard, obviously relieved to get away. She returned to DS Cameron. "Where's the guy who found her?"

"He's in there. That leads to the back of the pub. He indicated a battered-looking door that was opened onto the yard, its black paint flaking around a rusted, metal bar. She and Cameron entered and found themselves in a cellar that housed a number of beer kegs. A short set of stairs led them to the bar area. There were few customers at this time of night, though Shona thought the Wallace had a licence 'til 12.00. One or two of them looked over as they entered, their eyes sliding quickly away and their conversations becoming more hushed.

"That's him," said Cameron, indicating a tall youth behind the bar who was filling two glasses from the optics, while an equally youthful barmaid put glasses in the dishwasher.

"I'll speak to him, Garry. You have a word with the punters, see if any of them know anything." Cameron went up to the far end of the bar where a few drinkers had gathered. They didn't look delighted to see him. Shona approached the barman and showed him her warrant card. "I'm Detective Inspector Patterson. Is there somewhere we could talk?"

He called over to his co-worker. "Terri-Anne. Just be a minute." He led Shona back down the stairs to the cellar where he stood leaning nonchalantly against a beer keg. The discovery of a dead body didn't appear to have phased him.

"I understand you found the woman in the yard, Mr.?"

"Bamforth, Colin. Aye. I'd just gone out with a crate of empty bottles, like, to the skip, like. I saw her lying there. I thought she was maybe drunk, like. I'd noticed her earlier in the pub, like. No' drinking that much, like, but they might have been on a bit of a pub crawl, like."

13

"They?"

"She was with another woman, like. Kind of reddish hair. Noticed them because they were a couple of MILFs, like. Sorry. So I emptied the bottles into the skip and went over to see if she was a' right like. That's when I noticed the blood, like."

"Did you touch her?"

"No' me. I kent no' to, like. I've watched 'Midsomer Murders' and that, like." Spare me from people whose knowledge of police work was based on a television series in which some rural villages have a higher murder rate than Glasgow, Shona thought. At least it kept them from messing up crime scenes.

"Did you phone the police right away?"

"Had to go into the pub to get my mobile, like. Told Terri-Anne on the quiet, like, and she came out with me. Had to stop her from goin' over to her. She wanted to pick up her bag and, you ken, cover her up, like. You could see the woman's pants and that, like." He seemed unembarrassed by this revelation.

"What happened to this woman she was with?"

"She'd disappeared when we got back to the bar, like."

"Thanks, Colin. I'd like you to give a description of the woman to my sergeant and we'll probably have to speak to you again but here's my card in case anything else occurs to you."

"You think she was mugged in the yard, like?" For the second time that night, Shona had to roll out the cliché about it being too early to speculate. She went back out to the yard. Dr. Lawrence spotted her and came over. Shona was five feet six but she towered over him as he pulled down his hood. It was chilly in the yard but sweat stood out on the doctor's brow.

"Massive, blunt-force trauma to the back of the head looks like the cause of death but I'll know more when I get her back to the morgue. She hasn't been dead long - couple of hours at the most, I would say. No sign of a weapon yet but we'll do a sweep of the yard. Might have been improvised - a heavy-based bottle perhaps?" he said, looking over at the skip. Lovely job for someone, sifting through that lot for a murder weapon, Shona thought.

"I'll check for signs of sexual assault obviously."

"Thanks, Dr. Lawrence. Let me know when you'll be doing the PM." He walked back to the victim. What was a woman in designer gear doing in a squalid yard at the back of a pub at this time of night? She hardly looked the type to choose a place like this for an assignation. Slumming it? A knee-trembler against a skip on a cold, autumn night after too many drinks? That seemed a remote possibility but Inspector Lockwood always warned her about not eliminating any scenario, no matter how unlikely it seemed, 'til all the evidence had been gathered. And what had happened to her companion?

Funny she should think of Brian at this time. She had been a sergeant on his team and if he hadn't mentored her she might not have got her promotion. She missed having him to bounce ideas and theories off. His clear-eyed pragmatism tempered her sometimes over-emotional reaction to cases. He had certainly taught her a great deal before he retired to care for his sick wife. But more than that she felt a connection to him and she was sure he felt the same.

Her own relationship with Derek had ended after she had caught him playing away, a few months before Brian's wife died. Maybe she had been partly to blame. Derek wasn't a snake by nature and she had been so caught up in the job that they weren't just ships that passed in the night - their lives were so far apart they could barely see one another's signal lights. She had met Sandra, the woman with whom he had started an affair. She was a rather mousey, bespectacled temp in his office. Nobody's idea of a sexy secretary but then she probably at least gave him some attention.

She felt guilty about not keeping in touch with Brian after the funeral. She even caught herself entertaining some romantic fantasies, usually after she was on the wrong side of a bottle of Cabernet Sauvignon. She would go round to touch base and talk about the job now that he had had some time to heal and at some point they would fall into each other's arms.

The cynical copper in her usually didn't take too long to chide her. For fuck's sake, she was forty-seven not fifteen and she had seen too much of the wreckage of people's lives to believe the world was full of Disney princesses riding unicorns. Besides, she wasn't exactly central casting as a romantic heroine. She was a middle-aged woman who, let's face it, could stand to lose a few pounds, wore unflattering clothes and rarely had time to get a hairdressing appointment. What would the Brian of her fevered imaginings think when they had torn off each other's clothes in the throes of passion and he discovered her knickers were not so much Agent Provocateur as Primark?

Nevertheless, it was him Shona thought of as the chill of night seeped into her bones in a yard that stank of stale beer and piss, where a woman who was probably not much older than she was had come to the brutal end of any romantic hopes she might have had for her future. She owed it to her to find out her story.

Then

Chapter Two

Brian Lockwood

"Do you miss having sex?" said his eighty-year old neighbour as he had a cup of tea with her after having dutifully cut her front lawn. The question made his chocolate hobnob go down the wrong way and brought on a prolonged coughing fit during which she pounded unhelpfully on his back.

When he had got his breath back, she said, "Sorry, I didn't mean to shock you. It's just that when my Bill died - gosh it's twelve years now - I remember how much I missed it and when you get to a certain age there aren't many options on that front. How old are you now, Brian?"

"Fifty-two."

"Tragic for a young man like you to lose his wife." There seemed no adequate reply to that.

"Well, do you?"

"I - don't tend to think about it, Mrs. Brown," he stammered.

"Edith, please. It's been, what, nearly two years since Candice died? You're a good-looking man. Maybe you ought to find someone. Pornography is no substitute for the real thing, is it?"

"I don't ... I mean I ..."

"Don't be embarrassed. I may be an old woman but I know what goes on behind the curtains. You've gone all red. Do you think I should get a leaf-blower?"

The abrupt change of subject made him realise he had been gaping like a hooked fish. As he attempted to regain his composure, they managed to make polite chit-chat about her garden, her grandchildren who rarely visited her these days and her arthritic knee. As he parted with her at her front door, she said, "You'll never forget her, Brian, but I know she wouldn't want you to be on your own."

He raised his hand in a brief farewell and turned away before she could see the unexpected tears that sprang into his eyes. The truth was that she had hit a nerve. He was still grieving and he had been feeling increasingly lonely over the last few months. Candice and he had tried for children but, though both of them had tests - the memory of masturbating into a sample container still made him squirm - it never happened. He had been retired from the police for two years. His retirement had at least given him some time with his increasingly sick wife. Despite going to the pub, the gym, the church and volunteering at the local Children's Hospice charity shop, he realised he was spending an increasing amount of time alone. None of his 'social activities' were satisfying.

The pub provided him with some company but most of the men there talked about football or darts - subjects that had as much appeal to him as sumo wrestling or synchronised swimming - and his pub-going reminded him that he was drinking too much. He did his repetitive routine in the gym unenthusiastically, nodding a greeting at other exercisers, showering and coming home.

As for church, Candice had been the one with faith. The jury was still out for him - what was all that stuff about a vengeful God killing people's first-born children or ordering poor old Abraham to sacrifice his son and then popping up at the crucial moment to say, 'Had you going there didn't I?' He continued to attend out of habit and because he had to admit he quite enjoyed the tea and biscuits with the other parishioners after the service. Besides, the Reverend Moir had always been kind to him and Candice. The volunteering work mainly consisted of him driving the van to do pick-ups that involved minimal social contact.

He still missed his wife. She had fought hard for two long years against the cervical cancer that eventually killed her. Her radical surgery, spells of chemo and frequent hospitalisation had taken over both their lives during this period. Often, in his solitary moments, the memory of his last words to her when he was alone with her in the hospice reduced him to tears. He had said, "My poor darling. You're great." And she died.

After he had left Mrs. Brown he couldn't get her words out of his head. Did he miss sex? He certainly missed the companionship of women and as Mrs. Brown had intuited he did resort to the internet on occasion and not just the adult sites. He had some promising matches on the dating website he had eventually tried after some soul-searching but he hadn't had the courage to take the next step. Perhaps he could give Shona a call and see if she wanted to go out for a drink to talk over old times. He wondered how she might react to hearing from him out of the blue after all this time.

The next day was Sunday so he donned a dark suit and headed for St. Stephen's church. Most of the congregation wore casual clothes but Candice and he had always dressed more formally. She had said her father always insisted on the family turning up to church in their Sunday best and she wanted to maintain the tradition. "Dad would birl in his grave if I turned up in a fleece and jeans," she had once said, looking disapprovingly at a woman in the pew opposite.

The sermon this Sunday was centred around the story of Joseph and his brothers. Joseph starts off as an arrogant, young man swanning around in his fancy coat and happy in his position as daddy's favourite. Later he becomes this profoundly wise advisor. His brothers were guilty of his kidnapping, enslavement and attempted murder but later Joseph forgives them. The minister concluded that the story teaches us about the importance of considering our behaviour in relation to others and about the necessity for forgiveness.

Try telling that to a grieving mother after her son has been beaten to death by a gang of toe rags, he thought. All in all he preferred Rice and Lloyd Webber's funkier version. At least it had catchy tunes. As his attention wavered during the sermon he glanced around the church. Most of the congregation seemed absorbed in the story or were making a passable attempt at pretending to be. A woman at the far end of the pew in front of and opposite him caught his eye.

He was sure he hadn't seen her in church before. He prided himself that he still had the observation skills that had made him a decent detective but the woman stood out. She wore a brightly patterned dress that contrasted with the clothes of her drab neighbours and her hair was a startling ash blonde, cut into a neat bob.

As he took in her appearance, she suddenly turned around and looked at him. Rather embarrassed by being caught staring at her, he quickly averted his gaze. After a few more minutes of biblical cruelty, he glanced at her again and was surprised to find her looking back at him. A knowing smile played on her lips before she turned back to face the pulpit.

In that brief moment he took in her even, almost elfin, features and her startlingly green eyes. It was difficult to estimate her age. She might have been anything from late forties to early sixties. She appeared at the tea and biscuits session afterwards and he was able to study her surreptitiously as he made polite conversation with a few of the regulars. Her dress complemented her trim, almost boyish figure and she carried herself with a quiet confidence that contrasted with the nervous body language of the one or two members of the congregation who approached her to make small talk.

He tried to catch her eye again but she seemed oblivious to his presence. He noticed the minister stopping to talk to her as he moved around the room greeting his parishioners. "Brian?" He realised that Andy had asked him a question. He knew he was a groundsman at a local private school and his wife was a dinner lady there.

"Sorry, Andy, I missed that."

"You were miles away, neebs. I was just asking if you were available next week to take round some of the food contributions to the old folk."

"Sure. Give me a bell and let me know the arrangements."

"Cool. Thon's a fine-looking lassie Moir's talking to. Haven't seen her here before."

"I - hadn't really noticed her."

"If you say so." Andy smirked sceptically. "About time you were getting oot there again, man. You're a long time deid."

What was this? Was everybody worried he was turning into a monastic recluse? He resolved to leave and was just turning from putting his teacup on the table when Reverend Moir appeared at his elbow with the 'fine-looking lassie' by his side.

"Brian, This is Mrs. Tyler. Mrs. Tyler, Brian Lockwood."

"Isabel, please," she said, as she shook his hand. Did he imagine it or did she leave her well-manicured hand in his for a shade longer than social convention demanded? She appraised him coolly with those remarkable, green eyes.

"Mrs. Tyler - Isabel - has just moved into the area. I thought I'd introduce her to some of the flock."

"Nice to meet a you. You, I mean."

"Bah! " she said and laughed throatily. Moir looked bemused. He didn't think the minister understood his slip of the tongue and her response. There was never any evidence of a sense of humour in his sermons.

"So - em - what brings you to our lovely town, Mrs - Isabel?" Moir said awkwardly.

"I had just been through a messy divorce and I needed to make a clean break." Moir looked discomfited. Brian knew he was one of those old-school Presbyterians who didn't really approve of divorce - in fact, he refused to marry anyone who was looking to remarry after having been divorced. Brian knew he had a hardliner's attitude to female ministers and was appalled by the church's acceptance of gay clergy.

"I sincerely hope you settle in here. There are some nice parts of the town - the park is lovely and some of the historic sites like the Abbey and the castle ruins are worth a visit. Like any urban environment these days, of course, there are some less salubrious areas. Brian could tell you all about them."

Isabel looked curiously at Brian. "I meant in a professional capacity. Not because he frequents them." He laughed embarrassedly.

"Professional capacity?" said Isabel.

"From his work with the police. So you had better be a law-abiding citizen or he'll break out the handcuffs."

"What fun," Isabel replied with a grin that somehow managed to be both innocent and salacious.

The minister looked around uncomfortably, clearly looking for an escape as Isabel said, "Do you have contact details, Reverend Moir? Perhaps a mobile number? I'm trying to build up a bit of a network in the area."

"Of course. I'll give you my card. Ah, Mrs. Lorne, could I have a quick word about the church women's group? If you'll excuse me. I do hope to see you next Sunday, Mrs. - Isabel. It's David and Bathsheba next week." He departed hurriedly.

"Not sure I remember that one," said Isabel.

"As I recall, David sees Bathsheba bathing, has her brought to him so he can sleep with her, impregnates her and arranges for her husband to be killed in battle."

"I'm impressed with your biblical knowledge. So it's another everyday story of voyeurism, lust and murder by proxy."

"Something like that, though I'm sure the Reverend Moir will find some wholesome, moral message in it all."

"So - you're a policeman?"

"Ex. I retired a couple of years ago."

"You seem young to have retired."

"It's pretty standard in the police."

"Married?"

"Widowed."

Interestingly, she didn't offer the usual response to this which was apologetic sympathy accompanied by a suddenly serious expression.

"I'm starving," she said. "Must have been all that Old Testament famine stuff. Is there anywhere around here that does a decent brunch?"

"Giamatti's café is just up the road. It does a decent all-day breakfast. It's within walking distance."

"Sounds like just the job. Well, Mr. Lockweed?"

"Lockwood. Brian, please."

"It was nice to meet you, Brian. Perhaps I'll see you next week."

31

She retrieved her handbag from the chair where she had placed it and they moved together towards the vestry door, stopping at a set of pegs to get their coats. Rather self-consciously he helped her into hers, noticing the Burberry label and trying to avoid too much contact. Outside, it was a bright autumn day, though there was a stiff breeze. "Which way?"

"End of the railings there, turn right and keep on going straight up the hill. You can't miss it." She smiled, raised her hand in farewell and began to walk away, while he just stood there in a knot of uncertainty. Should he have offered to walk with her and show her the way to the café? She had only gone a few yards when she turned and made her way back to him.

"I was going to ask if you'd care to join me but I was afraid that might seem too forward."

"Not at all. As you said, nothing like tales of famine to give you an appetite. Not to mention all that bread-making." She didn't join in his own weak laughter at his sparkling wit but turned gracefully and began to walk away. He had no time to reflect on how glib and insensitive his remarks had been about what, after all, had been intended to enlighten them spiritually, as he hurried to fall into step with her.

She maintained a brisk pace up the steep hill that was Cairn Row. On the corner was the Old Tavern, long boarded-up with a tattered For Sale notice in what had been laughingly called its beer garden - a stretch of paving stones where a few mildewed wooden tables and benches had once sat, now studded with forlorn-looking weeds. He explained to Isabel that the town of Dunmalcolm boasted so many pubs it was a miracle that more of them didn't go out of business.

Halfway up the hill they passed a nail bar and undertaker's window - well-placed, he said to her, for when the hill proves lethal for the unfit. He thought to himself, Shut up, Brian - black humour and banal comments on the state of the local hostelry industry; really making an impression.

Further up was the recently reopened New Lyric Theatre advertising forthcoming attractions - stand-up comedians who had finished a stint in

Edinburgh; tribute bands; dancers made famous by television shows like 'Strictly Come Dancing' that Candice used to watch at the weekend while he sloped off to the pub. Isabel stopped to look at the poster of one such show which depicted one of the male professionals from the show on a solo tour, with a glistening, naked upper torso in a paso doble pose. Next to it was an advertisement for a show called 'The Dream Boys - Steps to Heaven', that again featured improbably-muscled, young men clad from the waist up only in bow ties.

"I'd like to see both those shows," said Isabel, with an impish grin. "Really intellectually stimulating." They moved on up the increasingly steep hill 'til they arrived at the entrance to the café and looked in its window.

"Busy, but there might be a few tables through the back," he said, trying to conceal how out of breath he was. Shit, Brian, you'll be sucking in your stomach next, he thought.

The café was, indeed, doing a roaring Sunday trade - groups of young people probably looking for hangover cures in the traditional Scottish heart attack breakfast; a few older couples and families perhaps decanted from the local churches; and solitary men apparently absorbed in the Sunday papers. He empathised with the latter, having frequently found himself uncomfortably eating solo meals in cafés and restaurants.

They found a table at the back in the corner and a young waitress brought over two menus, which they perused in a silence that he found slightly uncomfortable. The waitress returned and asked if they were ready to order. He was surprised when Isabel ordered the full Scottish - but no tattie scones, please - and a pot of tea. He went for the eggs Benedict and coffee. As he handed back the menus, he noticed the waitress eyeing him curiously. "It's you, isn't it, Chief Inspector?"

"It was just Inspector. Do I ...?"

"Ah'm Donna Dolan - Jamie Dolan's sister."

"Ah yes, Donna. I didn't recognise you there."

"Ah wanted tae thank ye for everythin' ye done for him. Thon gang he ran wi' were a right bad lot. Ye got him oot jist in time or wha kens where he would hae ended up. Well we ken really - daein' wan prison stretch efter anither. He's daein' great noo - haudin' doon a job in that wee computer shop in Guild street. Ye ken the wan that does repairs, unlocks phones and sells second-hand stuff. The owner's lettin' Jamie go to college two days a week to study IT. Puttin' him through his SVQs and that.

As he looked at her more closely he began to recall the plump-faced girl with bad skin and inexpertly dyed blonde hair. A fresh crop of pimples peppered the skin around her mouth but she showed even white teeth as she smiled at him. That was something of an achievement, he thought, growing up in an estate where toothbrushes were in short supply and where many children graduated from sugar on their dummies to Irn-Bru and sweets and later crack or heroin addictions that rotted teeth faster than spoiled fruit left out in the sun.

"I'm no' surprised ye didnae recognised me, sir. I expect I've changed a bit." With a wider grin, she indicated her stomach that swelled largely above the elasticated waist of her trousers.

"Congratulations," he offered tentatively, having been embarrassed on one or two occasions by congratulating women whose apparently pregnant bellies were the result of too many fish suppers. "Are you married now?"

"No. The faither's no' on the scene." A look that was difficult to read crossed her face. There was grief and anger in her eyes before she smiled. "But I'll manage fine."

"Great. And I'm glad Jamie's doing so well." She moved off to fetch their food.

"You have a fan," said Isabel. He explained to her how Jamie Dolan had been part of a gang that hung around the Chapel View estate committing petty thefts and minor acts of vandalism. When they kept having their collars felt, and their community service sentences escalated to the point where if they continued to offend sheriffs would have to put them inside, he introduced a scheme where he arranged for them to visit Saughton prison for uncompromising talks by long term inmates. The old lags' tales of the slippery slope from minor offences to serious criminality and the horrors of even short term incarceration put the fear of god into the budding Scottish Goodfellas.

"And despite your obvious initiative, you never rose through the ranks," she said.

"I had chances but I always enjoyed front-line policing and couldn't be bothered by the political games you had to play to advance."

Their food arrived and she attacked her bacon, sausage, egg, haggis and mushrooms with gusto.

"I'm surprised you manage to stay so slim." He was cringing even as he said it.

"I have a very efficient metabolism. Besides, this is a rare treat and I exercise like a bastard. If it's not too cheeky, how do you make ends meet now that you're retired?"

"I have my police pension and my late wife's father left her a substantial estate, which I inherited after she had - passed."

They made small talk as he picked at his breakfast and she wolfed hers down. She told him she was between jobs but was waiting to hear back after a couple of interviews. She didn't go into detail about the breakdown of her marriage except to say she had discovered that her husband turned out to be not the man she had thought.

In fact, she appeared to change the subject when the conversation drifted towards anything personal. He told her about Candice, trying for an unemotional account of her illness and death and she didn't offer the usual platitudes.

When her plate was empty she said, "Will you excuse me while I nip outside for a cigarette? I know it's a filthy habit and I am trying to cut down."

"I'll come with you. We've finished here so might as well get the bill and go." She opened her bag. "Please - let me get this," he said.

"Thank you."

He paid the bill at the counter and left a generous tip for Donna, who gave him a cheery wave as they left. Outside, Isabel lit a cigarette and attempted to waft the smoke away from him as he hovered indecisively. "Did you leave your car near the church?" he asked.

"No. My old Fiesta gave up the ghost eventually - I'm sure it had been round the clock twice - and I haven't got round to replacing it yet."

"Mine's in the car park of the bank across the road from the church. Could I drop you somewhere?"

"I'm actually meeting someone in an hour or so. I'll just have a wander around whatever shops are open on a Sunday here. Thank you for breakfast." She touched his arm and moved to go, then stopped and took out an envelope and pen from her bag. "Why don't you write down your number? I don't have my phone with me - I never remember to switch it to silent and I was afraid it might go off in the middle of the service." He jotted down his mobile number.

"Perhaps I'll give you a call." She walked off quickly. He watched her 'til she reached the corner of the street, where the breeze caught her coat, billowing it out behind her. He caught himself admiring the trim muscles of her calves and, not for the first time that day, chided himself for his ill-disguised lechery.

Chapter Three

Brian Lockwood

The following Wednesday he received a call on his mobile from an unidentified number. He recognised Isabel's voice at once. He had thought on Sunday that its deep huskiness was unexpected in someone so petite.

"Hi, Brian. Remember me? I'm looking for a favour. A friend of mine lost her husband fairly recently and she's struggling to get over it." I know the feeling, he thought.

"I thought it would be good for her to get out a bit more - she's been spending an unhealthy amount of time on her own at home. I realise that people need time to grieve but it's been over a year since he died and I think she needs a distraction. I don't want to sound heartless but I feel she's been rather wallowing in her sadness."

Again, that sounded rather too familiar to him.

"So, I thought to get her to dip her toes into the social waters as it were, she could come with me to church on Sunday. Not so much for the religious experience perhaps, but I thought when I was there last Sunday the socialising aspect was quite nice. I hope you don't think this is a bit of a cheek but I wondered if you might pick us both up. She lives a bit out of town. After some arm-twisting I persuaded her that it would be nice if I went over there on the Saturday night with a bottle of wine and stayed over to keep her company."

"Yes, of course, no problem."

"I'll give you her address. Her name is Mrs. Smith. Have you got a pen and paper handy?" He noted the address she gave him. "Actually, Isabel, I'm glad you got in touch because I was thinking ..." But she had rung off.

He realised that his hand was shaking and his face was flushed. Was he really about to ask her out? Then he thought, why not? After a short period of internal debate, he screwed his courage to the sticking place - was that Macbeth? - and called her back on the number in his phone. Disappointingly, there was no answer and again when he tried later.

He partly consoled himself with the thought that at least he'd see her on Sunday and there might be an opportunity to arrange - what - a date? He hadn't had the nerve to ask anyone out even though he knew Candice would have encouraged him. And when he contemplated the prospect, the first person who sprang to mind was always Shona. After all, they had a lot in common.

But the thought of going out with Isabel both excited and appalled him; so much so that he went to the cupboard and poured himself a large glass of Tanqueray with a splash of tonic water.

On the Sunday, he set Google maps for the address Isabel had given him - 15 Sycamore Road. The soft, cultured voice of the app took him to the outskirts of town passed increasingly affluent-looking estates until he found himself on Sycamore Road, a poplar-lined street with only a few houses set in their own grounds. The poplar trees had shed most of their leaves but still possessed a skeletal beauty. Mrs. Smith's address was an imposing faux Georgian building with a large, sculpted lawn sloping down to neatly kept herbaceous borders. He made his way up her drive and parked outside in an area that could have accommodated several cars comfortably. Clearly, the late Mr. Smith had left his widow well provided for. He sounded his horn. He waited for a few minutes before giving a more prolonged blast.

When no-one appeared he got out of the car and made his way to the front door, which had an elaborate stained glass panel inlaid with what looked like a Rennie Mackintosh design. When the chimes of the doorbell produced no response, he gently turned the handle. It was unlocked. He found himself in a large hallway. Its luxurious, antique carpet in patterns of red and grey made him itch to remove his shoes. Through the three doors leading off the hall, he caught glimpses of antique furniture and expensive looking ornaments and vases. In front of him was a wide staircase whose intricately carved, oak banister curved upwards to the landing above.

"Hello. Anyone home? Mrs. Smith, Isabel? It's Brian Lockwood. I've come to pick you up for church. Hello. Can you hear me?"

As he dithered there, he thought he heard a creak from upstairs. Still calling her name, he began to climb the first few stairs tentatively. As he hesitated, he heard Isabel's voice. "We're up here, Brian. Just come up."

"It's okay. I'll wait down here in the hall."

"Come up. We're nearly ready for you."

Reluctantly he made his way up the stairs. On the wall of the upstairs landing was a large reproduction of a Caravaggio, the well-known artist and, reputedly, murderer. He recognised it from a book about him and his paintings that Candice had bought. She was fascinated by art and had attended watercolour classes at the local college.

The painting was Judith Beheading Holofernes. It seemed gruesomely out of place amidst the tasteful soft furnishings there, with its depiction of an almost matter of fact looking Judith slicing through the neck of her agonised victim with his own sword, as a crone-like servant looks on in sadistic pleasure holding a bag in which to place the severed head.

Four doors led off the landing, one of them standing slightly ajar. He approached it and tentatively pushed it open further. He found himself in a high-ceilinged bedroom. The heavy, brocade curtains across the bay window at the far side of the room were partially drawn so that some sunlight enabled him to see large, solid-looking, antique furniture similar to what he had glimpsed downstairs - a large dressing table with an ornate mirror, an enormous oak wardrobe, a chest of drawers a couple of armchairs and, in the centre of the room, a king sized four-poster bed.

To his surprise, he saw a figure lying on the purple counterpane. Muttering apologies, he began to withdraw but hesitated and said, "Mrs. Smith? Are you all right? Mrs. Smith should I get ..." He found himself approaching the bed. The woman lying there looked as if she had been laid out for a funeral.

She wore a black blouse and pleated skirt and a dark, chiffon scarf was draped around her neck. Her expensively highlighted, auburn hair spread out on the pillow appeared to have been styled professionally recently. Her eyes were closed but her makeup was immaculately applied. He noticed her light blue eye shadow and her full mouth was accentuated by startlingly red lipstick. It was difficult to guess her age from her even features in repose but she was what used to be called a handsome woman. She looked tall, probably around five feet nine and he caught himself admiring the swell of her breasts and curve of her hips beneath her clothes. He thought, Get a grip, Brian. She may be ill.

"Mrs. Smith." As he reached out to touch her shoulder, Isabel appeared behind him as if from nowhere.

"Isn't she lovely, Brian?" He jumped back startled, pulling his hand away as if he had been burned.

"Isabel. You nearly made me jump out of my skin. What's going on? I came to collect you for church. Is that Mrs. Smith? What's wrong with her?" He realised that he was gabbling.

"It's Angela and what's wrong with her, Brian, is that she's been grieving for too long. She misses her husband still. But she's not entirely ready to move on and - well - engage with someone new. She feels she would be betraying him somehow; that guilt would spoil everything. But she does miss being touched - human contact; physical intimacy."

He lowered his voice.

"But why is she lying there like that?"

"You know the Sleeping Beauty story don't you, Brian? She's waiting to be awakened by a kiss."

"Look Mrs. Tyler - Isabel - I don't know what's going on here but I really think I ought to leave. I only came here to give you both a lift to church." Isabel came right up to him. She touched his face and gently ran her hands down his chest. "Yes. The church. It always did equate sex with sin and I think my friend here has been heavily influenced by that. She's only pretending to be asleep, you know. Then afterwards she can tell herself that it was all a dream."

"Afterwards?"

"She wants you to make her feel alive. She's waiting for you. Why don't you kiss her and see?"

"I really don't think that's a good idea."

Her hand moved downwards over the front of his trousers. He started back as if she had stung him.

"Really, Brian. I wouldn't have thought you'd be so inhibited. I saw the way you were looking at me last week."

"I'm not - you were - this is different. It could be construed as some kind of sexual assault." He was stammering and blushing like a teenager who had just been caught wanking by his mum. She lifted her head and kissed him lightly on the mouth.

"Don't be silly. She wants this. Don't disappoint her. You've no idea how much it took her to get her to this stage. Kiss her." She took his hand and led him to the bed. "Go ahead - she wants you to."

He leaned over the woman on the bed. He could feel Isabel gently pushing his head towards her and as if in a daze he touched his lips to the full, red mouth beneath him. He could smell her perfume. It was Elizabeth Arden. He recognised it because his wife used to wear it. That made him come to his senses but before he could draw back, the woman Isabel had said was called Angela opened her mouth beneath his. He pulled back and looked at her in surprise. Her eyes remained firmly closed.

"You see. She likes it. Why not touch her?" Isabel took his hand and placed it gently on the scarf at Angela's throat. It lay there like a stone as a sea of conflicting emotions washed over him. Isabel reached below his hand and began to undo the buttons on the blouse. She reached the last one and pulled the blouse from the top of the skirt so that Angela's breasts were visible, pushing out whitely from a lacy, red bra.

It had a clasp in the front which Isabel deftly unfastened so that Angela's breasts were fully exposed. They were remarkably large and firm, her nipples like small thumbs on large, dark aureoles. Blue veins stood out against her milky skin. Isabel took his hand again and placed it firmly on Angela's right breast. Almost in a daze he began moving his hand lightly over first one breast then the other.

"Kiss them." He lowered his lips to them, kissing them lightly and running his tongue around her nipples which stiffened in his mouth. Her breath quickened. "That's right. You can tell she likes it."

Though that seemed to be true, he was suddenly aware of how weird and wrong this felt. He stood abruptly. "Come on, Brian. If she hadn't wanted this don't you think she would have stopped you by now? Why don't you take just a little peek under her skirt?" She placed his hand on the hem of the skirt.

In a kind of surreal slow motion, he began to raise the skirt, first encountering the tops of stockings attached to suspenders that were the same colour as her bra. "She's dressed up especially for you." Isabel went down on her knees, unfastened his belt and slid his zipper down. This is like a strange fantasy, he thought, as he pushed Angela's skirt higher 'til it was around her waist revealing red knickers that matched the rest of her lingerie ensemble.

"Don't stop now. Take her panties off." I shouldn't be doing this, he thought but Isabel pulled down his trousers and underpants and began moving her hand up and down his burgeoning erection. In a fever of sexual curiosity, he grasped the waistband of the still supine woman's panties and worked them down over her thighs to her ankles. Beneath a neat nest of dark hair the pendulous lips of her vagina were clearly visible.

Isabel moved away to sit in the large armchair. "Go ahead - touch her," she said, as she pulled up her tartan dress and began to run her fingers over the crotch of her white knickers. The cliché, 'He didn't know where to look', became reality as his gaze moved back and forward between the erotic spectacle of the woman on the bed and that of Isabel on the chair. His hand moved onto

Angela's right leg tracing a line from her stockings to her suspenders, then tentatively between her thighs. Was it his imagination or had they parted more?

He ran his fingers over and between the plump lips of her sex pushing upwards onto her clitoris. She was undoubtedly damp and she was taking increasingly short breaths. "Why don't you taste her, Brian?" He glanced over at Isabel, who had pulled her panties to one side and was massaging a completely shaved vulva. He gasped involuntarily.

He became self-conscious that his penis was poking up under his shirt. As he leaned over in a futile attempt to conceal it, he found himself hovering over Angela's vagina. In a kind of lustful fever, he lowered his head and began to run his tongue first over her labia then between them. He was strongly aware of her musky smell and taste as his tongue probed her and her breathing quickened. He gently pushed two fingers inside her as his tongue flicked around her clitoris. Obviously she was finding it difficult to maintain her lack of movement and her hips began to rise from the bed.

She emitted a low moan. He realised that this was the first sound she had made since he had entered the bedroom. She hadn't asked him to make love to her. She hadn't given him permission. Isabel whispered, "Now fuck her, Brian." He looked at the woman on the bed and it was as if the heightened erotic heat of the scene had been cooled by a sudden shower. Her heaving breasts lolled slackly and between her open legs, her labia resembled two damp slugs emerging from dark undergrowth. With his mouth and chin wet with her juices, he started back and tried to retreat, hampered by the pants and trousers round his ankles. Clumsily trying to pull them up, he stumbled to the door.

"Where are you going, Brian?" Still doing up his trousers, he hurried down the stairs and as he went out through the front door, he thought he heard laughter. It was only when he was in his car and halfway back down the street that he regained some composure, though his hands still shook on the steering wheel and he felt sweat cooling on his brow.

What had just happened? At a distance none of it felt real. Yet he could still taste the woman on the bed on his tongue and he felt certain her scent was on his hands. When he got back to the town he pulled into a Starbucks in the leisure park. He ordered a flat white coffee and, leaving the cup on a table, went to the toilet and washed his hands and face.

He looked at himself in the mirror. He thought of Jamie Dolan and his mates. He looked like them. He had the same guilty, fearful looks they had in the interview rooms at the nick - looks they could hardly conceal as they pathetically tried to maintain an air of tough bravado.

Looking at the pale, wide-eyed man in the mirror he wished that he had some of the insouciant sang-froid of the hardened criminals he had come across. They knew that you knew they had done the crime but their expressions of innocence and hurt pride were as practised and convincing as a professional actor's performance.

As he sat nursing the cup of coffee, he tried to reflect logically on the incident in the bedroom of the house, though he was still sickened and unnerved by guilt. In his career, the crimes that had appalled him most were those perpetrated against women and children. Had what happened this morning been sexual assault and - the thought made his stomach spasm - near rape?

As he went over it again he thought that the whole thing had been engineered. Isabel Tyler had lured him to that house under false pretences. She had - literally - taken pleasure in the situation. Besides, Angela Smith, if that was her real name, could have stopped him at any time and she too seemed to be enjoying the experience. Perhaps Isabel's story about her sexual guilt did explain the oddness of the scenario. Or was he simply seeking to justify his own less than moral behaviour?

It was too late for church now, though absolution might not be a bad idea in his current state, if he believed in such things. He bought a couple of Sunday papers on the way home but he was still so perturbed by his morning experience that he found it impossible to concentrate on them. However, one article about a prominent Scottish MP who had resigned after allegations of sexual harassment by his female colleagues caught his eye and made him shiver inwardly.

He had always thought that prominent figures, deservedly pilloried for this sort of inappropriate behaviour, either let their dicks rule their brains or were so deluded by their own imagined power and charisma that they thought their attentions would be welcomed. Deluded indeed, he thought as he looked at the press photograph of the flabby jowls and ill-judged comb-over of the overweight MSP in question.

But hadn't he behaved just as badly? He should have walked away as soon as he saw the woman lying on the bed. He couldn't escape the fact that his better judgement had been overruled by his sexual arousal. How acceptable was it to undress and make love to a woman who hadn't opened her eyes during the whole process? She had reacted physically in other ways, it was true, but still. And what about Isabel's part in it all?

For the rest of the day his conscience pounded his psyche relentlessly. It was like an uneven contest between a heavyweight boxer and a seven stone weakling who could only raise his hands in token resistance. He slept very badly.

Chapter Four

Brian Lockwood

On Monday morning he resolved to get in touch with Isabel to discuss what had happened, no matter how painful that might prove. After all, he told himself, her own behaviour had been provocative and extraordinary. Unbidden, his last image of her on the chair, dress raised and underwear pulled aside sprang into his mind. He was almost overwhelmed by remembered arousal, shame and guilt.

Steeling himself, he phoned her number but his mobile failed to connect. After two more attempts he gave up. He made himself a coffee and took it out into the garden. Absent-mindedly, he pulled weeds from the chipping stones around the lawn while he tried to work out what to do. In his present state of mind there was no way he could wait 'til the following Sunday for the off-chance he might see her at church. What if she came with Angela Smith? In that event, he imagined his guilt would be obvious to the whole congregation. It would be like standing in front of the altar naked.

He had to pick up one or two things at the supermarket but as he made his way back with his purchases, he found himself taking the road out of town. He hadn't started off with the intention of going back to the house on Sycamore Road but he found himself driving passed there anyway, with no idea of what he hoped to achieve. The old saying about criminals revisiting the scenes of their crimes he had always found to be a myth. It might have made his old job easier if they had. And anyway, he hadn't committed a crime, he reasoned, failing miserably to convince his conscience.

The street was quiet as he parked his car across from the entrance to the drive and looked up towards the house. There was no sign of life. A man walking a large German Shepherd dog glanced over as he passed the car, so he pretended to be searching in his glove compartment, unwilling to let him see his face. The thought that In a neighbourhood like this,

61

inhabited by the seriously well - heeled, a man in an unfamiliar car behaving suspiciously might attract attention made him drive off unnecessarily quickly so that his wheels spun.

After several more futile attempts to phone Isabel, he spent the rest of the day in a turmoil of self-recrimination. Around eleven that night he was watching a documentary on television about prisoners on Death Row in US prisons. The irony of his choice of viewing wasn't lost on him. As his attention wandered, he checked his phone for e mails. There was one headed: Cupid. He was about to delete it, thinking it was probably an unsolicited ad from one of these online dating agencies but lazy curiosity made him open it.

He felt as though someone had plunged him into an ice cold bath, the shock almost stopping his heart and making him struggle for breath. The image was unmistakably of him captured in Angela Smith's bedroom. Hand shaking, he pressed the arrow to start the recording.

The face of the woman on the bed was in shadow but there was enough light to see her body and the face and body of the man who, erection bobbing absurdly from beneath his shirt tail, pushed up the woman's skirt. He watched as he pulled down her underwear and touched her intimately before going down on her. The video stopped at the point where he had stood abruptly and turned. His confused and panic-stricken face was framed perfectly by the camera lens.

He wasn't sure how long he sat there staring at his image frozen on the screen. Rousing himself from his fugue, he watched the recording twice more, all the while swallowing down his horror and revulsion. The logical part of his brain registered that the camera appeared to have been positioned above and to the foot of the bed. He noted that it had focussed on him and there was no footage of Isabel.

He crossed to the window and peered out of the blinds as if he thought someone might be watching the house. The wind had got up and by the streetlight, he could see the leaves tumbling by as chaotically as his thoughts.

His phone pinged with a message from an unfamiliar number. It read, 'Hey, Brian. Want to star in your very own porno? Contact Izzy and Ange for details and costs'. What the fuck was going on here? Was this a kind of elaborate practical joke? He was certain he hadn't seen either of these women 'til last week but that didn't mean they might not perhaps be wives or sisters of someone he had put behind bars in the past, seeking some sort of sick revenge. Or was all this a preamble to blackmail? If so, presumably he'd have some kind of demand soon.

When the next couple of days passed without further contact one thing became clear - he couldn't stand much more of the fearful anticipation and dread that prevented him from focussing on anything and kept him from sleep. He was like someone who discovers a sinister lump beneath the skin and waits anxiously for the results of medical tests. The haunted face that stared back at him as he shaved in the morning, dull smudges beneath his eyes, convinced him that he had to do something. He was an ex-cop after all, used to taking a practical approach to cases.

So it was that he found himself heading back to the house on Sycamore Road. This time he drove boldly up the drive, determined to confront the situation head-on. A brand new top-of-the-range Volvo estate was parked outside the house. Before he lost his nerve, he marched up to the front door and rang the bell. He could hear the familiar chimes sounding inside. There was a long pause so he rang again.

The door was pulled open suddenly. A middle-aged man stood there dressed in a white, towelling robe. His hairy chest and skinny legs looked deeply tanned and his greying hair stood up on his head like a cock's comb. Shading his eyes against the light as if it gave him pain, he peered at Brian suspiciously. Behind him he could see three pewter coloured, hard suitcases, some of their contents strewn across the floor as if someone had stopped in the middle of unpacking.

"Yes?"

Who the hell was this? It took him a moment to find his voice, during which the man looked him up and down as if he wanted to remember him for a police line-up.

"Sorry to bother you but I was looking for Mrs. Smith - Angela?"

His scowl deepened. "Never heard of her - think you have the wrong address."

He made to close the door. "Perhaps Mrs. Tyler then? Isabel?" He hastily interjected.

"Never heard of her either."

"Who is it Dennis?" A woman had appeared behind him standing halfway down the stairs. She was wearing a bath robe matching his, only hers stopped mid-thigh revealing dimpled legs that looked like they had been dipped in mahogany.

"Go back to bed, Babs. It's just some guy who's got the wrong address."

She came to stand behind him. Her face was as tanned as her legs and, unlike the man, her blonde hair looked as if she had just brushed it. She pulled her robe up over her dark, wrinkled cleavage. "Who is it you're looking for?" she asked.

"Mrs. Smith? Or Mrs Tyler? One of them is quite short and slim with ash blonde hair and the other is taller with auburn coloured hair."

She looked thoughtful. "I don't recognise the names and they don't sound like anyone I'd know from around here. Wasn't someone moving into number eleven while we were away, Dennis?"

"How the hell should I know?" Dennis was looking increasingly disgruntled.

"You must excuse my husband. We only got back from three weeks in Florida in the early hours of the morning and we're both a bit tired."

"And if you don't mind we'd like to get back to bed," said Dennis.

"Now, now," said Babs, giving her husband two playful slaps on his bottom. "Sorry we can't help you, Mr.?"

"Brown," he lied. "And you are?"

"What's it to you?" said Mr. Warm and Cuddly.

A firmer slap from Babs and then, "Coulter - Dennis and Babs Coulter. Well, good luck finding them, Mr Brown." He stepped back quickly as the door was slammed unceremoniously in his face. He could hear Babs's voice remonstrating with her husband. "Honestly, Dennis, you were really rude to that man."

As he moved away, he could only make out the low rumble of Dennis's reply but he could guess that he wasn't expressing remorse. As he sat in his car wondering what the hell was going on, he felt his phone vibrating. It was a message from yet another unknown number. It said, "Fiddling with a woman while she's asleep, Brian. Tut, tut. You of all people should know that constitutes a criminal offence. We'll be in touch."

Though the autumn sun had warmed the interior of the car, he shivered. He looked up at the house, trying to make sense of this. He had noticed a fancy, old-fashioned Bakelite telephone on a table in the hall. He called up the telephone directory on his mobile, on the slim chance that the phone wasn't an ornament, that the house still had a land line and it wasn't ex-directory. He was surprised to find a number for D Coulter, 15 Sycamore Rd.

He drove off, conscious that he had stayed in the drive too long and worried that the said Mr. Coulter might appear at the door any minute to chase him off at the end of the barrel of a shotgun. He looked the type.

The Coulters were evidently the registered occupants of the property. Were they involved with Isabel and Angela? Perhaps their just-got-out-of-bed demeanour was an act. On the other hand, had the two women known that the Coulters were on holiday and somehow accessed the house in order to lure him there as part of their scheme? If so, what scheme? He had certainly made enough enemies over the years to make revenge a possible motive. Perhaps they intended to discredit him publicly or - the thought chilled his blood - have him arrested. And then there was blackmail.

As it happened, he didn't have to wait long to find out.

Chapter Five

Brian Lockwood

Early the next morning he was awakened by his mobile ringing. He had slept fitfully after hitting the gin bottle hard the night before and had only just fallen into a proper sleep. He didn't notice the display as he answered it groggily, his voice thick with sleep and booze.

"Mr. Lockwood? We met recently and I'm pretty sure you'll remember me given the - intimate - nature of our encounter."

He was instantly awake and sat bolt upright. "Who is this?"

The voice carried on in what sounded like an educated Fife accent. "You know who it is, Brian. You would surely recognise me if we met again, though as I recall you weren't paying much attention to my face the last time."

"Mrs. Smith? Angela?"

"You'll be sent the details of a bank account. We'd like you to transfer £50,000 into it. You have two days. Be assured this is a one-off payment and we won't be coming back for more. We're not cruel and it's a sum you can well-afford. As you know, we have some interesting video footage of you which we're sure you wouldn't want to appear online. At the very least I have no doubt it would go viral causing you a great deal of embarrassment. At worst, it might even lead to legal enquiries but because of your former occupation you'll know about such things."

"Now hold on ..." But she had rung off.

So it was blackmail after all. He didn't know how long he lay there paralysed by a mixture of fear, outrage and anger. Certainly he was angry at Angela and Isabel - if those were their real names - but he was furious with himself. How could he have been so gullible?

His lack of sexual activity over the last couple of years was no excuse for what had happened in the bedroom of the house in Sycamore Road - a house he now knew belong to Dennis and Babs Coulter. His mind struggled to take in all the implications of what must have been an elaborate plan - the apparently casual meeting with Isabel in church; the 'rich widow' waiting to be aroused amidst the opulent trappings of the house; a camera obviously planted in advance. How had they singled him out as a victim? Were there other victims?

Eventually, he rose and went into the shower, punishing himself by having the water so hot that it turned his skin red. When he returned to the bedroom there was a message on his phone with the numbers of a bank account in the name of A and I Smith.

The woman on the phone had been right. He had sufficient funds in his account to meet her demand. Perhaps that was why Isabel had taken such an interest in his income last week. And they had said it would just be a one-off payment.

More self-delusion, Brian, he thought to himself. He had been involved in a few cases of blackmail in the past. Latterly, it had been mainly cases of cyber blackmail - often young men persuaded by nubile, teenage girls to get their penises out for them on web cam. The 'lovely girls' usually turned out to be men, frequently based in places like the Philippines, who soon demanded cash transfers to stop them posting the revealing images.

The bottom line though in all cases of blackmail and extortion was that they always came back for more. He was in a fever of indecision. On the one hand, the thought of his what?: indiscretion, crime? being made public was too shameful to contemplate. On the other, he knew he couldn't live constantly looking over his shoulder, fearful that any day another e mail might appear from an unknown number demanding another pay out. And where might that end? Perhaps when he had been bled dry.

His memories of former cybercrimes reminded him of someone - Ali Olsen, AKA Ali Oop. He was the archetypal computer geek whom he had first encountered around ten years ago when Ali was a tall, under-nourished looking nineteen year old. His skin was so white it looked as if he had spent his life in an underground bunker. Brian suspected at the time that he only left a computer screen to eat and go to the toilet and probably not even then.

Despite having dropped out of school with no qualifications, he had the IT skills of the best employees of Silicone Valley. It was as if he had appeared fully-formed from the womb of a mainframe computer. He was a complete loner, which was no surprise given that he had the social skills of a badly brought up warthog. Brian immediately reproached himself for his insensitivity. The young man clearly had a mental illness. When Brian had first encountered him he had so many physical tics that it looked as if someone was administering electric shocks to him at regular intervals. His vocabulary was as rich in expletives as a Cowdenbeath squaddie. Brian suspected the symptoms and coprolalia of Tourette's Syndrome.

He had been up on charges related to computer hacking but Brian suspected he had been more motivated by curiosity and the challenges to his abilities afforded by some system's firewalls than by any nefarious political

74

ambitions or the desire to commit fraud. He knew the shambling, foul-mouthed youth would do himself no favours in court and that prison would probably finish him so he had called in a favour from an advocate he had had some dealings with and she managed to secure a non-custodial sentence.

Perhaps Ali had been grateful but he certainly showed no outward sign of it. However, they had kept in touch over the years, Brian consulting him on IT problems and using him clandestinely to cut the odd corner in investigations. He resolved to call him the next day.

That night he dreamt he was in freezing seas drifting away from a sinking ship. Every time he tried to hold onto a piece of wood or ice, it disintegrated in his hands. When he opened his mouth to scream for help the salt water rushed into his mouth to choke him. He jerked awake and sat upright.

You didn't need to be a Joseph to interpret that particular dream, he thought. He could only hope the piece of flotsam known as Ali Oop that he planned to cling to would prove more resilient, or the stormy seas would close over his head.

Chapter Six

Angus Moir

The Reverend Angus Moir was in his study contemplating the text for his sermon in two weeks' time. He always liked to be at least a fortnight ahead in case parish business was particularly demanding in any one particular week. He gazed at the blank screen. Perhaps he ought to do something uplifting from the synoptic gospels. He typed 'Something from New Testament'. The old testament stuff always had interesting stories and even in those cases when its heroes behaved badly, he usually managed to find an inspirational moral lesson there but Christ's life and ministry was more suited to the liberal sensibilities of his congregation.

Besides, the latter was undoubtedly thinning out. He had to find something to engage its remaining members and perhaps find new additions to his flock. After all, word of mouth was a proven advertising tool and he needed to believe that if his regulars could be enthused they might tell friends and neighbours. He wasn't so blind that he couldn't sense his audience's dissatisfaction with his recent performances. It wasn't so much that they looked bored or distracted, if anything they seemed to be hanging onto his every word. This to him was a sure sign that they were having to put on a great show of feigning concentration.

Rachel, his sixteen year old daughter, had suggested introducing more modern music instead of the usual diet of traditional hymns. She was in a music group at school and had even volunteered their services on the odd Sunday, which was a remarkable offer from her considering that she usually claimed to have so much homework and projects on Sundays she couldn't spare the time to go to church. His attempts to persuade her of the importance of regular worship usually ended in a row, with his wife, Marian, generally defending their daughter.

Pop music at the services indeed. He was determined to resist such innovations. He had seen these bands on TV in 'Songs of Praise' and it seemed to him they were diluting the word of God for the sake of entertainment. And don't get him started on these gospel meetings where a congregation predominantly made up of people of colour were all on their feet clapping and swaying and somehow singing in joyous harmony. Religion wasn't all about enjoyment and celebration; it had to address the hard questions of death, suffering and sin.

A tap came to the door and Marian appeared. "Sorry if I'm disturbing you, dear, but I'm just heading out to my quilting group. I'll be back by lunchtime."

"Fine."

"Why on earth are the blinds drawn? It's sunny outside." She bustled to open them then moved behind him, one hand on his shoulder. "Oh, dear. Having problems?" she said, looking at the meagre fruits of his labour.

"I have to formulate it in my mind first," he said tetchily.

As she planted a dry kiss on his cheek one of her hair grips fell out. She bent to retrieve it and he viewed her enormous backside with distaste. She was definitely putting on weight. She had always been on the plump side but all those cakes she consumed that she made ostensibly for coffee mornings, cake and candy stalls and similar church events, were taking their toll. He was relieved that she had taken to undressing for bed in their en suite bathroom so he didn't have to see her. Probably, he thought, because even she was aware of her - embonpoint? - was that the euphemism for giving Billy Bunter a run for his money? Or more aptly a puffing shuffle for his tuck.

She gave him a curious look as she left. He detected in it disappointment, disapproval, perhaps even hurt. He turned back to his desktop as he heard the front door closing. Rachel was at school so he was alone in the house. He rose and closed the blinds once more and Googled one of his favourite internet sites.

He unzipped his trousers as two young men appeared on his screen, one dark and dressed in a formal suit, the other blonde in jeans and a tee-shirt. They enthusiastically kissed, slowly stripping one another 'til they were both naked. He hardened as the blonde youth took the dark one's penis into his mouth, one hand cupping his testicles. As Angus's excitement rose, passages from the bible ran through his head. The two men on screen were engaged most definitely in 'dishonourable passions' as St. Paul described them. As the blonde took the full length of his partner's penis into his mouth, Angus wondered if indeed this was what the saint had had in mind. Certainly there was all manner of debauchery around in those times.

Angus mouthed the words from Romans 1 verses 18 - 32 quietly to himself, as the dark one rubbed his erection with lubricant and the blonde youth got on all fours. 'And the men likewise gave up natural relations with women and were consumed with passion for one another.' He was breathing in short bursts as the dark one inserted his penis carefully into the puckered rose of the other man's anus. 'Men committing shameless acts with men.'

The two men were making grunting moans suggesting pain as much as pleasure. Angus called out the words from Leviticus, "You shall not lie with a male as with a woman; it is an abomination," as he suddenly ejaculated before he could reach for a handful of tissues from his desk. His dark trousers were spattered with semen.

In a paroxysm of shame, he closed down the website, deleted his browser history and rushed upstairs to clean up. He scrubbed ineffectually at his trousers before deciding to change them. As he donned an identical pair in the bedroom, he thought that he couldn't risk putting the stained pair into the laundry basket in case Marian noticed.

He went to the full basket in the bathroom and sifted through it for clothes that he could put into a dark wash with his trousers, handling the darker coloured underwear of his wife and daughter with distaste. He knew that him doing a washing would arouse Marian's suspicions. Household duties were her responsibility. She was untroubled by modern feminist thinking about the traditional division of household tasks and she knew he was a fastidious man who would be uncomfortable with cleaning the lavatory or handling dirty underwear.

As he loaded the washing machine, he resolved to tell her he had noticed the washing basket was overflowing and decided to intervene in the normal chores. He thought that if he presented it as a gentle reprimand, she might be too chastened to question it. When he had started the machine - though he never switched it on; he had followed the instructions when it was first installed to demonstrate to his wife how to use it - he went back to his bedroom and threw himself onto his knees and fervently begged God's forgiveness for his sinful behaviour and for the strength to resist temptation in the future.

He decided that as penance for the rest of the day he would do a round of pastoral calls to those parishioners whom he was normally most reluctant to visit. People like old Mrs. Seaton who was in the latter stages of a terminal illness and with whom he struggled to pray in her room as he tried to breathe shallowly against the stink of decay, urine and excrement there.

Or the recently widowed Major Carter whose stiff upper lip frequently trembled as he sought reassurances that indeed he would be reunited with his wife in the next world. Or the Misses Cruikshank, spinster sisters who were convinced that the majority of the town had one foot in hell already because these young people cursed so foully at the bus stop, even the girls who also exposed far too much flesh; and their mothers and fathers - if they had any - were too interested in the pub or bingo hall to bring them up properly.

Yes. He would go now before his wife got back. He would leave her a note about the washing and try to explain his sudden zeal for household duties later.

In the event, his anticipation of the unpleasantness of his duty visits was unfounded and he completed them more quickly than usual. Mrs. Seaton was too frail and addled by the heavy doses of painkillers she was taking, to be able for more than a short prayer and blessing and he had taken the precaution of rubbing some Olbas Oil on the inside of his nostrils, to minimise the stench of her sick-room.

The Major was anxious to get to his golf club, where he was meeting friends for lunch. The Cruikshank sisters were more subdued than usual in their diatribes against the sinful behaviour of the inhabitants of the town, so perhaps Dunmalcolm was saved from the fate that had befallen Sodom and Gomorrah for another week. He even enjoyed the homemade Victoria sponge they offered him with his tea.

He decided to delay his return home to face Marian's questions about his encroachment into her domestic domain by popping into St Stephen's. As he walked up the stone path, he waved to Harry Westwater who was chopping the longer grass at the edge of the cemetery in the church's grounds with an old fashioned long-handled scythe, like a dungaree-clad Grim Reaper. Harry had been the gravedigger and general keeper of the church grounds since Angus had come to the parish. There were no burials in the graveyard anymore so Harry was more or less retired but he still worked there for a couple of days a week.

Angus entered by the main entrance and made his way between the pews to the pulpit. He usually savoured the atmosphere in the church when it was quiet like this - the fusty smells of old stone and wood and damp hymn books mixed with the scent from the large floral displays created by the ladies of the church flower-arranging group soothed his spirit. Today, however, he was still too unsettled by his morning lapse into sin to find peace there.

He mounted the steps to the pulpit. On Sundays he felt so powerful here as he stood gripping the solid oak with its elaborate carvings This was his place; he was master here - above the congregation, looking down on their heads (mainly grey or balding now it was true) as he translated the bible stories for them, finding modern truths and allusions in the scriptures. He stood with his head bowed, seeking some of that strength now.

A sound from the back of the church made him raise his head. A young man entered and moved to a pew halfway down the aisle. Angus was nonplussed for a moment. He had the irrational feeling that he had been caught out in an act of wrongdoing by standing in the pulpit of the empty church.

Angus recalled his conversation yesterday with Harry. The caretaker had caught a young man sleeping rough next to the east corner of the church, presumably finding a modicum of shelter from the wind among the buttresses there. Harry had said, "I told him he was trespassing but he looked that bedraggled that I gave him a cup of tea and a couple of biscuits before sending him on his way, Hope you don't mind, Mr. Moir." Angus had reassured him by muttering some platitudes about Christian charity. Perhaps this was the same man.

But as Angus made his way down the pulpit steps and cautiously up the aisle, the closer he got to the man who sat openly watching his approach, the more obvious it became that he didn't look like any rough sleeper that Angus had encountered. He looked too clean and well-fed for one thing. He was dressed in black jeans and a black, leather blouson jacket over what looked like a freshly laundered, white shirt. His dark skin, full lips and tight, black curls suggested mixed-race and he was extraordinarily handsome. He was broad shouldered and his tight jeans revealed muscular-looking thighs.

As the man appraised him with a faintly amused expression, Angus found his voice. "Can I help you? Are you in need of some help or spiritual guidance? I'm the Reverend Moir."

"Aye, the dog collar was a bit of a giveaway. Look, I hope you don't mind but I saw the church and just fancied a bit of a nosey around. I love these old churches and this one has the most amazing tower. Kind of gives it a medieval look."

"It was actually built in 1903 and, as you can see, we have some good examples of decorative artwork and craftsmanship dating from around that period. Please feel free to look around."

"Thanks - Reverend. I'm Leon," he said, as he stood offering his hand. His height and broad, muscular physique made Angus feel small. He self-consciously straightened his round shoulders as the man grasped his limp, bony hand in a firm, dry grip before moving off down the aisle, looking up at the beams of the roof and taking in the stained glass window at the front depicting the Last Supper.

Angus admired the animal grace with which he moved. His easy gait reminded him of a young Sean Connery. When he reached the pulpit, he ran his hand over the ornate wood carving then turned to regard the minister. Conscious that he was standing in the same position staring at the visitor, Angus moved briskly to him.

"I'll just be in the vestry if you need anything and if you want more information about the history of St. Stephen's we have leaflets at the door where you came in." Angus hoped the young man would not notice how flustered he was by his rather knowing gaze. In the vestry he stood behind the desk blindly perusing some of the paperwork there. After a few minutes, a peremptory knock came to the door and Leon put his head round. "Thanks for letting me poke around."

"Next worship is on Sunday at 11.00 a.m. You would be most welcome."

Without replying, the man smiled and withdrew, leaving Angus feeling foolish. There was no way he was going to come to the service, Angus thought. He shook his head and hurried back out into the nave to see if he could perhaps catch a glimpse of Leon's lithe form as he left the church but he had gone. 'Leon', thought Angus. The name suited him because there had been something feline about his features and movements.

He imagined him returning so that Angus could impress him with his knowledge of St. Stephen's. Of course, he realised why he was so anxious to make a good impression on a complete stranger. He knelt before the altar, head bowed, exposed in the hair shirt of his sin; his thoughts scourging him for this perverted attraction in God's house.

Chapter Seven

Archie Macdonald

The place had undergone some renovation since the last time he had been here, Archie reflected as he sipped his Kronenbourg and obviously it was attracting a younger and hipper clientele. Did people still use words like 'hipper'? He was very much out of the scene, if indeed he had ever been in it. In order to conceal the fact that he mainly drank on his own these days, he tended to spread his custom around the local pubs. Nothing spelled out sad loser more than a man drinking alone every night. But it meant that he didn't have the opportunity to strike up friendships.

Those friends he had socialised with in the past had been mainly Diane's and so had evaporated like steam when she left him. He still missed her terribly. He shuddered when he recalled the night he had come home from work to find her sitting stony-faced at the kitchen table. When he had asked her what was wrong the words had come tumbling from her. She had made up her mind to leave him, she said. Even he must see that their relationship had become routine and dull. They never did anything together anymore except watch television and there had to be more to life and she wanted to find it before it was too late. He probably needed to move on to pastures new as well, she had said.

She had arranged to spend a month in New Zealand with Monica their daughter and she would like him to be gone when she got back. He squirmed as he remembered how he had pleaded with her. He would try to change; think of exciting activities they could both enjoy together. Clutching at straws, he had even suggested that they could go to New Zealand together, though even as he was saying it part of him was wondering how on earth he would get so much time off at such short notice.

He realised how pathetic he must have sounded and Diane had looked fixedly off to the side so she didn't have to see his desperate, tearful face. But she had looked him in the eye when she replied to his declaration that he still loved her with four words that thrust into his gut like a cold blade. "I don't love you."

Later that night he had phoned his daughter in Auckland. It was morning there and she was trying to get the kids ready for school. He hoped she could intervene; perhaps persuade her mother she was just having some kind of temporary, mid-life crisis. It proved to be a vain hope when it became clear that Monica had spoken a great deal over the past few months to her mother, who had relayed her unhappiness with him and their marriage. Monica had at least sounded sad when she said, "It's probably for the best, Dad."

And so he had found himself in a one bedroom flat in the new western expansion with a divorce on the horizon from a woman he still loved, who couldn't stand to live with him anymore because he was apparently so boring. To stop himself wallowing in self-pity and depression, he had thrown himself into his work. He was co-ordinating more and more of the work of the outlets for the Children's Hospice Charity he worked for and his remit now extended as far south as Edinburgh and as far north as Dundee. Again, work gave him very little opportunity for forming friendships.

He had spent that afternoon on his home turf in the Dunmalcolm shop, discussing turnover and examining their accounts and had come straight to the bar after work. He looked around. There were some good-looking women in here. He ran his hand over the bald spot at the back of his head. It was becoming an increasingly large, round clearing in a thinning forest. As if any woman would be interested in him - a sad, solitary man sitting at the bar wearing his middle-age like a moth-eaten jumper, who according to even those closest to him was as interesting as watching flies on a turd.

He became aware of two women sitting at a table off to the left of the bar. They seemed engrossed in their conversation but he thought they glanced his way from time to time. Probably discussing how out of place the miserable-looking guy at the bar was among the other younger and trendier customers. Did people still use the word 'trendier'?

Though they were both seated he could see that one was petite with long, blonde hair and the other was fuller-figured with a rich mane of auburn hair and startlingly red lips. Definitely out of your league, Archie, he thought without rancour. He had never been successful with women and he remembered how surprised and delighted he had been to find that Diane had been prepared to commit to him.

At least 'til she couldn't bear to live with a man whom she didn't find exciting anymore. He reflected, had she ever? The physical side of their marriage had become increasingly mundane 'til it eventually ceased altogether. He still desired her after all these years but he should have heeded the warning signals, when she continued to rebuff his half-hearted advances with weak excuses.

It had got to the stage where he couldn't bear to hear about another headache or how she was really tired after a hard day or see how her eyes shifted away from him, embarrassed by her own dishonesty. Yes, lack of honesty. He realised too late they should have talked more but he had always been a man who shied away from confrontation. So here he was, cast adrift by his own cowardice, helpless to stop the current taking him onto the rocks.

He was swallowing the bitter dregs of his pint and wondering whether to order just one more when he realised the blonde woman he had noticed earlier was standing beside him, trying to attract the barmaid's attention. She was close enough for him to smell her perfume, something sweet and subtly floral. She had small features and even this close it was difficult to guess her age. Her hair was immaculate and he wondered if it might be a wig.

Thinking that she could see the gloom and melancholy that surrounded him like dark clouds, he offered her a tentative smile that probably looked more like an idiot's leer. She turned remarkable green eyes on him and said, "Hi. My friend and I were just talking about you. You're the man from the charity shop, aren't you?"

"Yes. I mean I might be. That is, I do work for a charity," he stammered.

"We were in the Children's Hospice one this afternoon and we saw you there. You were going over something behind the counter. We thought you looked too formally dressed to be one of the assistants there."

"No I'm more of a kind of boss." How pathetic was he sounding? "That is, I have responsibility for a few outlets." He wondered why someone like her would be in a charity shop. The dress she was wearing looked expensive so she didn't seem the type to go in for second-hand clothes.

"We always look round the second-hand books," she said, as if she had read his mind. The barmaid arrived so she ordered a gin and tonic and a spiced rum and coke. "Can I get you one?" she asked, indicating his empty glass.

"Well, all right, yes please, as long as you let me buy the next round for you and your friend."

"Deal. Would you care to join us?"

He was so surprised by the invitation that he stared at her for a moment before stumbling from his bar stool. I must look like a startled goldfish, he thought, an impression no doubt reinforced by his gawping at the women as they introduced themselves as Izzy and Angie. His contribution to the initial conversation was limited to monosyllabic responses to their polite questions, though they didn't seem to notice his tongue-tied awkwardness as they continued to chat animatedly.

After another few rounds he began to lose some of his inhibitions and found himself talking about his work. They both wore expressions of sympathetic sadness and the one called Angie even squeezed his arm, as she said how proud he must be to be making such a meaningful contribution to a really good cause. Izzy said at one point, "I always think Children's Hospices make you question the existence of a God that would allow such horrible things to happen to children and at the same time, remind you that the essential goodness of the people who work in them and those who donate money and time is maybe proof He exists after all."

As he struggled to wrestle with this philosophical conundrum, Archie realised that perhaps he ought to slow down his alcohol intake. But then Izzy persuaded him to switch to shorts and he found himself telling them about the breakdown of his marriage, making sure he emphasised his wife's unreasonable behaviour. They listened to him with rapt attention, as if he were some honey-tongued raconteur imparting the wisdom of the oracle. He caught himself thinking at one point if only Diane could see him now with two attractive women hanging on his words, she would recognise what a huge mistake she had made. Not so boring after all, eh?

As closing time approached he asked them if they would like to come back to his for a nightcap. He had plenty of booze in the flat, having toyed with the risible idea of having a flat-warming party when he moved in, only to get cold feet when he knew he would be hard-pushed to find enough people to invite. He was pleasantly surprised when they agreed to come back with him and the three of them jumped into a cab.

A particularly violent snore woke him up, or rather brought him round, in the early hours of the next morning. He was momentarily disorientated before he realised he was sitting upright on the settee in his flat, the light from the table lamp making him wince and feel nauseous. Hell, how much did he have to drink last night? The central heating had switched itself off and in the chill of the room, he realised he was naked from the waist down. The cold in the room was nothing compared to the icy hand that gripped his heart, as the events of the night before began to come back to him.

Screwing up his eyes, he began to take in his surroundings. An overturned bottle of spiced rum lay on the coffee table at the other end of the room still dripping its contents onto the rug. Next to the bottle a broken wine glass stood, its jagged end poking up menacingly. His hazy memories of the night seemed like some kind of erotic dream.

After a few drinks he had put some music on and the women had started dancing with one another. Izzy, or perhaps it was Angie, had given him her phone and asked him to take some photographs of them as he sat on the sofa watching them. They had posed, faces together, pouting in exaggerated sexiness and then one of them had come over and switched the camera to video mode. As he filmed them they had started dancing slowly together, their arms around each other. As they began to kiss with some passion he had put the camera down in shock 'til one of them broke from their clinch to exhort him to keep filming.

Despite the booze he had consumed, he remembered becoming increasingly excited by the spectacle especially when Izzy slowly pull her friend's skirt up to her hips to caress her ample bottom that was barely covered by the black g string she was wearing. Then they had come over and started kissing him. He remembered Angie saying to him, "You like to watch, don't you, Archie? This one of your fantasies?" How could she have known that they were enacting a scene from his favourite genre on Porn Hub?

As they kissed one another in turn, the women making soft, erotic sounds as they ran their hands over one another's breasts, he became aware that one of them had undone his trousers and a hand was caressing him through his pants. He felt a stab of embarrassment as he recalled his reply to Izzy's question, "What else do you like, Archie?" It must have been a combination of alcohol and arousal that had made him confess to some of his more lurid fantasies.

When he had mentioned spanking, Angie had pulled the smaller woman across her lap, lifted her dress and unceremoniously yanked down her white knickers. She had then vigorously smacked the pale cheeks of her squirming and giggling companion's bottom. A kind of madness must have overcome him, he thought, as he remembered how turned on he was by the sight of Izzy's backside turning redder under Angie's ministrations.

Either a brain befuddled by alcohol or by its reluctance to remember his own depraved behaviour made what came after a series of blurred snapshots, so that he was unsure what was real and what was fantasy. His crumpled up trousers were lying half off the armchair next to the sofa, his boxers on the floor beside it as if they had been tossed there carelessly.

He looked down at his white, mottled legs and his sorry-looking penis that had retreated to the size of an acorn in the cold flat. He couldn't even recall how his clothes had been removed. Confused pictures flickered in his mind.

A voice: 'Oh look, Izz, I think Archie likes your bum'. The scent of a sickly, seductive perfume. A tongue wriggling in his mouth like a small worm. Another voice: 'You need a hand, Archie?' An unnaturally red mouth sucking his penis and his mixed desire and sadness as he thought of his wife. He wiped his hand across his face as if he could erase the images 'til one made him jerk upright, sharpening the stab of pain behind his eyes. A figure looming over him, holding a phone.

God, had they been filming him? Why? Did they get some kind of kick out of it? That would hardly be surprising given the rawness of their uninhibited performance last night. Their untethered sexuality had been alarming and provocative in equal measures to someone like him - a man who had only been with two women in his life, who had rarely departed from the missionary position and who normally kept his sexual thoughts and fantasies firmly under lock and key in his head.

He roused himself to retrieve his abandoned clothes and headed for the bedroom, half-fearing he would discover the women in his bed, naked and in each other's arms. He felt both relief and a flicker of disappointment when he saw his bed was empty and still neatly made.

In his dressing gown, he carefully tidied up the broken wine glass and upturned bottle and took them to his small kitchen. The bright, overhead strip light there made his head throb but it also helped him to think of the events of last night in a less condemnatory and sinister way.

After all, no harm had been done. They were all consenting adults having fun and it had been a long time since he had used that word about his life. Perhaps it had even demonstrated that he, buttoned-down Archie Macdonald, could be adventurous. For the first time in his life he felt less invisible. Not just one but two glamorous and sexy women had seemed to find him attractive. He still loved Diane it was true but she could hardly be described as glamorous and sexy.

Perhaps this would be just the beginning. He would be transformed from plain, old Archie in his cheap supermarket suit worrying about his bald patch to a more dynamic character that men noticed and women admired – a monarch butterfly emerging from its dark chrysalis in all its colourful glory. He swallowed two paracetamols and went to bed where he moved around restlessly in a clammy sweat of shame, disbelief and hope.

The next day the video message on his phone crushed the new butterfly he had thought to become under a heavy boot.

Bruce Adam

Chapter Eight
Angus Moir

That night he was locking up the church hall after the meeting of the church ladies' group had dragged on 'til after nine. Pulling the collar of his jacket up in a futile attempt to ward off the soaking drizzle he could see illuminated by the streetlamps, he hurried for the vestry to retrieve one of the umbrellas that he knew were there.

A figure was sitting on the steps underneath the arch at the entrance to the church. Angus saw the glow of a cigarette and his first thought was this was the rough sleeper Harry had mentioned. The figure stood as he approached and Angus recognised him as the young man who had been in the church that day.

"Hi. Remember me from earlier? Leon? Sorry for turning up again but I was walking up to the High Street for a drink when the weather turned shitty. Oh, sorry, Rev. Just grabbing a bit of shelter 'til it goes off a bit." He tossed his cigarette off to the side as if he was conscious that it was probably as out of order as his language. "Or maybe something drew me back. Told you I love these old buildings. If it wasn't for the streetlights you could imagine yourself in any century here." He touched the stone of the arch almost reverently.

Angus didn't know how to respond. He gazed at the rain sparkling on the man's dark curls and eyelashes. Finally he found his voice, "I could lend you an umbrella. I was just heading in to get one for myself."

"No you're all right. Seems to be easing off a bit. Hey, you don't fancy a drink do you?"

"I ... I ... don't really think ..."

"Come on, Mr. Moir, there's nothing in the bible that forbids drinking on a school night is there? Anyway, you get to be a wee bit naughty sometimes."

Angus was trying to work out if there was an edge to this statement. He looked over at the graveyard to avoid the knowing challenge in Leon's eyes. "Well, I'd better ..." He knew he should go but he felt as immobile as one of the headstones he could make out indistinctly. Leon followed his gaze. "Daft thought but doesn't it make you feel alive being surrounded by death," he said. He touched Angus's shoulder. His hand seemed to burn him through his thin jacket.

The next moment he had pulled Angus into the shadows of the arch and kissed him fiercely. Angus's head swam as he tasted the cigarette on his breath and felt the rough grain of his beard against his cheek. His brain told him that this was wrong on so many levels. The act itself, of course, but here at the church it felt like a desecration. He caught his breath and tried to pull away but Leon held him firmly.

"Come on, Mr. Moir, you're not going to be struck by lightning."

"We mustn't ...someone might ..."

Leon held him against the arch with one hand, holding him at arm's length while he unzipped his jeans. Angus could see his dark penis curving upwards from them. It looked huge. It reminded him of the large phalluses he had once observed in the work of Robert Mapplethorpe, Andy Warhol and Louise Bourgeois as he had browsed rather shiftily through a book in the library about contemporary art representations of the male figure. Leon took Angus's hand and placed it on the jutting cock - when had he started thinking in these crude terms? He found himself moving it up and down its length. Despite its twitching hardness, he could feel soft skin and the contours of veins.

He felt that the devil must have possessed him when he didn't resist, as Leon forcefully pulled down his trousers and underpants and thrust him face first against the arch. The other man's hand grasped Angus's own more modest erection and he was simultaneously embarrassed by his comparative inadequacy, startled by the alien touch of another man's hand and enveloped by his mounting desire.

A high-pitched cry escaped him as he felt a stab of pain in his anus. He tried to shout out that he wanted it to stop but the combination of pain as Leon thrust into him and pleasure as his hand tugged more insistently on his penis, stopped his voice in his throat. His climax was a kind of exquisite agony.

He felt Leon withdraw wetly and heard him zipping up his jeans as he remained with his face against the stone unable to turn and face him. "It's been a pleasure, Rev. I'll be in touch. Maybe we'll have that drink, eh?"

He was gone by the time Angus pulled himself together, suddenly conscious that someone might come by and be met by the shocking sight of the minister's skinny, white buttocks. He had experienced enough humiliation for one night. As he adjusted his clothes, he noticed that the drizzle was continuing to fall. Nevertheless, he abandoned his plan to get an umbrella and such was his dazed stupefaction that he was surprised when he arrived home, his clothes soaked and water running down from his hair into the top of his collar.

Marian greeted him with, "Heavens, look at the state of you. Where's your coat? Didn't you have an umbrella?" He mumbled something about not thinking the rain had been too bad when he set out and told her he was going to have a shower before she could look closely at his face, where he was certain the trauma of the night must be etched.

He undressed in the bathroom. When he peeled down his pants he could see they were a mess of blood and semen. Leon hadn't used a condom. What if he had given him some horrible disease? Well, it was only what he deserved.

He would have to get rid of his underwear somehow. Perhaps he could sneak out and bury the pants in the outside bin. If he showed any more interest in the laundry Marian would definitely smell a rat. As he scrubbed at his skin in the shower he had the despairing thought that no amount of water could cleanse him of his sins.

After his shower he searched the bathroom cupboard for one of Rachel's sanitary pads - he found the thought of menstruation distasteful - and placed it inside his pyjama bottoms to soak up the blood that continued to seep from him. He stayed up 'til he was sure everyone was asleep and slunk out furtively to the outside bin with his soiled underwear.

Later, as he lay in bed next to a gently snoring Marian, he began to weep at the ache from his body and soul and for the loss of the man he had thought he was. That man lay buried in the stained shroud of his shame.

The next day he was up early after a fitful sleep and thought he would do some paperwork at the church. He couldn't bear the thought of staying at home with Marian prattling on innocently, as he wrestled with his guilt. It was bad enough that he would have to sham interest in the conversations of strangers at a charity reception he was expected to attend later at the town hall. As he sat gingerly behind his desk and opened up his tablet in the vestry, Angus had an absurd vision of Moses on Mount Sinai with another kind of tablet. His tablets had been made of stone. How much easier it would have been if he had been able to simply carry something like this down from the mountain and, indeed, to smash it when he saw the fickle Israelites cavorting in front of a golden calf. Some scholars thought the stone was lapis lazuli, at least in their second appearance. The mind was a strange thing, he thought, as his sought refuge in absurd wanderings to distract it from the night before.

These thoughts exploded and he had to clap his hand across his mouth to stop the sickness that rose in his throat, as soon as he opened the e mail from someone calling themselves Cupid. The images were grainy and moved in and out of focus but what they depicted was only too clear. He could easily discern the churchyard, the two figures rutting there and the unmistakable image of his own pale face contorted into a gargoyle's grimace of lust and pain. Attached were pictures of his wife and daughter, obviously taken as they were leaving the manse.

The accompanying text said that they wanted £50,000 to be left in a bag in three nights' time, beside the cherry tree that grew at the back of the graveyard. Angus bit back a cry as he read the last sentence. 'No police if you don't want to feature in your own little movie online. And you don't want your nearest and dearest to find out.'

He didn't know how long he sat there, numb with shock. He felt that the ground had opened up beneath him and revealed a vision of Hell. Eventually, some rational light began to penetrate the fearful darkness into which he had descended. Where had this film come from? Someone else must have been there last night unnoticed by him. Not surprising perhaps when his face had been pushed against a stone arch and he had been overwhelmed by his visceral cravings and pain. One thing was evident. These people were dangerous. He stared sightlessly into the abyss.

Chapter Nine

Archie Macdonald

He could envision the headlines: 'Head of Children's Charity a Secret Pervert'. His career would be in the mud. The Hospice could hardly keep him on if this became public. And where did they expect him to get the kind of money they were asking for? He realised what a fool he had been.

He should have known that women like that would never be interested in someone like him. This was simply another step on the path that was paved with his humiliations at the hands of females, that had begun when he was sixteen, with his rejection by Daisy Gallagher after he had asked her to the high school prom. He could still hear the derisive tittering of her friends as he made a flame-faced retreat. Then there had been his first drunken sex with a college friend at a party where he had climaxed as soon as he had fumbled a condom on and entered her. He had seen her the next day laughing with a group of friends and he imagined she was telling them about his pathetic performance.

And it hadn't ended even when the only woman who had shown any interest in him and whom he had loved so much had left him. Now there was this. The camera had captured the dazed, lascivious expression on his face as he watched the reddening arse of the squirming, laughing woman called Izzy and he was tormented by the image of his cock standing up finally, as the one called Angie worked on it as if she was trying to suck the remains of a particularly viscous drink through a straw.

With a heavy heart – he now knew exactly what that cliché meant – he dragged himself along to the town hall. A reception had been organised there for some of the local businesses that had sponsored the charity over the last year. There was a buffet and speeches in the oak-panelled, old court room. His second glass of sparkling wine had the same cloying sweetness as the first and the curled up egg mayonnaise sandwich that he picked at to counteract its taste had a faintly sulphurous taste.

He barely registered the speeches by the Provost and a so-called local celebrity who had enjoyed a brief run in some dire Scottish soap opera he had watched once. The brief thought crossed his mind that the fee for her shiny presence was hardly the best way to spend the charity's money, but then soon that would be none of his concern once he had been forced to resign. As he automatically joined in the applause for the rehearsed platitudes of the speakers, inside he twisted helplessly on the rack. He could see no way out. Even if he managed to scrape together enough money to pay his tormentors off, there was no guarantee they would destroy the footage. They could hold it over him forever.

He could just let them go ahead and put it out there. After all, in this age where any kind of pornographic perversion was available at the click of a mouse, it would hardly cause a ripple. But he thought how humiliated Diane and Monica would be if they saw it.

He looked to the front of the audience at Derek and Sally, his colleagues whom he had so far managed to avoid. His head filled with their imaginary conversations behind his back. Derek, the office comedian: 'Old Archie eh. Who'd have thought he'd be into a bit of S & M and threesomes? Was going to say butter wouldn't melt in his mouth but that might give him ideas. Ho ho'. And Sally: "Makes my skin crawl, thinking all the time we were having an innocent conversation he was fantasising about smacking my bum'.

He thought he must be attracting attention as he stood there in stunned silence while everyone around him reacted dutifully to the wit and wisdom imparted by the celebrity in a speech someone else had written for her. He made his way out to the hall fighting a feeling of nausea. A heavy weight on his chest made him breathless. He remembered taking part in a conducted tour of the building years ago. The guide had pointed out the magnificent, crystal chandelier beneath which he was presently standing and the ornate carvings on the banister of the wide staircase that curved upwards to the next level.

She had led them out on the rooftop up there to admire the clock tower. His feet seemingly climbing of their own volition, Archie began to ascend the stairs. He was surprised when he tried the door that he was sure led out onto the roof area and found it was open. He found himself high above the town, looking down on the roofs of the pub, café and offices across the street. Above him, the hands on the town clock moved towards one. He peered over the chest-high railings that ran around the roof area to the cobbled street far below.

At least he felt he could breathe up here, though his discomfort with heights made him dizzy. He registered vaguely that the railings could do with a lick of paint. How easy it would be to climb them and stand on the edge. Then what? Plunge to the cobbles below? He pictured his broken body lying there, his head smashed open, red and grey matter spattering the stones. Perhaps his stomach would burst open and disgorge a mess of cheap fizz and half masticated egg mayonnaise. The image made him giggle incongruously at the same time as his nausea returned.

He had one hand on the railing and a foot on the ledge when a voice behind him said, "Lovely view from up here." He turned to see a thin, gaunt man in dark clothes and a dog collar. The man came over and stood beside him to peer over the edge. "Long way down."

Archie wondered if the man had intuited his half-formed intention. "You're with the charity, aren't you? I'm Angus Moir, the minister at St. Stephen's. We met before when my church raised some funds for the Hospice. Great work you do. God's work. Suffer the little children." Archie thought the minister was oblivious to his unfortunate pun.

"Archie Macdonald." He shook the other man's bony hand.

"Reception's finishing. They're just clearing up but there are a few people still queuing up to get that young woman's autograph. She's quite famous apparently, though I've never come across her before."

"I expect you don't watch many soap operas, minister."

"Dear me, no. Mind you, if everyone had the never-ending crises and emotional intensity of these characters in real life my church might be a bit fuller on the Sabbath." Archie noticed that the smile that accompanied his weak joke didn't reach his eyes.

"Well, perhaps I'd better ..."

Moir showed no sign of moving but said instead, "I like it up here. The view, of course, but also being close to that old clock. How many generations have watched its hands turning and heard it chiming out the hours? And it will go on measuring out the lives of this town's inhabitants when we and our fears and worries have passed. And there's peace and quiet up here. Especially peace." He continued to look around at the view but his voice was strained and strangely wistful.

"Closer to God up here perhaps." He probably thinks I'm taking the piss, thought Archie, feeling uncomfortable both at his own crassness and the irony of his comment, given his own morbid imaginings.

As they both moved together awkwardly towards the door leading to the stairs, Moir said, "It's none of my business but you appear troubled." Archie's first instinct was to attempt to laugh it off. After all, God was more likely to cast him out for his sins than help him. However, something about the minister's demeanour made him pause. "I know how unbearably bleak some of our problems can seem, believe me."

And how would an upright minister of the Kirk know that? Archie thought.

"I don't know about you but I found the buffet food rather unpalatable and I've never liked the tea and coffee at these things. Perhaps you could join me for something at that café across the road."

Despite his misgivings, Archie found himself seated across from Moir a few minutes later, sharing a pot of tea and talking about the Hospice. Archie was relieved that the minister avoided bringing God into the conversation at every opportunity and occasionally he thought he detected an undercurrent of hopelessness in the man's face, as his professional, caring expression faltered. He appeared to be as worried as Archie was.

"Those poor parents. What they must be going through? Makes one's own problems pale into insignificance." Moir had a distracted air as he said this. Perhaps he's contemplating God's place in it all, Archie thought.

"Are you all right? When I saw you on the roof, I thought ..." Moir let the sentence hang in the air and Archie was surprised and embarrassed by the sudden tears that sprang into his eyes. "If there's any way that I can help, my son." Moir reached out a hand to touch Archie's then hastily withdrew it.

Before he could stop himself, Archie found himself blurting out his sorry tale to the minister: his despair at the breakdown of his marriage; his encounter with the women in the pub and its aftermath at his flat. He omitted much of the detail of the latter to spare his own and the clergyman's blushes. Besides, the formality of, "I engaged in sexual activity with them," made his admission seem less damning and sordid than a story of blow jobs and bared bottoms.

He knew that confession was not part of the Church of Scotland's practices but he began to understand the relief of unburdening oneself to a stranger, and he realised he was unworried about the man's possible reactions - disgust, condemnation, an exhortation to throw himself on the mercy of the Lord?

In fact, the man of the cloth appeared to be sympathetic and non-judgemental. However, when Archie told him about the existence of the video evidence and the subsequent demand for cash Moir's face blanched. To Archie he seemed shocked and fearful.

His voice fell to a whisper as he said, "They're blackmailing you?"

"Please don't suggest that I go to the police. I couldn't bear for this to come out."

"No, no. I understand. Trust me. I do understand."

They regarded one another in silence. He doesn't know what to tell me that will make things better, thought Archie; after all this must be completely alien to him. He probably hasn't even read about experiences like mine, he thought, however much he had censored them in the retelling.

But Moir looked as if he had come to a decision and when he spoke it was Archie's turn to listen with open-mouthed incredulity. Unbelievably, they were both in the same sinking boat and Moir believed God was going to bail them out.

Archie was a lapsed Catholic and he remembered the stations of the cross. He thought that he and Moir were at the tenth station, stripped of their garments and stage eleven looked likely to follow inevitably - both nailed to their own crosses. Before he left the café, the minister outlined a plan that he thought would give them salvation - that was the word he used. He couldn't have known it would lead both men to decide on a course of action that would leave them standing side by side on the precipitous ledge of their own destruction.

Chapter Ten

Angus Moir

Angus had met the man at the reception before and knew he was someone connected with the charity. Despite his three piece suit, the man still had an unkempt look and in the bright courtroom he seemed to be standing under his own personal rain cloud. An impulse made him follow him out of the reception and up the stairs and to call out to him when he saw him holding the rail, one foot on the ledge.

Now as they sat in the cafe, Angus could hardly conceal his stunned disbelief at Macdonald's story. On the surface, their experiences were different but there were too many similarities for it to be a coincidence, particularly the existence of a film and the revelation of blackmail to conceal sexual impropriety. Angus was aware that the other man's account of the activities in which he had been recorded indulging had omitted many sordid details that he no doubt regarded as shameful enough to be tempted to give in to his oppressors' demands.

Was there even more of a connection? After all, Leon - if that was his real name - couldn't have been working alone. Someone had to be there recording their encounter in the churchyard. He would have to take the chance on Macdonald's discretion. Perhaps their mutual guilt would bind them together and that might give them both a glimmer of hope.

But how could he broach his suspicions about the possibility that there was a group of people in this town conspiring together to extort money, without exposing his own reprehensible conduct? He decided he would take his lead from the other man and tell him just enough to convince him they had to work together to find a way of thwarting these people.

"I'm being blackmailed too, " he blurted. He told Macdonald that he had been visited at the church by a thug who said there were people who knew he watched pornography sometimes. He didn't elaborate on what sort. They would expose him if he didn't pay them money. He was too ignorant about the technology to know how they would go about this but he was certain they could carry out their threat.

"I don't get it. Watching porn's not that bad nowadays."

"But I'm a man of the cloth. Something like this could ruin me. How can I set people on the right spiritual path if they know I do - that sort of thing - and the thought is as bad as the deed in God's eyes?" The throbbing between his buttocks mocked his half-truths and equivocation.

"Like you, I don't want to go to the police and I don't think paying them off is a good idea. I suspect we've both read or seen enough fictional thrillers to know that blackmailers tend to come back for more."

Macdonald looked as if he was struggling to comprehend this new development. "But how do you know that your visitor and, my two women are connected?"

"You think this is a coincidence? I think they're all part of a group of criminals blackmailing people in Dunmalcolm. I'm sure we're not the only victims."

Angus's words appeared to hit home. "Then what do you suggest? How do we stop this nightmare? I'm at my wit's end."

"How are you supposed to pay them?"

"Electronic transfer. These - women - sent me bank account details."

"They want me to leave the money in a bag in the churchyard the day after tomorrow. No police or they'll tell people close to me."

"Fuck. Oh, sorry."

"Here's what I suggest. I could probably scrape together about a quarter of what they ask. You?"

"The same. Maybe a little bit more."

"Okay. We pool our resources and leave the money as they've asked. But we'll be watching. I know the churchyard so well they'll not spot us."

"And then what? Confront them? With respect, Mr. Moir, you're nobody's idea of Jack Reacher and the only black belt I have is round my dressing gown."

Recalling Leon's muscular animalism, Angus acknowledged the truth of this. He could overcome them both easily.

"Look, they don't know we've met. They'll be wrong-footed when we both approach whoever comes for the money. We'll leave a camera running to record the meeting as a bit of extra evidence. Give them a taste of their own medicine. We'll persuade them to take what's on offer from both of us or we go to the police and face the subsequent damage to our reputations and careers. We'll convince them we'd still be better off than they would be because they'll go to jail."

"And what if they beat the shit out of us - sorry - seriously assault us or worse when they realise we're onto them? Or they could just take the money on offer and ruin us anyway."

"Wouldn't you prefer to take the chance? We'll both lose money but it won't be the financial disaster that's the alternative. These are smart criminals - they won't want the fallout a violent attack on a church minister and a charity organiser would generate. They'll want to cut their losses."

"Maybe you're right but this is so risky. If they've threatened you that means they may not stop at blackmail. These are seriously scary people, Mr. Moir."

"You know what the alternatives are. Financial and professional ruin. At least consider my suggestion. I think we were meant to meet. I think God put us together to offer us some hope of salvation from this. I'll give you my mobile number. Let me know what you decide."

As he left the café his would-be accomplice remained staring into his cup. Across the road, the young woman from the reception was standing on the steps of the town hall posing for photographs for the press, her smile carefully practised, chest pushed out, one leg artfully crooked in front of the other. He thought of the vacuity and futility of the pursuit of fame. Yet, bizarrely, they were alike. Her outward glamour was manufactured to conceal the unyielding hardness of her ambition, just as his public garb of piety and righteousness hid the ugliness in his soul.

Now

Chapter Eleven

Shona Patterson

She sat down behind her desk clutching a Starbucks' coffee. The stuff in the station tasted like a mixture of diesel oil and poo. Hadn't she seen a programme about this really expensive coffee that they actually extracted from animal poop? Kopi something or other and they got it from the shit from civets, those weird-looking creatures that looked like a mangy hybrid of a dog and a cat. Focus, Shona.

She should never have had wine and a carry-out curry so late last night. Her tongue felt as furry as her head and she had been late in this morning as she was unavoidably detained in the loo. DS Cameron came over. He was dressed in an immaculate, grey suit with a subtle, purple stripe running through it that was complimented perfectly by his lilac shirt and tie. He must spend most of his wages on clothes, Shona thought. When she first started working with him she had suspected he was gay but a steady stream of stunning girlfriends suggested otherwise.

In her navy jacket and trousers that were beginning to look rather shiny, she must look like someone he would normally arrest from the Church View estate. "Boss wants to see you." Christ, could this morning get any better?

"I'll just finish this."

"She said as soon as you got in."

"Okay. Thanks, Garry." She got up, turning her head so she wouldn't have to look at him pretending not to notice her coffee and curry breath and went upstairs to DCI Morton's office.

Alice Morton sat behind a desk upon which everything seemed to have been arranged by a geometrician. Her telephone and the two filing baskets at either side of it were perfectly aligned and the files in them looked as if they had been ironed. A brass paperweight in the shape of an elephant sat on a single sheet of paper, aptly looking as if it had been told to stand to attention.

If an interior designer had been looking for the perfect accessory to accentuate the neatness of the room, the woman behind the desk fitted the bill in her crisp, tailored suit, with her dark helmet of hair sculpted around a subtly made up face. Shona had barely had time to hastily apply some lipstick and drag a brush through her tousled curls. Morton made Shona feel like the before part of one of those rubbishy reality shows she sometimes watched, where some fat frump was transformed by an army of personal trainers and make up and dress designers into Cinderella at the ball before the glass slipper incident. Alice Morton was the after in that scenario.

Shona thought that she and DS Cameron must be conspiring to lower her self-esteem. Thank God for DC Buckle, thought Shona, or Fatty Arsebuckle as he was known affectionately. At least compared to him she was a model of clean living and sartorial acceptability. He would only have seen the gym if it was next door to a chip shop. She sometimes suspected that he had run out of plates at home and just decided to eat his dinner out of his lap then give his trousers a quick wipe down with a tea towel.

"Sit down, Inspector." She didn't actually say 'You're making the place look untidy', but Shona thought that was the subtext. "Where are we with this woman who was found murdered behind the High Street? I have the Super breathing down my neck so I'd like to be able to report some progress."

"We found the murder weapon, ma'am - a broken brick. It was found in a pile of rubble in the yard where the body was discovered. The victim's blood was on it but unfortunately there were no fingerprints, which strikes me as odd if it was a spur of the moment act of violence perpetrated either by a stranger or someone she knew. Another odd thing - we found what we think was her phone too. Smashed to pieces in one of the skips in the yard."

"No trace of the woman she was seen drinking with?"

"Not yet."

DCI Morton rose and stood at the window looking out onto the station car park. Shona looked enviously at her trim, athletic figure. She knew her boss had run various marathons and half-marathons and most lunch times she donned her training gear to go on a short run', which would have led Shona to have a cardiac infarction if she had attempted it. The woman's buttocks looked like billiard balls in her perfectly tailored slacks.

"Had she been sexually assaulted?"

"No."

"Have you been able to trace her family? Friends?"

"Here's the thing, ma'am. Isabel Tyler seems to be a ghost. Her ID is fake and we haven't been able to find out where she lived or worked. We've put out a photofit and a 'has anyone seen this woman? She was probably using the name Isabel Tyler', etc. So far no responses."

"So, we have an unidentified woman's body and no clues," Morton said, continuing to look out of the window. Shona understood her frustration because she felt it too, though hers stemmed from her desire to find justice for the unknown victim, whereas Morton's was probably a result of seeing her foot slipping on a rung of her ladder to greater promotion.

"Don't let me keep you, Inspector. You have a lot to do."

The implicit, barbed criticism stung Shona. She had a sudden urge to move the neatly arranged objects on Morton's desk into awkward angles and scatter some files. "I'm sure we'll make more progress once we identify her," she said, with more conviction than she felt and her attempt to make a dignified exit was somewhat marred by the loud animal growl that her stomach emitted.

The rest of the morning was spent going over reports of the case to see if they might have missed something, while her guts churned. As she headed for the toilet, she noticed Cameron holding up a finger as he talked on the phone. She went over. "That was a guy called Andy Linklater. He's a groundsman at the local private school. He reckons he saw our mystery woman at

Your Sin

St. Stephen's church a couple of Sundays ago. That's his address." He handed her a scribbled note.

"Let's go and talk to him."

St. Stephen's church. That was where Brian's wife's funeral service had been held. She was sure they had both gone to church there when Candice was alive. Perhaps he still did. She tried to suppress the ripple of excitement she felt at the thought that there was a chance she might see him. They might have to interview some of the congregation if this guy's information proved to be accurate. She chided herself even as she anticipated it. She was thinking like a schoolgirl with a crush on her geography teacher for God's sake, when she ought to be concentrating on solving a murder.

After they had spoken to Linklater they decided to swing by St. Stephen's. The church had the familiar smell of wood, dust and mildew that immediately reminded Shona of her Sunday school a lifetime ago. Part of her still missed the innocent confidence of those days when Jesus

141

loved her and wanted her for a sunbeam. When had she lost that?

Perhaps it was when she watched her mother turning into a desiccated husk, wrung out by all the angry tears she had shed as Shona's older sister Maggie succumbed slowly to the leukaemia that had killed her at the age of fourteen. Or the stinking smell of putrescence in a flat on the Chapel View estate she had entered as a young PC, where a young mother had slipped into a diabetic coma and died. She hadn't been discovered for three weeks and Shona had never really got over the sight of her child in its play pen, a lifeless doll among the other toys there. Then there were the constant reminders every day of her working life, of the darkness at the heart of people's lives.

Yes, all of the above had chipped away her fragile faith and swept up the fragments, she thought, as she stood in St. Stephen's feeling like an impostor. "Never really feel comfortable in places like this," said Cameron, standing at her side as if he had read her mind. She was surprised to see a man in a dog collar watching them from the pulpit. This was Monday. Were ministers like actors, rehearsing on a stage all week and imagining their performance in front of an audience?

He hastily came down the steps of the pulpit as if he had been caught with his hand in the collection plate and appeared to be even more jittery when they produced their warrant cards. When they had introduced themselves, Cameron said, "We have reason to believe that a woman calling herself Isabel Tyler attended this church, Reverend Moir. Attractive, petite, blonde?"

"Calling herself?" When he received no response, he went on tentatively, "I do think I remember someone of that name who fits that description, yes. But I only met her once at the meet-and-greet after the Sunday service. Why are the police interested in her?"

"I'm sorry to inform you that she's been found murdered, sir," said Shona and she observed Moir's sudden pallor.

"My word - how dreadful. You don't expect that sort of thing to happen in Dunmalcolm, do you? I mean, I'm sure it does and I daresay you see more of it than most but ..." He looked increasingly flustered as his voice tailed off.

Cameron cut in, "Did you notice her with anyone, Mr. Moir?"

"She appeared to be alone but I did introduce her to one or two members of my flock. She didn't stay long as I recall. I think she left with Mr. Lockwood. He was one of you 'til a couple of years ago."

Shona hoped Cameron didn't notice her reaction to the mention of Brian's name. "If you could give us a list of people she talked to that would be helpful," she said, handing Moir her card.

"I'll certainly do my best, though as I said I only met her once. I'll give it a bit of thought and hand the list in later."

As they left, Cameron said in a low voice, "He was as jumpy as if we'd accused him of buggering the choir boys."

"They don't have choir boys here, Garry, and you know as well as I do how nervous some folk get when they're being questioned by the police. I don't suppose a minister comes across a murdered church-goer every day, even though they profess to be experts on sin."

Inwardly, she wondered if perhaps Angus Moir was familiar with sin in more than just a professional capacity.

Chapter Twelve

Brian Lockwood

Later that morning he phoned Ali. Eventually a rough voice answered. "Inspector. What dae you want, ya cunt? That fuckin' piece of shit you cry a laptop fucked again? Tak my advice and get a fuckin' abacus."

"Ali, I'd like your expert advice. I'll pay you, of course."

"Too right ye will, ya cunt. Last time ah checked ah hadnae registered as a fuckin' charity."

"Could we meet later for a drink and a chat?"

"Meet me at wan in the shit-catcher." And abruptly he rang off.

The pub was across the road from the grey, sandstone building of the Town Hall, huddling in its shadow as if being bullied by its more imposing neighbour. The flaking paintwork of its exterior and its filthy window advertising Caledonian 80 Shilling further emphasised its shabby meanness. It was a run-down boozer called the Nappy, the Robert Burns reference to strong ale lost on Ali and, he reflected, probably on most of the bar's regular clientele, who probably wondered about its association with babies.

Inside it was busy. He took in the threadbare seats and bar stools, one of which was lying broken at the corner of the semi-circular bar. The walls were a dirty shade of nicotine yellow, as if they hadn't been cleaned since the smoking ban came into force. An ancient ceiling fan whirled dust motes around.

As he looked at the customers, he thought that Ali's appellation had been accurate. A few of the punters looked as if they had been there since the eleven o' clock opening time. One or two of them looked at him directly with a kind of curious hostility as he made his way to the bar but the majority ignored him, some of them staring gloomily into their pints as if they saw the sad dregs of their lives floating there; others reading the sports section of tabloid papers.

A few couples sat across from one another in silence, finding more interesting company in their phones. The eighties rock music that sounded from the music system switched to 'The Final Countdown' by Europe. How apposite, thought Brian as he looked at the bar's customers.

They all had the everyday ugliness of a modern Hogarth painting. Fashions consisted of shiny, nylon jackets or anoraks with washed-out polo shirts under them or the strip of the local football team from three seasons ago. And who still wore white shell suits?

He ordered a pint of Tennent's lager and a tonic water and lime from a scowling barmaid. Her shock of dyed, black hair was shaved at the sides. Both her arms sported sleeve tattoos and the elaborate ironmongery in her ears, nose and lip must have thrilled anyone queued behind her in airport security. He had just seated himself at the window when Ali appeared, his height, gaunt skinniness and convulsive twitching attracting the attention of even the pint-gazing punters and the taciturn barmaid.

He clocked Brian and came over. When he sat, his legs continued to move up and down spasmodically and as he took a swig of lager his shaking hands spilled some of it on the table and down his black AC/DC tee-shirt and jeans. His fashion choices at least fitted in with the other drinkers. He stretched his mouth into a wide grimace, making him resemble one of the monkeys from a wildlife documentary. Brian estimated that Ali must be nearing thirty but he still looked like a particularly awkward teenager with his pale, spotty complexion, bum fluff and unblinking stare.

"What can I dae for ye, ya cunt?" was his opening pleasantry. Another simian grimace. Brian had decided that he was going to tell Ali the whole story, no matter how sordid it seemed or how bad it made him look. One thing he had learned in his previous dealings with the gurning, quaking man across from him was that, despite his eccentricities, his discretion could be assured and very little seemed to shock him.

In a voice lowered to avoid eavesdropping by any of the denizens of the Nappy, he gave Ali an account of events from his initial encounter with Isabel up to the demand for the money transfer.

During the narrative, Ali took sloppy gulps from his pint and went through a series of odd tics such as tapping his left shoulder several times with his left hand, raising his right knee and grasping it fiercely and more open-mouthed jaw cracking. He interrupted the flow of Brian's story with random phrases uttered in a low grunt. Brian tried not to be distracted by his ejaculations, of which 'arse fire, pineapple chunks, fudge packer, clean holes, Soapy Souter and raspberry tits' were the less expletive-strewn examples.

He interrupted only to ask what colour knickers the two women were wearing as Brian red-facedly recounted the incident in the bedroom and to interject in a too loud voice, "You mean tae say you licked her fanny, ya dirty cunt." This last was accompanied by more frenetic yawning as Brian glanced around in alarm to see if any of the punters had heard.

When Brian had finished, Ali said with his usual delicacy, "Ah felt ma cock gettin' stiff there, ya cunt." He waved his empty pint glass. As Brian made his way to get him a refill a man at one of the tables said, "Is your mate the full shillin'?" His hairstyle wouldn't have looked out of place in the seventies and he was wearing a muscle tee-shirt exposing meaty arms and a belly that had succumbed to the wrong kind of six packs. He was sitting with a skinny, nervous-looking girl in fishnet tights and denim shorts who looked as if she should be at school at that time of day.

"Special needs. I'm his carer," Brian replied, continuing to the bar. When he returned with the lager Ali said, "How the fuck dae ye think I can help? Ye ken fine ye should go tae the filth, ya cunt. Sorry, nae offence." Brian wasn't sure if he was supposed to take offence at being called a cunt so regularly or at being ex-'filth'. Ali filled the ensuing silence with some choice non-sequiturs like 'Kiss ma crack' and 'Dipped in shite'.

"I suppose I get why ye wouldn't want your ex-mates sniggerin' at ye in the fuckin' station canteen, though. Have ye thought aboot jist payin' these two hoors off? Then again they might squeeze ye till your ba' bag bursts."

"Look, Ali, I thought you could use your magic a wee bit. Maybe find out something about these two women's identities online or trace this bank account." Brian handed him a typewritten sheet with the women's names, a brief description of them and the numbers of the accounts; plus five hundred pounds in cash. "The money is to retain your services. Obviously there's more, depending on the length of the job."

"Hang on to your phone for now in case they contact ye again but I might need tae tak a look at it later. Get a fuckin' pay-as-you-go."

Mr. Beefy and his twig-like girlfriend suddenly loomed over them. "Look ya lanky freak, I don't like the way you were starin' at my girlfriend."

The girl looked embarrassed. "Come on, Tam, leave it. Let's go."

Brian thought it was entirely possible that the big guy was right – Ali stared at everyone.

"No' my type, pal. I prefer them a bit older like wi' a bit more meat on the bones." Wide grimace and several tics.

"What are you sayin' and what's with the monkey impressions? Are you takin' the piss?"

Brian stood up. "I'm sure this is just a misunderstanding, mate. My colleague meant no offence. He has – issues."

"Andy, come on," said his companion. The threat of violence hung in the air for a few moments more as Tam clenched both fists, his hands like anvils.

Then with a parting shot of, "Fucking spastic," he allowed himself to be pulled away.

As they left, Ali said, "There was no need for you to step in. I can handle fuckin' apes like that," this ironically accompanied by an ape-like expression.

Since Ali looked as if he'd fall over if the guy had breathed heavily on him, Brian had to suppress a smile. He had a sudden cartoon-like image of a giant fist launching Ali's skinny frame through the pub window, jagged shards of glass raining down around him.

Ali gulped down the last of his lager, some of it running down his chin. "I'll be in touch if I have somethin'," he said, as he made a shambling exit.

Brian was surprised to receive a call from him two days later. "The fuckin' bank account's goin' tae tak time but might be a dead-end. The bank is based in a country that's on the FATF blacklist of NCCTs. What that shite means is the powers that be set up a Financial Action Task Force in 2000 that lists Non-Co-operative Countries or Territories. In other words, they don't shop money launderers or fuckin' terrorist financers. Havenae' got a handle on the Smith bitch yet but as for the other wan, you have a fuckin' problem. The polis are lookin' for information about somebody called Isabel Tyler. And a woman showed up deid in a yard in the toon. Somebody had caved her fuckin' heid in."

Chapter Thirteen
Shona Patterson

She tried to ignore the fluttering in her stomach as she rang Brian Lockwood's doorbell. Act like a fucking professional, she told herself. Cameron looked at her curiously as they waited. She knew how observant he was and he had no doubt noticed that she had taken more care with her hair and makeup than usual and had ironed her suit trousers and white blouse. They had just rung the bell again when an old woman appeared at the doorstep of the house next door.

"Are you looking for Brian? He's out but I don't think he's gone far. His car's still there. Oh look, here he comes."

Shona could see Brian along the street. Did she imagine it or did his casual stride falter when he spotted them? He walked up the path towards them.

"Shona. This is an unexpected surprise." He regarded Cameron. "Don't think we've met before." Brian held out his hand but the DS ignored it and produced his warrant card. "Detective Sergeant Cameron, sir."

"So, this isn't a social call then. That's a shame. I keep meaning to call you, Shona."

She felt ridiculously pleased at hearing this. "Same here, Brian. How have you been?"

"Oh, you know." He turned to the old woman who continued to observe them from next door. "Thanks, Mrs. Brown. "

"Enid," she said, as she rather reluctantly retreated.

"Come in." When Brian headed off to the kitchen to make the tea that he had offered them, Shona looked around the tidy, rather pristine living room. On the mantelpiece stood a framed photograph of Brian and his late wife that had obviously been taken on some holiday in the sun. Must have been a rare occasion, she thought, because the Brian she knew had been something of a workaholic.

She had been an attractive woman, Shona thought, as she looked at the woman's openly smiling face and her thick, blonde hair. The last time Shona had seen Candice had been at a retirement do for one of their team. She had been wearing a short, blonde wig at the time to cover the effects of the chemotherapy that she was undergoing and her smile at that time had seemed more strained.

Brian returned with a tray on which were three matching china cups, a teapot and a plate with biscuits. Bit of a change from the Brian she remembered from work who often just grabbed one of the mugs abandoned by the sink and, despite their typically toxic-looking brown stains, barely rinsed it before chucking in a tea bag.

Shona regarded him surreptitiously as he poured their tea. He looked in good shape and she found herself feeling relieved that, like his house, he hadn't let himself go. Though when his eyes met hers as he handed her a cup, she thought they had lost some of the brightness she remembered and there were dark rings under them.

She must have held his gaze a fraction too long because he cleared his throat, sat in the armchair opposite her and said, "You're looking good, Shona. Promotion must agree with you." Again she felt an absurd frisson of pleasure as she stammered,

"So do you. Still hitting the gym I see. I have to get back there." Why did she have to grab the fold of flab at her waist in front of him?

Clearly Cameron became impatient with this exchange and interjected. "I don't know if you follow the local news these days, sir."

"Brian, please. Been out of the game for a while now. But yes - you never lose your interest in the criminal doings of the denizens of Dunmalcolm."

"Then you'll have heard of the recent murder of a woman in the town?"

Brian said nothing. His face remained impassive but Shona noticed his hand shaking slightly as he lifted his cup.

She jumped in. "The thing is, Brian, we have reason to believe you might have come across her. She was calling herself Isabel Tyler but that wasn't her real name. We've spoken to the

Reverend Moir and he reckons you were speaking to her in church recently and he remembers you leaving with her."

Brian looked as if he was searching his memory for her but to Shona it looked too elaborate to be convincing. "My God, yes. We actually had brunch together in Giamatti's cafe." Shona fought down a pang of jealousy. "And she's been murdered?"

"Anything you can tell us about her, sir - Brian?" said Cameron.

"We only exchanged some small talk really. I didn't think it odd at the time but afterwards I realised that she had hardly told me anything about herself: where she lived; what sort of work she did; that kind of thing. She did say she had just come out of a messy divorce, which I surmised must have left her reasonably well-off. I'm no expert in women's clothes but she looked to be wearing designer labels." Shona felt self-conscious in her M&S suit.

"Have you seen her since then?"

"No."

Shona was too relieved by this to notice his hesitation.

"Well, if you can think of anything that might help you know how to contact us," she said. As they were leaving, Brian put a hand on her arm and said quietly,

"Listen, Shona, I know you're in the middle of a murder enquiry but I'd really like to meet up again." Shona tried to read his expression which looked both fearful and pleading. Was he so keen to ask her out and scared she might refuse? The thought thrilled her.

"Of course, Brian. I'd like that. Give us a chance to catch up." Cameron had turned away during the exchange, apparently having found the hanging baskets at Brian's door fascinating suddenly.

As he drove them away he was quiet. He glanced at her.

"What?"

"Nothing."

"Spit it out."

"Is everyone we interview today going to be so edgy? I mean he's ex-police so he's hardly going to feel intimidated by our presence."

"I think he was embarrassed at seeing me again. We both were. Brian was a big influence on my career and we hadn't really seen each other for the last couple of years. I suspect we both felt - remiss. I know I should have been more supportive after he lost his wife."

"Aye maybe it's that. Only did you notice he looked a bit shifty when you asked him if he'd seen the victim again after their little date in the cafe?"

"No." She wanted to say that it hadn't been a date but she bit her tongue.

"Must have imagined it then." They were stuck at a set of temporary traffic lights. He turned to her with a cynical gaze. "You think it's wise to see him at the moment?"

"I've known Brian for a long time. There's no way he'd kill anybody." She knew she sounded defensive but the implications needled her. The sergeant must have sensed the undercurrent between her and Brian.

"We still have to treat him as a suspect, Inspector Patterson."

She felt reprimanded by his use of her formal title.

Chapter Fourteen

Shona Patterson

Shona felt an absurd flush of pleasure as she received Brian's phone call the next day. He wanted to meet at Giamatti's cafe for a coffee. The thought that maybe he took all of his first dates there flitted across her mind before she mentally slapped herself. This wasn't a date and she was a police officer looking to garner information about a murder from a member of the public. She almost convinced herself.

She told Cameron she was following up a lead and would tell him about it later. As she left the station, he gave her a look that she had seen before when they were interrogating suspects who were lying through their teeth.

The cafe was quiet and she spotted Brian immediately in a corner by the window. He was nursing a coffee and staring down at the chipped Formica table as if he was studying a road map to hell. He rose when he saw her and his clumsy kiss aimed at her cheek caught the side of her mouth. She wondered if she was blushing as much as he was.

"Thanks for meeting me, Shona."

"I was pleased to hear from you again so soon."

"The thing is this isn't a meeting to reminisce over old times."

Shona felt a flicker of disappointment.

"It's about the woman who was murdered." Typical of Brian, she thought - come to the point unembellished by social niceties. A pregnant, young waitress materialised at her side.

"What can I get you?"

"Just an Americano, please."

"They do amazing cakes and scones here. You should have one. On me," said Brian.

"Better not - they go straight to my bum." Shut up, Shona.

The girl gave Brian a warm smile before retreating.

"I know who this woman is. Her real name is Irene Dunlop."

Shona took out her notebook. "How do you know?"

"You remember a computer hacker called Ali Olsen?"

"Ali Oop? How could I forget? I think the last time we met he called me a few less than complimentary names. 'Whore sandwich' sticks in my mind for some reason."

"He can't help it. It's his condition."

"You used to use his services on the quiet as I recall. If Morton had found out she'd have set Internal Affairs onto us quicker than she could order us to drop down and give her twenty."

"Keeping up her exercise regime then?"

The waitress arrived with her coffee. "Can I get you something else, Inspector?"

"Brian, please, I'm okay thanks, Donna."

"Friend of yours?" Shona asked, as she went back to the counter, carefully avoiding contact between her bump and the tables.

"Yes."

Since he didn't seem inclined to elaborate, Shona asked him the question she had been dreading, "Why? I mean what makes you so interested in this woman that you would go to the trouble of getting Ali Olsen involved?"

Brian hesitated and looked out of the window for what seemed like an age. He appeared to come to a decision and looked into her eyes. His piercing gaze contained a mixture of determination, shame and guilt.

"She was blackmailing me."

Shona couldn't have been more startled if he had suddenly confessed his undying love for her.

"Her and her accomplice. I have to warn you that what I'm about to tell you doesn't exactly picture me in the best light, Shona, and the last thing I want is to lose the respect of someone whose opinion I value so much but I feel I have no choice." His words both warmed and chilled her.

She tried to retain an impassive demeanour as he told her about his dealings with the woman she now knew was Irene Dunlop, scribbling notes partly to avoid looking at him. But when he got to the bedroom incident, she was so startled that her notebook fell from her hand into her lap, where it lay forgotten. He didn't seem to notice as he stared fixedly at a point above her left shoulder as if he were studying someone behind her.

She knew he wasn't telling her all the gory details but what he did tell her was enough to tear away her mask of objectivity and stare at him, stricken. She retrieved her notebook and opened it distractedly as she attempted Canute-like to push back the waves of conflicting emotions that engulfed her.

When he had finished his account he sat silently like a guilty prisoner in the dock, awaiting the inevitable sentence of the jury.

"Did you ..." Her question stuck in her throat. "Did you have sex with these women?" "Not - as such. I did have - intimate contact - with the woman on the bed while Isabel or Irene - spectated," he said haltingly.

"Spectated?"

"She was - touching herself." He spoke so quietly she had to lean forward to hear him. He shook his head as if he was trying to dispel the remnants of a bad dream. She had once seen him facing down a woman brandishing a kitchen knife she had just stabbed her partner with after too many years of black eyes and broken bones. She remembered him quietly removing the knife from her hand as she held it at his chest. His opening up to her like this must have taken even more nerve than he had shown then.

She tried to throw him a lifeline. "But surely all of this was consensual. You might have done something stupid and, okay it doesn't exactly enhance your reputation, but it's not criminal."

"You have to see what it looks like in that film." He took a shuddering breath. "In it, I partially undress and - am intimate with - a woman who to all intents and purposes seems to be at best, asleep and at worst, unconscious. It could be construed as an assault. You can only see me and her in the film. Would anyone really believe I had been persuaded that it was all part of an erotic role-play instigated by a third party - a woman I'd met in church - ostensibly to help her friend move on from a bereavement? Even as I'm telling you this I realise how ridiculous that sounds. And now the stakes have risen even higher. Someone's murdered her."

He unexpectedly reached over and grabbed the hand that was still clutching the notebook so that it fell from her grasp once more. He immediately withdrew his hand and apologised.

"You must believe I could never have done it."

She suddenly felt a flash of anger. "You fucking fool, Brian. What have you got yourself involved in?" She knew her reaction was fuelled by more than concern for him. There was an irrational jealousy at work too. Certainly she was furious that he could risk his reputation like this but another thought poured petrol on the fire - if he was so fucking sexually frustrated why hadn't he come to her before now? She had been waiting for him only too ready and willing to - how did he put it? - be intimate with her.

"You can't be any angrier with me than I am with myself, believe me. I know I'm asking a lot but could you keep me in the loop with the investigation?"

"Brian, you said yourself you're on the other side of the table now. I have to let the team know what you've just told me. You'll be hauled in for questioning."

"I would expect that and I wouldn't ask you to compromise yourself. Frankly, it's a relief to tell someone. This has been a constant ache like a particularly bad tooth. If my reputation suffers, so be it. The important thing is to get to the bottom of this cess pit, however much stench it raises."

"Where did your meeting with these women take place?"

She noted the address Brian gave her. "But it's a dead end. The owners of the house have never heard of them."

"You've been back there?" He nodded sheepishly.

"For fuck's sake, Brian." She said this more loudly than she intended and several customers cast disapproving looks their way.

"I thought if I confronted them there ... I don't know what I thought. I wasn't thinking very clearly."

Shona fought to compose herself before allowing herself to speak. "Well, we have this woman's real identity now thanks to your potty-mouthed friend and the location where you were - compromised. That's a start."

"Shona, I know this is asking a lot but before you call this in could we go round there together?"

"Christ, Brian, that is so contrary to procedure that if I did that I'd feel I should arrest myself."

"It's just that with your authority I could get inside the house. I never got passed the doorstep last time."

"And then what exactly?"

"I might pick up something I missed. Then you can drag me to the station in handcuffs if you like. It would be a personal favour to me."

Shona read the subtext. He had covered her arse many times in the past. Now he was asking her to return the favour.

"I hope all this hasn't made you too disgusted with me, Shona. What you think of me is really important to me." The appeal in his eyes was so naked and sincere that it halted the refusal on her tongue. She had seen him this vulnerable only once before.

One night she had come across him sitting immobile in his car in the police station car park. He had reluctantly rolled down his window when she tapped. His phone was in his hand. He had said simply, "Bad news," and she could tell he was fighting back tears. She knew it was about his wife but the armour that everyone in the job wore to protect them from feeling, made her hesitate to reach out to him. She should have got into the car and put her arms around him but she was afflicted with the same cop's macho bullshit that made him try to suppress his emotions in front of her.

The way he was looking at her now was like a punch to her gut and she knew she might be about to make the biggest mistake of her career.

"Who did you talk to there?"

" A couple - the Coulters. They said they'd just got back from holiday."

"If they're telling the truth it begs a couple of obvious questions - how did these women know the property was empty and how did they access it?"

"That's been bothering me too."

"All right, Brian. We'll go there but I do all the talking and if they're not forthcoming we back off immediately and Cameron and I go back later in a more official capacity."

"Thanks, Shona." He touched the arm that she was resting on the table and again she felt ridiculously flustered. She rose awkwardly and began rummaging in her bag for her purse.

"I'll get it," he said.

She waited for him by the door as he paid at the counter, cursing herself inwardly. She was being a sentimental numpty but worse than that, her professional instincts were screaming at her not to do this.

The pregnant waitress gave them a curious look as they left but waggled her fingers in a child-like gesture of farewell.

Chapter Fifteen

Brian Lockwood

Brian found that his confession to Shona did little to assuage his feelings of guilt and shame. It had taken a real effort to swallow back the bitter taste of humiliation as he exposed his dirty laundry to a woman whom he both liked and respected. How different could it have been if he had acted on the impulse he had felt many times to call her? Perhaps they might have had a chance of settling into a relationship that was based on shared experience and affection - a relationship that was, above all, normal.

He stole a look at her as she drove them to the house in Sycamore Road. He was conscious that he had always found her attractive with her tousled hair and warm smile, though he had suppressed these feelings when they were colleagues and he was still a married man. One of her most endearing characteristics was that she was unaware of her own appeal and was self-effacing to the point of near invisibility. Well, he had taken a sledgehammer to the walls of trust and mutual regard they had built up together brick by brick over the years.

He wondered what was going through her mind as they drove in silence. He was surprised she had agreed to allow him to accompany her, so perhaps she was now regretting that decision. And of course, she was no doubt trying to come to terms with her new unsavoury knowledge of him. Perhaps she was thinking he was no better than those creeps at the station who, prior to the new workplace regulations, used to find sexual innuendo in the most innocent remarks of their female colleagues and who openly commented on their breasts.

"That's the house, on the left." He felt a nervous cramp in his stomach as they entered the drive. Shona knocked and after a few moments Barbara Coulter answered. She was wearing a tight running top and leggings that Brian thought showed a little too much of her generous figure. Her mahogany face was sweaty and her blonde hair was pulled back into a topknot that exposed the beginnings of dark roots.

She looked at them curiously 'til recognition seemed to dawn as she looked at him. "Back again, then. Mr. Brown."

Shona cast him a look of exasperation and annoyance. She hastily produced her warrant card. "Detective Inspector Patterson. Would you mind if we came in and asked you a few questions?"

"What's this about? I already told this man that I didn't know the people he was looking for." Brian and Shona stood there in silence so she said, "I suppose you'd better come in."

She guided them into the room on the right. It was evidently a public room, presumably used for entertaining. Brian's earlier impression of its elaborate furnishings were confirmed when he saw the whole room. Light streamed in from one side from the enormous bay window that looked out to the front of the house and from the other direction from patio doors, through which he could discern a landscaped garden to the rear. It was a long room with high ceilings - Brian thought he could fit his entire house into it and still have space for an extension.

It was furnished with what at first looked like a random and eclectic mix of antique and mock antique furniture that on closer observation had been artfully chosen, probably under the eye of a professional interior designer. A dark, leather chesterfield sofa sat in front of a dark, wood coffee table with a floral inlay. The table was so wide you couldn't reach across it. Next to it was an armchair that wouldn't have looked out of place in the living quarters of Louis IV.

Brian's eye was particularly drawn to an unusual-looking cabinet on a stand with elaborate colour veneers and marquetry inlays. After Candice's death he had watched far too many day-time antique programmes on TV and he thought he recognised its 18th century style, perhaps modelled in the manner of Robert Adam. Even as a reproduction it probably cost somewhere north of ten grand.

"I'm sorry the place is such a mess but I've been doing a yoga session," said their host, as she led them to the far end of the room where a long dining table with twelve chairs sat in front of the patio door. Brian thought the only thing out of place in the immaculate room was the yoga mat that had been placed in a space next to the doors.

Babs gestured for them to sit at the table while she took a chair near the open doors. "We'll sit here if you don't mind while I cool down." There was an impressive chiffonier sideboard at the head of the table on which some photographs were displayed in fancy frames. Brian felt a chill that had nothing to do with the breeze that was coming in from the garden as he looked at the painting above it.

It was another reproduction of a Caravaggio that instantly took him back to that fateful day and the painting he had seen upstairs. This one was Salome with the Head of John the Baptist. Brian reflected that someone in the house had a thing either for this artist, Baroque art in general or for depictions of severed heads.

Babs noticed his rapt interest. "Impressive isn't it? Not my choice for the dining area but my husband loves the artist and it's certainly a conversation piece for our guests. You never mentioned you were with the police when you came here before, Mr. Brown."

She emphasised the "Mr." and Brian's attention snapped back instantly to the woman. "No. It wasn't really official police business as such." He stumbled over the words as he spoke and saw that Shona was looking at him with knives in her eyes. He knew he was putting her in an uncomfortable position.

"Mrs. Coulter, we have reason to believe that the two women my - colleague - was looking for somehow managed to gain entry to these premises while you were away."

"But the house was all locked up when we got back from Florida and there was no sign of a break-in. We have some valuable possessions here so my husband had a state-of-the-art alarm system installed. And I think I would have noticed if anything was missing."

"Did anyone else have a key?"

"My housekeeper, Mrs. Gunning. But she only came in a few times to water the plants and to give the place a once-over just before we arrived home."

"What does she look like?" Brian interjected. Shona shot him a warning glance.

"Why would you want to know that? She's quite old - in her sixties, a bit on the plump side. She used to be a cleaner in my husband's firm before she retired. He thought she was a good worker and absolutely trustworthy. I mean there's often a fair bit of petty cash lying around in his office so she had to be. He approached her after she left to see if she would like to do a few days' work for us to supplement her pension."

Brian was disappointed. From this description she was certainly neither Isabel nor Angela.

Shona went on, "Perhaps you could give me her details. I'd like to check that she didn't give the keys to anyone else."

"I'm certain she wouldn't but hang on a second. We could ask her now." Babs crossed to the coffee table to retrieve her phone.

Shona whispered fiercely to Brian, "Stay out of this. Let me deal with it."

Babs returned, putting her phone to her ear. Brian rose and went over to the sideboard and pretended to be fascinated by the photographs on it both to avoid eavesdropping and to escape Shona's wrath.

"Hi, Mrs. Gunning, Babs Coulter here. Look, this may seem like a silly question but did you give our house keys to anyone while we were away on holiday?"

Brian observed that the photographs had been taken mainly in this room and depicted groups of people in fairly formal clothes, apparently enjoying a series of jolly social gatherings. There were no family photographs here. Perhaps they were in another room in the house. He wondered idly if the Coulters had children.

"No, I was absolutely certain you wouldn't do that, Mrs. Gunning. No don't upset yourself, dear.

It's all a bit strange. The police think someone was in the house while we were away."

Brian was thinking that this Mrs. Gunning sounded as though she wouldn't welcome a visit from Shona. "Yes, of course, we knew you were here as we'd arranged. Don't worry yourself. I'm sure it's all a bit of a misunderstanding. We'll see you on Thursday as usual."

She rang off and turned to Shona. "Just as I thought, she said there was no way she would ever give our key to anyone else without our permission. I just hope I haven't upset her too much."

"I'm sorry, Mrs. Coulter, but we may have to interview her anyway."

"But why? I don't understand. Why on earth do you think these women were here? What do you think they were up to if nothing's been stolen?"

Brian barely registered the women's fractious conversation. His attention was fixed on one of the photographs on the sideboard. It depicted a group of people round the dining table raising their glasses in a toast to the camera. But it wasn't the celebrating group that had caught his eye and clutched at his gut with a frozen hand. Standing in the background, watching the scene, was a woman that he recognised. Her hair was a darker colour than he remembered but it was undoubtedly the woman he knew as Angela Smith.

"I said we're leaving," Shona's voice made him aware he had been standing there as if he had been turned to stone. Absurdly, the image of Medusa flashed into his mind - more Caravaggio and more severed heads. He took the photograph over to Babs who was now standing impatiently willing them to be gone. "Can you tell me the name of the woman in this photograph?"

Shona fixed him with a stare of disbelief.

"Which one?" Babs turned the frame towards her impatiently.

"The woman with dark hair who's standing in the background."

"That's Eleanor Thomson our old housekeeper before Mrs. Gunning. Unlike her successor, she used to help out occasionally if we were entertaining a big party. Serving the food, tidying up afterwards and so on."

"What happened to her?"

"Brian - Mr. Brown." Shona still looked as if she might drag him out of the house in handcuffs but she also looked puzzled and curious.

"My husband let her go, I'm afraid. Never told me why. Just said it was better if I didn't know the details. I assumed he'd caught her doing some petty pilfering. Why do you want to know?"

At that point, the man whom Brian remembered as the choleric Dennis came in through the patio doors. His hair was wet and he was carrying a sports bag from which jutted the handle of a squash racket. The Coulters clearly liked to keep fit, Brian thought. He looked as equally pleased to see Brian as he had in their initial encounter.

"What's going on?"

"This is Inspector ..."

"Patterson."

"And you remember Mr. Brown. I'm sorry I don't think I got your rank. They're asking about Eleanor."

Brian thought that Dennis had gone pale under his tan.

"Anyway, I'm not sure how much more I can help you so if you'll excuse me I'm going for a shower. Dennis will show you out." She left, pulling the tie out of her hair as she went.

"Excuse me for just a moment." Dennis followed his wife. Brian thought he looked flustered. Shona turned to Brian angrily.

"What the hell are you playing at?"

"It's her." He pointed to the woman in the photograph. "It's the same woman I ... who was on the bed upstairs." Shona was staring at the photograph as Dennis returned. He obviously noticed her interest but was trying unsuccessfully to appear casual.

"Look, I'm not sure why you're interested in Eleanor - Mrs. Thomson but we haven't heard from her since she left our employment."

"What is it that you do, Mr. Coulter?"

"I'm a hedge fund manager. I'm based in Edinburgh but fly down to London two or three times a week."

Brian had no idea what hedge fund management entailed but looking at the Coulters' lavish lifestyle he deduced that it had little to do with gardening.

"Why did Mrs. Thomson leave?"

"I had to sack her I'm afraid. She had become unreliable."

"In what way?"

"Not turning up for work - that sort of thing." A look passed between Brian and Shona. They could both tell he was lying. "Why are the police interested in her?"

"We have reason to believe she may be involved with others in blackmail and extortion and she may be a suspect in a murder enquiry." Brian was surprised by Shona's candour but if she was trying to provoke a reaction from Coulter it certainly worked. He looked as if someone had suddenly pierced him and let all his air out. He moved quickly to the other end of the room and stood listening for a moment at the door before closing it and returning to slump into one of the dining chairs.

"A murder enquiry?"

He looked round furtively. "Listen, she - she blackmailed me too." As if they were synchronising their movements, Brian and Shona sat down simultaneously. "Initially I enjoyed having little chats with her when I was at home and she was going about her work here. She was quite flirtatious you might say and I enjoyed her attention. It was little things at first. Straightening my tie with that mischievous gleam she always had in her eye when we were alone; her - her chest brushing my shoulder when she gave me a coffee; asking me to hold the ladder as she dusted the ceiling cornices so that when I looked up ... Her dresses were shorter than were practical for housework." He looked as if he had swallowed something particularly unpleasant.

"One day I came across her in a bedroom upstairs. She had been vacuum cleaning and making the beds and so on. Before I knew it we were ... look it just happened. There had been a - tension - between us and something snapped. Over the next few weeks there were several opportunities for us to be alone. I always felt dreadful afterwards. I love my wife, Inspector, and nothing like that had ever happened before."

Brian noted that Shona had difficulty in concealing her cynical disbelief. He could almost read her impressions - rich guy, away from home a lot, able to afford some leisure and recreation that wasn't listed in the activities available in the up-market hotels he no doubt stayed in.

"Anyway, to cut a long story short, she came to me one day and asked me for money. Unless I paid up she'd tell my wife about our affair. That's what she called it. She had recorded our - liaisons - on her phone." He sat in wretched silence 'til Shona prompted him.

"So what did you do?"

"I gave her the money on the condition she left her job and left us alone. But she got back in touch recently and asked for more. I didn't know what to do."

"You could have come to us."

"Then it would all have come out and my wife might have left me. I couldn't bear the thought of that."

"When was the last time she contacted you?"

"Just before we left for Florida. It cast a pall over the entire holiday I can tell you. I've been so stupid. My wife doesn't have to find out I've told you this does she?"

"I can't make any promises, Mr. Coulter. Could she have kept a key to this house?"

"I insisted she handed back all her keys before she left." A thought seemed to strike him. "I suppose she could have made copies. My God, perhaps she intends to come back and rob us."

"We'll have to talk again. Could I borrow this?" She indicated the photograph that Brian was still holding unconsciously. Coulter removed it from its expensive frame and handed it to her. "If you hear from her or think of anything else, here's my card."

They left him with his head in his hands, a forlorn figure out of place in his opulent surroundings. Brian had little time for men like Coulter. There was a coldness and a whiff of amorality about him. The little puddle of misery he sat in now was probably nothing compared to the wide pool of it his everyday dealings created for others.

And yet part of him felt sorry for the man. He had sounded sincere when he said he loved his wife. Besides, hadn't Brian been just as guilty? Hadn't he also succumbed to the taste of forbidden fruit that had been presented to him on an elaborately crafted plate? As they walked to the car in silence, Shona looked up at the sky as if she expected to see thunder clouds gathering there. He thought she must be beginning to hate him. So her next words came as a surprise. "I don't know about you but I could do with a drink."

Chapter Sixteen

Shona Patterson

I need my head examining, she thought as they drove away from the Coulters' house. Bunking off to go for a drink in the middle of the day was the least of her misdemeanours. She had actively involved a suspect in an investigation and instead of taking him in for further questioning, she was inviting him to the pub.

Nevertheless, it was difficult to regard Brian as a potential murderer. She had known corrupt policeman over the years: some of them now serving a stretch inside; others forced to resign; and still others whom she suspected were even now taking back-handers and flying below the radar. Brian had never been like them. His journey through the ranks had been a straight line guided by an unwavering moral compass.

She supposed he had been something of a hero in her eyes. He had been driven by a need to root out wrongdoing that seemed noble to her

191

and he had always shown unfailing compassion for the victims of crime and those suffering collateral damage. Inwardly she gave herself a shake. For God's sake, he was hardly going to sneak up an alley and rip off his suit to reveal a blue outfit with red underpants over his tights.

Didn't this business demonstrate he was just as weak as most of the men she had encountered? Throw enough temptation at them and they succumbed. They were like dogs following a bitch in heat, unable to resist their own basic instincts.

Then again, part of her was aware that her jaundiced view of the male gender was conditioned by her everyday dealings with the detritus of the town; the bottom-feeders who, when eventually caught in the net, were ugly and squirming in their futile attempts at self-preservation.

Her impressions were hardly enhanced by her own failed relationships with inadequate men. And perhaps this had been an aberration for Brian. After all, grief and loneliness damaged people, even those who seemed resilient and strong.

She was so preoccupied by her own thoughts that she was hardly aware that they had travelled to the town centre in silence. Brian probably thought her lack of conversation indicated her condemnation of his behaviour, while for his part he no doubt thought that he ought to keep quiet in case she changed her mind and drove him to the station.

She pulled into a space outside the Wallace Arms, ignoring the double yellow lines. She noticed Brian raising a questioning eyebrow as they went into the pub but only spoke to ask her what she wanted.

"Guinness."

"Half pint?"

"Pint."

Again that raised an eyebrow but he knew better than to remind her she was driving. He ordered two pints of Guinness from the young barmaid, who gave Shona an awkward smile.

"Is Colin working today?"

"He's in the cellar changing a barrel. Be up in a minute."

Brian carried both their pints to a table across from the bar. She took a long swallow and wiped her top lip self-consciously. She didn't want Brian to see her with a moustache of white foam.

He looked around at the lunch time customers of which there were a reasonable number. The Wallace had a good reputation for reasonably priced, hearty pub grub. "Why are we here?" he asked.

"Mrs. Tyler's - sorry, Irene Dunlop's - body was found in the yard behind here. We think this is the last place she was seen alive." He looked around as if he might see her ghost sitting at one of the surrounding tables. She saw Colin emerging from the door to the cellar and go to the bar where the barmaid - it was Terri something she remembered - said something to him and nodded towards their table. He affected a nonchalant air as he sauntered over to them.

"Inspector? You found oot who killed that woman, then?"

"Not yet." He looked questioningly at Brian but she wasn't going to offer any introductions. "Colin, you told us she was drinking in here with someone. Would you recognise her if you saw her again?"

"No sure like. Mebbe. As I said they were good looking for their age, like, if you ken what I mean." He smiled at Brian as if he would understand the masculine appreciation of attractive women. Brian remained stony-faced. She took out the photograph from the Coulters.

"Do you recognise the woman standing in the background of this photograph?"

He stared at it for a few moments, turning his head to the side as if that would help him to see it more clearly. "Braw place."

Frustrated, she said, "The woman in the photograph. Could that be who you saw in the bar that night?"

"Could be. Her hair was different, like, from what I can remember. Colour and that. And you can't see her that well in this, like." He handed the photograph back. "Do you think she done it, like?"

"We're just trying to identify possible witnesses at the moment. Thanks for your help."

"You havin' food? I can recommend the steak pie, like."

"No - just a quick drink." He strolled back, collecting a few empty glasses as he went.

Brian waited 'til he was out of earshot. "You think he might be a suspect?"

"Unlikely, but we can't rule anything out at the moment. He claims to have found the body, though given his predilection for older women - don't they call them MILFs? - he might have ..." She halted and took a sip of her drink.

"Come on, Shona. What are you not telling me? I know I've put you in an impossible position but you must know me well enough to realise all I want to do is help. I'm not trying to cover my own back."

She hesitated. Her logical mind told her that she shouldn't involve him any further. She had compromised the investigation already. But she had always trusted her instincts and she was convinced he was being honest. He would never have confided in her otherwise and admitted to behaviour he must know she would find reprehensible. Besides, part of her longed for their old partnership, putting their heads together and tugging at the threads of cases until they unravelled. His clear-eyed insights and her emotional intelligence had made them a formidable team.

"At first, we thought this might be a random attack, though if it had been a mugging her bag would have been stolen. Then there's the mystery surrounding her identity and what we now know about her involvement in blackmail. Then there was the way the body was discovered. Her skirt was pulled up."

Brian took a sip of his drink, obviously to disguise his discomfort. "Couldn't that have been accidental? The way she fell. And her assailant would have been too busy covering his or her tracks to have been bothered by a detail like that."

"You've heard of pencil skirts? They have a straight narrow cut and are tailored for a close fit. That's what she was wearing. It wouldn't just have flipped up when she fell. Someone must have pulled it up deliberately."

"Maybe it happened before she was killed - someone who'd misread the signals, was trying it on with her and then striking out when she resisted. Or perhaps she was with someone willingly and was attacked then."

"There was no evidence of sexual activity. And if someone else had been with her what happened to them? Anyway, a sudden impulse to have sex in a filthy yard surrounded by rubbish skips. It just doesn't fit somehow."

Brian glanced over to where Colin was bringing over lunch to a couple a few tables away, holding two plates with a cloth in each hand. "So you think our young barman might have interfered with the body?"

"It's possible. I don't know though. He wasn't giving out those kind of signals when I interviewed him."

"And what do you think happened with the woman we now know as Eleanor Thomson? Had she left before it happened? Or when Irene didn't come back to the bar did she go looking for her, discover the body and take to her heels, afraid of what might come out about them? There's always the possibility that she did it, of course, but what possible motive did she have? A falling out of thieves?"

The doubting voices that were clamouring in Shona's head were quieter now as she and Brian fell back into their old rhythms of questions and likelihoods.

"What next?" he asked. She thought she detected a note of trepidation.

"You'll have to come in and make a statement. And now we know the identities of these two women it should be easier to trace their activities and track Eleanor Thomson down." Her mobile rang. It was Sergeant Cameron. "Garry, I was just about to come in." She listened in disbelief before telling him that she was on her way.

"What's wrong? What's happened? Brian asked, concerned, as she failed to hide her stunned reaction.

"They've discovered a body in the grounds of St. Stephen's church."

She registered the fearful look in his eyes,

"I know what you're thinking but it's not Eleanor Thomson. It's the body of a man."

Chapter Seventeen

Angus Moir

He examined his face in the bathroom mirror as he tried to staunch the blood pouring from his nose. He thought it might be broken. Already bruises were beginning to discolour his face, a particularly livid one on the left of his jaw. His tongue tentatively probed a tooth that was loose in its socket.

What had possessed him and Macdonald to think his idea would have any more chance of succeeding than a lost soul's prayer in hell? Yes, he reflected, hell had become only too real and familiar to him over the last couple of days. Tears of self-pity rolled down his battered face. He had left Marian crying downstairs. Her face had gone ashen at the sight of his bloodied face when he returned home. At least Rachel had been out when he returned, but how would she react when she saw the state of him?

A mugging, he had told his wife. He had only just managed to persuade her not to phone the police. He would do it in the morning, he said. Anyway it would be pointless because he hadn't got a good look at his attackers. It had happened so quickly and after the first punch to his face he had been too dazed and too preoccupied in trying to prevent further damage. He had just laid in the road as they robbed him.

That reminded him. He would have to dispose of his wallet and cancel his credit cards to make his lie more credible. And how was he going to explain the money he had taken out of their joint savings account that morning? Layer upon layer of lies. They were like handfuls of earth pouring down on him 'til he felt they would bury him alive.

Despite the distraction of his throbbing nose and aching jaw, his brain kept replaying the scene from the churchyard. He and Macdonald standing among the trees after they had deposited the sports bag with their collected cash. Macdonald setting up a camera on a tripod he said he had bought years ago second hand from one of his own outlets. Both of them standing in the damp chill of the night 'til the unmistakeable figure of Leon appeared eventually and he alerted Macdonald.

He had been examining the contents of the bag when Angus approached him. He had looked up, his handsome face contorted in fury. "Are you having a laugh, minister?" The last word delivered with ironic venom. Then he had spotted the light from the camera and raced towards it. Macdonald had been struck violently to the ground before Leon smashed the camera again and again against the trunk of a tree. When he had begun to hit the supine man on the ground with the tripod, Angus had simply stood there shivering, rooted to the ground by his craven helplessness. He felt warm urine running down his leg when Leon turned and began to move back to him.

His memory then became more blurred, though the shock of Leon's fist exploding in his face was vivid still. He had read about people seeing stars when they had been almost knocked out but all he could recollect was the way the pain seemed to overwhelm him so that it blotted out the cherry tree and the dankness of the churchyard. His legs had folded beneath him as if they had suddenly been made of paper and the earth seemed to rise to meet him. When his vision cleared he had seen the man looming hugely above him, fist raised. He recalled the coppery taste of warm blood as it ran down his throat mingled with the salt of his tears.

He had scrambled to his knees, his hands raised in supplication, his only thought to avoid being hit again as Leon grasped his throat and leaned towards him. His face was so close he could smell his alcohol and tobacco breath.

"No more of this shit from you and your new pal. You have the rest of the cash here by tomorrow night or I guarantee you will suffer. You know all about the agonies of hell, minister. If you try to fuck with me again, I promise you I'll visit them on you in this life."

Leon had left him grovelling on the ground as he grabbed the bag. As he moved away, Angus had struggled to his feet, grasping the trunk of the tree as dizziness threatened to overcome him. He saw Macdonald on all fours trying to get up as Leon stood over him, no doubt issuing similar threats to him. He watched as Leon launched a kick into Macdonald's midriff that lifted him onto his back. The sight galvanised Angus into a staggering run from the scene, moving as swiftly as he could through the gravestones, falling several times.

As he stripped off his filthy clothes in the bathroom, he could hardly bear to look at himself in the mirror. His legs and arms were covered in scrapes and bruises but they were nothing compared to the damage to his own sense of self. Even as he had watched Leon administering a further series of kicks to his erstwhile accomplice as he lay among the trees, the thought of trying to intervene never entered his head. His one desire had been to get away as quickly as he could to save his own skin - a shambling, stumbling coward who had wet his pants and cried. He was transported back to childhood memories of the school playground where he had handed over his lunch money to the bullies without putting up any resistance.

Ironic thoughts raced randomly through his mind - the words to the hymn 'Onward Christian Soldiers'; the Lord helps those who help themselves; the courage and sacrifice of Christ Himself and all the martyrs who had come after Him. He wasn't fit to wash their feet. At this moment, he felt too miserable and despicable even to attempt to pray.

And what now? He would have to find out how Archie was tomorrow and decide what they were going to do. Thinking of the man whom he had abandoned so readily by his Christian name turned the screw of his self-loathing even more.

He quickly dressed in his pyjamas and had just got into bed when Marian appeared. "I'm worried about you, dear. Don't you think it would be better to call the police tonight? And you ought to go to A and E. You might have a concussion."

"No!" He realised that he had shouted at her. To hide his vehemence, he said more quietly, "Tomorrow will be time enough for the police and

I'm okay, Marian, really. Just a few cuts and bruises. It looks worse than it is. They only hit me once and knocked me down."

She looked doubtful so he grasped her hand. "Thank you for worrying though. A couple of paracetamols and a hot drink would be just the thing. Do we have any cocoa?"" She seemed unconvinced by his attempt at a reassuring smile but patted his hand and bustled off to get him his drink and pills.

When she had gone he suddenly remembered his wallet was still in the pocket of his jacket that was hanging behind the bathroom door. He leapt out of bed to retrieve it, aggravating the throbbing pain in his head and face. He retrieved the wallet and buried it under a pile of underwear in his chest of drawers. He would have to get rid of it tomorrow.

As he lay back down, his head felt as if it might explode. Part of him welcomed the pain. He deserved to suffer. Perhaps Marian was right and Leon had done some serious damage to his brain and he would die from it in the night. How much easier that would be.

The next day would bring no respite from his dilemmas; no escape from his lies; no balm for his soul. His jumbled thoughts turned to Shakespeare. How often his plays touched presciently on the human condition. Angus was even now drowning in Hamlet's 'sea of troubles'. And what had Macbeth said about being 'steeped in blood so that were I to wade no more, returning would be as tedious as to go o'er'? In his case, for 'blood' read 'lies'.

The more he wrestled with the serpents that writhed agonisingly in his brain, the more he saw the inevitability of his fate. He would have to see Macdonald and persuade him to go to the police with him. The consequences would be unbearable, it was true. The ignominy of their exposure would surely force them both to resign - he from his ministry and Macdonald from his post with the charity.

And then what? How would Marian and Rachel react? If by some miracle they stood by him, they would still have to uproot themselves from here. Obviously they couldn't live in the manse any longer but equally they couldn't live in the town either, having to bear the whispering and sniggering that would go on behind their backs. Perhaps some people would be openly hostile, only too glad to take the opportunity to throw his hypocrisy in his face. He would be seen as the man who preached goodness and committed evil; the man who railed against sin but was drenched in sin himself; the man of God who turned his back on God.

No. He had to cling to his faith. He would have to find a way to swim back, however much the current threatened to pull him under. He slid from the bed onto his knees, embracing the agony that jarred his head and limbs. "Dear Lord, I kneel before Thee in my despair and worthlessness. I welcome Thy punishment. I know I deserve to be cast into night. But I beseech Thee to leave one candle burning that I may seek it in the darkness and find my way back to Thee."

He heard Marian return. He looked up at her. He could discern the anxiety and rising panic in her eyes but she only said, "Here we are - a nice cup of cocoa to make you feel better."

Chapter Eighteen

Shona Patterson

She sped to St. Stephen's after leaving Brian in the pub. She had offered to drop him off home en route but he had insisted on walking. Cameron met her at the churchyard entrance.

"The body's round the back among some trees. The church is still locked up." He led the way as they went around to the rear of the building. She saw a forensic team busily at work and noticed the diminutive figure of Dr. Lawrence among them, looking like a child accompanying the grown-ups. They donned their protective suits, Shona reflecting that they didn't make these for the female figure as she struggled to pull it up over her backside. They lifted the police tape and approached the trees.

Lawrence had been leaning over the body but looked up and nodded to her as she stood a few feet away. The victim was lying on his back. He looked to have been young, well-dressed and muscular. Perhaps he had been good-looking but someone had done their best to obliterate his face. However, the first thing that she noticed was that his jeans had been pulled down to mid-thigh and he hadn't been wearing any underwear. Despite herself, she found her eyes being drawn to his penis, which was very large and lolled obscenely against the dark skin of his upper right thigh.

She caught Cameron noticing her gaze. "Don't get many of those to the pound," he said. She looked away quickly.

"When was he found and by whom?"

"Found this afternoon by a Harry Westwater. He works part-time maintaining the church grounds and graveyard." Lawrence approached. "Inspector, I hate to say this but it appears murders are like buses. None come along for ages then two appear together. What on earth is going on in the sedate little town of Dunmalcolm? If this keeps up I'm going to request a transfer to Glasgow for a quieter life."

"He was murdered then?"

"I'd say he's been lying here from sometime last night - around eleven or twelve o' clock. Mixed-race male, twenties, struck initially from behind with something heavy. By the look of the wound at the back of his head I'd say the weapon was club-like, perhaps a tree branch but my best guess would be something like a cricket or baseball bat. As you can see, he was also struck several times in the face."

"If he was struck from behind wouldn't he be face down?" Cameron asked.

"He's been dragged into this area where the trees are a bit thicker. Not much of an attempt to conceal the body and the injuries to the face suggest someone must have turned him over. As you can see his - er - clothing is also in some disarray."

"Yes. Hard to ignore the elephant in the room or rather the elephant's trunk."

"Stop with the inappropriate jokes, Sergeant."

"Sorry boss."

But even as she was admonishing Cameron she found her eyes drifting back to the man's cock. Act like an objective, fucking professional, Shona, she chided herself. "How come his - his - jeans are pulled down like that?"

"Several explanations come to mind. Perhaps he had been engaged in some kind of sexual activity and his partner struck him during or after the act."

Cameron interrupted, "Maybe he was caught short and came into the trees for a crap."

"Again, possible. Or the jeans were lowered post-mortem. I'll know more later."

Cameron turned to her and voiced her own unspoken thoughts. "Bit of a coincidence. Two bodies found within days of each other. Both left exposed in one way or another."

Lawrence interjected. There's something else. Come over here." Lawrence led them to another area among the trees where two members of the forensic team were engaged in gathering evidence. "This is where the initial attack took place. You can see some blood spatters and the area of flattened grass. There are drag marks leading over there to the body. The thing is there are signs of more than one body here."

"He fought back and there was a scuffle on the ground here?" asked Cameron.

"Unlikely, given that he was struck from behind with some force but someone else was on the ground here and there are small traces of blood leading away from the trees and out of the churchyard."

"That could be the murderer's. Maybe he was injured by this guy and when he turned away he took his chance to club him down," said Cameron.

"Possible. But another curious element is this." Lawrence pointed to what looked like pieces of plastic and electronic components lying near one of the trees. "Those are pieces of a camera."

"Camera?" Shona exclaimed. Cameron looked at her curiously.

"Looks as if someone smashed it against the tree with some force. The broken tripod is lying over there. And another thing. Over by that cherry tree there's more blood and signs that someone fell there."

"This guy and his attacker start a scrap over there. One of them tries to get away but the other one catches him and it all kicks off again over here," Cameron conjectured.

"Again another possibility. We're taking samples of the blood so I ought to get a better picture when they're analysed." Lawrence went back to his examinations as Shona stood silently lost in the tangled thicket of her own thoughts.

"What's up boss? Why did you look so surprised when the Doc mentioned the camera?"

She drew Cameron out of the earshot of the forensics team. "There's something else happening here. Two bodies; both with fatal head injuries; both partly undressed; and both somehow connected to this church."

"Might be a good idea to have another word with Reverend whatsisname - Moir. Remember how jumpy he was when we spoke to him. That would be a story for the tabloids if he turns out to be killing people for some kind of weird sexual gratification. Shit, that sounds far-fetched even as I'm saying it."

"Nevertheless, he might be connected to this somehow."

"Skeletons rattling around in his closet among the vestments?" He stopped as he noticed Shona's look of unease. "Do you know something you're not telling me?" She clearly hesitated for too long because he continued, "And you still haven't explained about what was going through your mind when the camera was mentioned."

Shona was perfectly aware that Brian's involvement would have to come out sooner or later so she quickly filled her Sergeant in on the bare bones of what he had told her. She found herself beginning to clarify her own thoughts, picking them up like cards that had been thrown up in the air and rearranging them.

Brian had been blackmailed by the first murder victim, Irene Dunlop. She had an accomplice, Eleanor Thomson, who was already guilty of extorting money from her rich employer. Wasn't it striking that a hidden camera was used in the Coulters' house and now, at the scene of a second murder, the remains of a camera had been discovered? Cameron listened with growing agitation. At last he could contain himself no longer.

"You should have brought Lockwood in right away. You know as well as I do that he must be in the frame for the Dunlop killing. I can't believe you took him to the Coulters' house."

"I know how this looks, Garry. Believe me, you couldn't beat me up about how far I went off the book any more than I have myself. But I've known Brian for years. Every instinct tells me he couldn't murder anyone."

"Listen to yourself. We both know the most placid and law-abiding citizen is capable of behaving like an animal if they feel they've been backed into a corner." He stopped as a thought occurred to him. "Did you say Lockwood first met the woman at this church?"

"Yes," she murmured.

"Christ, Inspector, this gets worse and worse. He's not only linked to one murder; he's linked to the scene of a second one."

"That's pretty tenuous as, I guess, is the camera thing. These two murders might not be connected at all. But you're right, we can't ignore the similarities. Something tells me the key to this is the blackmail element."

"We have to bring Lockwood in. Whatever relationship you two have had in the past, even you must see he's our number one suspect for Irene Dunlop's killing." She wanted to tell him that there was more to her conviction that Brian was innocent than their previous friendship. But she had to acknowledge that her feelings might be clouding her judgement. Those same feelings had made her behave less than professionally already and she knew herself well enough not to recognise that for her, this was hardly uncharacteristic conduct.

So she bit back her anger and frustration and simply nodded in agreement.

"And when you're in the DCI's office telling her about all this, I plan to be hunkered down in a bunker at a safe distance. When she explodes, you can scrape her off the walls and ceiling."

Bruce Adam

Chapter Nineteen

Brian Lockwood

As soon as he had got home from the pub, Brian called Ali Oop. He knew he should attempt to put the case aside - lock it in a box 'til Shona did her job and, Pandora-like, opened it up. His own troubles would then be exacerbated, beginning with the inevitable knock on the door and invitation to visit his old work-place.

But he knew he couldn't just sit there and wait for the storm. He asked Ali if he had made any progress in finding out more about Irene Dunlop. "Some interestin' shit there, ya cunt," Ali had said with his usual delicate phone etiquette. "Buy me a pint and I'll fill you in."

Brian arranged to meet him at the usual watering hole in a couple of hours but first told him about Eleanor Thomson, AKA Angela Smith. "Aye. That's the whoor whose pants ye were rootin' aboot in ya dirty bastard." Despite the fact that Ali couldn't see him at the end of the phone, he felt the blush spread over his face.

He set off to walk back to the town centre in plenty of time for his meeting with Ali. He probably could have taken the car since he had barely drunk half of his pint of Guinness in the Wallace but that was also one of the reasons he thought he might join Ali in a pint at the Nappy and besides, he wanted something of the numbness a couple of pints might provide.

The bar was quieter than it had been the last time he and Ali had met there, though what clientele there was would again hardly have graced the cocktail bar at the Balmoral. He ordered a pint of lager and a pint of Guinness from the tattooed barmaid who seemed to have acquired even more piercings and sat once more at the table by the window. He was half-way down his beer before Ali arrived.

The latter twitched and jerked into his seat and took a long swallow of his lager before grimacing as if he had just imbibed a draught of pig's urine. "Sorry I'm a wee bit late but I thought I'd do a preliminary search on that whoor you had your tongue up." Brian looked round the pub anxiously. He found Ali's predilection for bluntness was one of his least endearing qualities, though his companion was blissfully unaware of any offence he might cause others.

After a few of his customary verbal tics, that included random phrases like 'spaghetti hoopla', 'ice bandits' and an exhortation to 'lick ba's', Ali said, "First the Irene whoor. Used to live in Morningside - typical of you to want to go oot wi' posh cunts. She divorced Mr. Dunlop three years ago so that bit was true; no kids; maiden name Irene Walker. Worked in a real estate agents but after the divorce no employment history. But here's the interesting bit, ya cunt."

Brian leaned towards him to urge him to go on as Ali paused for more non-sequiturs, gurning, body tapping and sloppy lager sipping. "A few months before the fuckin' divorce, she was involved in a court case. Claims this rich cunt raped her. "

The revelation shocked Brian. "Who was it?"

"That local entrepreneur," - Ali pronounced it enterprenhoor - "turned multi-millionaire Arnold

Hastings. Made a fortune in double-glazing. Loads of friends in high and low places if you ken what I mean. Gives a substantial wedge to various charities so he's a fine fuckin' upstandin' member of the community probably on the way to his MBE."

"What happened?"

Ali uttered a few more bizarre phrases as Brian struggled to conceal his impatience. "She said this cunt had invited her up to his hotel room after some charity do because he was interested in discussin' some properties her agency had for sale. Then she claimed he jumped her. He didnae deny he fucked her but claimed the sex was consensual. His word against hers. Not guilty. She had nae chance against Mr. fuckin' citizen of the year and his expensive lawyers."

"But how did you find out about her? Isn't the victim in these cases guaranteed anonymity?"

"She waived it so she could have a right go at all the cunts she felt had cocked up the case. The legal system and that. But especially the polis. Said your lot had seriously fucked up the investigation from day one. First officer that had interviewed her apparently had treated her wi' a' the sensitivity of a fuckin' pimp demandin' a blow job. Well no' in so many words but that was the gist of it. Said there was a fuckin' conspiracy that protected cunts like Hastings."

Ali rattled his empty glass on the table so Brian left him fidgeting and uttering nonsense to head to the bar to get him a refill. He felt as if a nest of wasps had taken residence in his brain. He had always been methodical and loath to jump to conclusions 'til all the evidence was laid out before him. But he couldn't resist the thought that Isabel/Irene could have been motivated by revenge and a grudge against the police. Maybe that was why she had singled him out.

After Dennis Coulter's confession, Brian had no doubt that he wasn't the only victim of the two women. And Ali's discovery suggested Coulter and Hastings could both fit the profile of someone Irene and her accomplice would want to go after - rich, amoral men who pursued their own selfish desires, disregarding the damage they inflicted on others and thinking themselves untouchable.

Even as these thoughts swarmed through his brain, he realised he wasn't just jumping the gun, he was half-way to the finish line. He had to calm down and try to be objective. It was all very well to speculate on Irene's motives but he had to acknowledge that her anger at the system might not have been her only driving force. There was the money for a start. Perhaps the fall-out from the rape incident had left her strapped for cash.

Then there was Eleanor Thomson. How had she become involved with Irene? As he made his way back with the drinks, he couldn't rid himself of the nagging possibility that one of her blackmail victims may have been more powerful and ruthless than she estimated and that had led to her death.

It was as if Ali had eavesdropped on his internal monologue. "As for the other bitch, I havenae been able to get much on her in a couple of hours. Eleanor Welles before she became Mrs. Thomson. She's local. Went to school here. After that she did catering at the college. Then she had a wee cleaning business for a while. Her and her man had a flat in the town up 'til last year. Then here's the odd fuckin' thing. She disappeared aff the radar. I'll do more diggin' when I get back though."

"It's amazing you've found out so much in such a short time."

"Clever cunt, me."

"I don't suppose you happened to find a connection to Irene Dunlop?"

"For fuck's sake, gie me a break. One thing though - might be nothin'."

Brian felt a familiar tingle on the back of his neck and had to restrain himself from grabbing Ali's arm, as he took another long swig of his lager.

"Mr. Thomson wasn't the ideal fuckin' husband apparently. Get this - your lot had to go round to the Thomsons' flat a few times. Neighbours reported shoutin' and bangin' comin' fae the premises. Sounded as if someone was gettin' attacked. Down in the files as fuckin' domestic disturbances but nobody was charged. No' even so much as a caution. But one thing's for sure, she doesnae live there now. Flat was sold by a Ben Thomson last May. Her name's no' on the fuckin' property deeds. He seems to have moved to a one-bedroom flat in Kirkcaldy. No sign of her."

Brian didn't like to contemplate how easily Ali seemed to be able to access police and other files but he was certain it wasn't legal. He choked back his reservations. "So they appear to have split."

"Aye. Trail goes cold for her then. But nae fuckin' worries. I just need a bit more time."

"Okay, Ali, give me the addresses you have for Eleanor's old flat and her husband's new one."

Again, Brian couldn't stop his imagination from going into overdrive. If Eleanor was escaping an abusive marriage, she might want to pull a veil of secrecy over her whereabouts. And his instincts told him it was no coincidence that both the women in this case had a similar history of abuse at the hands of men. Another tentative thought occurred to him. Both women had received less than satisfactory treatment by the authorities.

Perhaps all of this could be part of a vendetta against the male sex and anyone in the system they thought had let them down in the past. That may have been what connected him and Dennis Coulter as victims. He was aware that he was making another massive leap of reasoning. For a moment he was back in his nightmare. Here he was once more clutching at flimsy wreckage to keep him afloat in a high sea.

He knew he ought to let Shona and her team connect the dots. But he wasn't driven simply by his impatience to find some kind of closure; to be able to sleep easily again, compelling as that was. He was a suspect in Irene Dunlop's murder and he had to clear his name, so his first port of call had to be police headquarters. He knew there was little they could do to hold him and after that, he wasn't prepared to back off.

After all, by using dark doorways and back entrances, he and Ali were ahead of the police already. The call Shona had received in the

Wallace had rushed her to another fatal incident. It was tempting to surmise that the location of the other body meant there was a link to Irene. Equally, however, the body discovered in the churchyard might be a separate case entirely and that would mean the police's attention would be divided between two separate investigations.

Ali was swallowing the last of his beer as Brian urged, "Give me what you have so far and keep digging."

"Will do. You'll get the bill. Your fuckin' pension must stretch."

Chapter Twenty
Shona Patterson

"The PM reveals that my first impressions were correct. He was struck with some force from behind with a blunt object. The initial blow didn't kill him but it would most certainly have incapacitated him."

Shona and Cameron were in the mortuary standing over the naked body from the churchyard as Dr. Lawrence laid out his findings. "Then he was bludgeoned repeatedly and that's what killed him. Oh, and he had engaged in anal intercourse recently, though his jeans were pulled down post-mortem."

Cameron looked appalled. "Christ, I wouldn't fancy something that size up my arse." Inevitably, Shona's gaze was drawn back to the man's penis before she pointedly turned to Cameron to conceal her embarrassment. "Does the ID in his wallet check out?"

Cameron looked at his notes. "Aye. He's one Liam Jeffries. A number of convictions for drug related offences, soliciting and a few assaults. It looked like he frequently operated as a male prostitute probably to feed his habit. Male and female clients apparently."

"What woman pays for sex?"

"Lonely women maybe, older women, ugly women, women who want a walk on the wild side?"

She knew Cameron was no doubt right but she still struggled with the concept.

"Though Jeffries' clientele were mainly men according to his record."

"So he might have been in the churchyard turning tricks," she said.

"Maybe. Certainly quiet enough there."

Lawrence interjected, "The blood samples we took showed evidence of at least two more people being at the scene. There was the victim's blood of course, but there was also someone else's blood close to it and leading out of the yard and neither sample matches the blood that was found over by the cherry tree. Also, the ground was damp so we have impressions of several footprints."

Shona looked puzzled. "This is weird. At least three people injured near the church. What was it? Some kind of mass brawl?"

"Who goes into a churchyard for a ruck at that time of night?" Cameron added.

As they left the mortuary to head back to the station, Cameron reluctantly broached the subject of bringing Brian in for questioning.

Shona fought to keep the irritation out of her voice, "Just let me give him a call and ask him to come in for interview. There's no need to make a public spectacle of going to his home and taking him away in a squad car."

"And what if he doesn't come in under his own steam?"

"I know him. He will." She hurriedly went on, "How much more do we know about Irene Dunlop? And have we tracked down Eleanor Thomson yet?"

"There's still a bit of mystery there. We know Dunlop was a divorcee. Worked for a while in an Estate Agents. You remember the rape allegations against Arnold Hastings a few years ago?"

"The double glazing guy?"

"Well-known businessman, benefactor and all-round solid citizen."

"And sleazy crook. That was her?"

"Jury found Hastings not guilty. Prosecution did their best but they were always on a hiding to nothing. Even the fact that bruising on her body seemed to indicate she had been involved in a struggle didn't hold up. His lawyers just claimed she liked it rough. She got divorced not long after the trial. Make of that what you will. Then she effectively disappears 'til her little church visit that we know about. Interestingly, her pal Thomson seems to have done the same. Had a flat in town with her husband but when they split, she seems to have gone to ground as well."

When they arrived at the station she was unsurprised to discover that she had been summoned to the DCI's office. As she waited outside her door she felt the same trepidation she remembered from her schooldays when she had been called to the headmistress's office. Morton threw open her door and curtly told her to come in. She didn't invite her to sit down. Morton's thin-lipped mouth was a straight line. Shona's first thought was that she didn't suit the pale lipstick she always favoured and that, with her colouring, she could afford to go for something bolder. Shit, she had to concentrate. Her career might be on the line.

Morton said, "So now we have two murders on our patch and we appear to have made little progress." Her passive face and quiet voice unnerved Shona more than if she had transformed into a snarling fury determined to rip her to shreds. The only sign of her anger was a slight tic she had under her left eye, that Shona had noticed before when she was tongue-lashing - albeit similarly sotto voce - some hapless officer for his or her perceived incompetence.

"On the contrary, ma'am. We now know the identity of the first victim and a possible motive for her murder. We believe that she, acting with a female accomplice, was involved in a blackmail scam. We're in the process of tracking down this other woman. We know too that the other murder victim was a rent boy called Liam Jeffries and we'll be investigating his recent contacts."

"The informant about the blackmail being your ex-colleague, Inspector Lockwood." She managed to inject a note of bitter reproach into her words.

"Yes."

"For fuck's sake, Shona, what were you thinking? Involving a suspect in an investigation? I know you two were close once but taking him along to interview possible witnesses? Who do you think you are - fucking Batman and Wonder Woman?"

Somehow, Morton's use of expletives delivered in her steady voice alarmed Shona even more.

"And why isn't he sitting in an interview room downstairs as we speak?"

The neatly placed phone on her desk rang. She looked at it as if it had just told her that her blouse needed ironing as she snatched it up. "Yes." The look she gave Shona as she listened could have frozen sea water. "Right."

"Brian Lockwood is downstairs asking to speak to Inspector Patterson." Shona didn't dare to look into her eyes. "Under no circumstances are you to interview him. Get Cameron and Buckle to do it under caution.

"But ..."

"And I'll have to review your role in this investigation." To signal that the discussion was over, she sat at her desk and became absorbed in the papers that had been stacked there with military precision.

Shona swallowed back the bile of her anger and disappointment and left the office. She ascertained that DS Cameron and DC Buckle were in interview room two, so she went into the adjoining room to observe them through the two-way mirror. Cameron and Buckle sat opposite Brian, the two detectives looking like a more sartorially elegant and better looking Laurel and a more dishevelled Hardy.

After he had cautioned Brian and he had waived his right to have a lawyer present, Cameron went on the attack immediately, aggressively interrogating him about his relationship with Irene Dunlop. Brian related the story he had told Shona already in a calm voice, though she detected a tremor in it when he reached the bedroom incident. She noticed Buckle shifting uncomfortably in his chair. When Brian revealed that he had received a film of the incident and a demand for money, Cameron asked him if he had believed he had committed an offence.

After a pause, Brian replied, "I've thought long and hard about this and I'm not trying to excuse my conduct but I don't think there was anything criminal about it."

Buckle chipped in, "Then why not come to the police?"

Brian smiled ironically and said, "Because stupidly I cared about what people would think."

"And you're not worried that people might think you went to the Wallace Arms with the intention of shutting Irene Dunlop up."

Brian was silent so Buckle asked him where he was between 9.00 and 11.00 on the evening of the murder. Brian's reply both stunned and infuriated Shona.

"I was next door at my neighbour, Mrs. Edith Brown's house. She often calls on me when she's having trouble with her Sky TV channels. Usually it's simple to sort out. She's around eighty years of age and the technology sometimes confuses her. That night was no exception but she insisted on me staying for tea and cake and we ended up watching two back-to-back episodes of 'Game of Thrones'.

"A bit racy for an old woman," Buckle offered.

"She's remarkably unperturbed by depictions of sex and violence on screen it would seem."

"And she'll confirm that you were with her at that time?" Shona saw that Cameron was trying to conceal his frustration.

"Yes. She may be old but she's sharp as a tack and there's nothing wrong with her memory."

"We'll be checking nevertheless."

There was no course of action left for the detectives but to wind up the interview with the warning that he might be called back for further questioning and to let him go. If Shona had been in their shoes, she would have had difficulty working out if Brian had committed any offence for which he could be charged.

Shona seethed. If Edith Brown confirmed his account, Brian had had an alibi for the murder all along. She exited hurriedly before the three men left the interview room and raced to the car park. It was raining heavily but she ignored the drops that peppered her jacket and her uncovered hair. She felt as if they might evaporate in the heat from her anger.

She waylaid Brian as he emerged to get his car. He was unsurprised to see her but regarded her remorsefully. "What the fuck are you playing at, Brian? Why didn't you tell me you had an alibi for the night of the murder?"

"I'm really sorry, Shona. I wanted to tell you but I suppose I desperately needed to know if you believed in me for myself. You probably know me better than any woman I've known apart from Candice and there were even things the two of us shared that I never took home to her. I needed to know we still had that bond of trust."

"Are you telling me you were testing our friendship?" Shona felt tears of indignation stinging her eyes. She wanted to shrug off the hand he placed gently on her shoulder but let it rest there as she fought against the current of her conflicting emotions.

"I'm sorry, Shona. There have been times recently that I've felt like something people scrape off their shoe. My instincts screamed at me that if anyone could see the good in me it was you. I should have listened to them."

He looked so contrite that for a moment she wished he would pull her to him and put his arms around her. But he patted her shoulder and said, "If you can forgive me for my lack of faith, not to mention compromising your position, I'd still like us to stay in touch. And if there's anything I can do to help ..."

He tailed off as if he was afraid of the wounds she might inflict with words of rejection. Before he turned away he gave her an intense look that was dejected and melancholy but also perhaps contained a hopefulness that neither of them felt they deserved. She felt forlorn as she watched his car driving off through the rain.

Chapter Twenty-One

Brian Lockwood

He glanced in his mirror as he left the station car park and saw Shona still standing there in the rain. She looked so lost and bedraggled, his first impulse was to turn the car around, go back and sweep her into his arms. He knew that would neither be wise nor discreet and under the circumstances it probably wouldn't be welcomed.

He felt guilty about not telling her about the evening of the murder that he had spent with Mrs. Brown and some visceral violence, nudity and dragons. Especially when his instincts had proved correct and she had believed him enough not to insist on pulling him in as soon as he has told her about his involvement with the dead woman. In fact, she had stuck her neck out for him so far he hoped fervently that someone didn't take an axe to it.

He decided to give it some time for the dust to settle before he contacted her and shared some of his, admittedly tenuous, theories about Irene and her accomplice. In the meantime, he persuaded himself that it could do no harm to do a little clandestine investigation of his own. If the police wanted to rap his knuckles later, well he would just have to risk it.

He managed to find a short stay parking space in the High Street and searched for the address Ali had given him for Eleanor Thomson's old flat. He saw the number above a close entrance that was between a fruit shop and a travel agency.

As he went along the close, he tried to ignore the pungent stink of stale urine. Why the fuck couldn't people, usually men but not always, use the pub toilet before they headed for home? The blue door halfway along had an intercom system. There was no response from flat 14C so he pressed the buzzer for 14B. "Yes?" The voice was male and sounded querulous.

"Hello. I'm an old friend of Eleanor Thomson who used to stay in 14C. I wondered if the new occupants perhaps have a forwarding address for her but no-one seems to be in."

"Come up." The door release sounded and he made his way up the stairs inside. The banister rails were painted the same shade of blue as the exterior door. On the first level he saw a bespectacled man above looking down the stairwell observing his ascent. When Brian reached him he was standing at the open door of flat 14B. "Sorry. Thought this would be easier than talking through that thing downstairs." The man looked to be a few years older than him and somewhat incongruously was wearing a shirt and v neck jumper with a pair of cargo shorts and suede slippers.

"You'll not get Gillian and Doug at this time of day. They both work. As far as I know they don't have an address for Eleanor or that bastard she was married to but if you call back later they might have his solicitor's details."

"Thank you Mr.?"

"Edmondson."

"Have you lived here long yourself?"

"Eleven years."

"Did you know the Thomsons well?"

"She was okay. Bonny-looking woman. But I couldn't stand him. You say you're a friend of hers?"

"Was. Lost touch. Decided to look her up for old time's sake."

"Well I hope I'm not telling tales out of school here but Thomson treated that poor woman like shite. Pardon my French. I had to call the polis a few times. Heard him knocking her about upstairs. Not that the law did anything. Shower of useless bastards. I even complained when he threatened me. Said he'd kick my teeth in if I called the polis again. What did they do? Fuck all. Pardon my French. It was a relief when I heard she'd left the bastard. The night she snuck out when he was at the pub, he went berserk. I could hear him chucking furniture about and smashing stuff. If you ask me that lass had a lucky escape. She could do a lot better than that arsehole. Pardon my French. If you do manage to find her, tell her John was asking for her. That's me."

"Thanks Mr. Edmondson. And thanks for looking out for Eleanor."

"I only did what any good neighbour would. I mean that bastard could have killed her."

"If by any chance you should hear from her could you let me know?" Brian searched his pockets for his notebook to scribble his number on but Edmondson said,

"Hang on." He disappeared for a moment into his flat and emerged with a post-it note.

When Brian was back in the High Street he crossed over and looked at the building from the outside as if it would render up some clue. The Thomsons clearly had occupied the top two storeys but they were long gone and he felt he had reached a dead-end. He stood there motionless, his thoughts chasing each other like ghosts in a maze, as pedestrians manoeuvred around him impatiently.

He was torn. He could see if the new occupants of the flat could give him information that could lead him by a circuitous route to Eleanor's whereabouts. Or perhaps he should give up and leave the police to piece it all together. Shona was too astute to miss the connections between the two women's past experiences. Domestic abuse and sexual assault were on the same spectrum as far as he was concerned. But was it a significant factor in Irene's death? He doubted whether paying Eleanor's ex-partner a visit would yield up anything useful but he was running out of options.

As he stared upwards he caught a glimpse of John Edmondson peering out from behind the blinds of a window on the floor below. He quickly dropped the blinds back into place when he spotted Brian looking up.

He got back into his car and took the dual carriageway to Kirkcaldy. According to Google maps, Thomson's new flat was situated at the north end of the town. It turned out to be in a new-build apartment block with views over the Firth of Forth. The river was a uniform grey with two tankers anchored near the Edinburgh side. A small fishing boat was making its way east probably heading towards Pittenweem or Crail.

As he moved towards the building, huddling his coat around him against the chill of the wind that always seemed to blow off the Firth here, he noticed a battered looking blue van parked in the space reserved for residents. It had 'B S Thomson. Painter and Decorator' painted in fading lettering on its side. There was yet another intercom at the entrance and Brian was about to press it when the door swung open and a heavy set man came out in paint-spattered, white overalls.

"Mr. Thomson?"

"Aye. Who wants tae ken?"

"Sorry to bother you but I was hoping you might have a contact address for Eleanor."

At the sound of her name, the man turned scowling aggressively and moved suddenly close to Brian. Even under his painter's whites he looked as if he spent a great deal of time lifting weights in the gym. His chest and arms bulged with muscle. An air of sullen menace surrounded him like a bad smell.

"What the fuck do ye want wi' her?" He looked Brian up and down with his head tilted to one side like a badly acted heavy in a gangster movie. Brian thought on his feet.

"I'm an ex-policeman. I do a bit of work for a solicitor's firm. They're trying to locate Mrs. Thomson to inform her she's inherited a small legacy from a deceased relative's estate."

"She never had nae close relatives. At least she never mentioned any to me."

"Well, this particular relative wasn't close. Second cousin, I believe."

Thomson still loomed over Brian eyeing him suspiciously, before growling, "Well I cannae help ye. Havnae a fucking clue where she is."

"When was the last time you heard from her?"

"Listen pal, I havenae fucking heard from her a' right? Good luck findin' her because Christ kens I've tried to find out where she is. I never had a chance to say cheerio properly." He managed to imbue this last statement with so much latent threat that Brian knew instantly why Eleanor would want to avoid coming anywhere near this man. A thought suddenly seemed to cross Thomson's mind. "You been round our old flat? Talkin' to the neighbours by any chance? Talkin' to that nosy bastard, Edmondson mebbe?"

"I can't reveal my sources. Well, thanks for your help." As Brian attempted to leave, Thomson moved to block his path. For a moment, an unexpectedly humorous thought crossed Brian's mind. He knew the man's first name was Ben but the initials on Thomson's van might as well have suggested his first name was Brick and his middle name was Shithouse. "You no' wantin' to leave me your name and that so if hell freezes over and I do hear from her I can let her know."

"That won't be necessary. We have your address and I take it that's your phone number on the side of your van. We'll keep checking in if we can't locate her."

Thomson looked as if someone had just told him his Artexing job on their ceiling reminded them of the Sistine Chapel. "You no' wantin' to write it down?" he snarled suspiciously.

"I have an eidetic memory. That's one of the reasons I'm so good at my job. I only need to see something once and I remember it. Don't worry, Mr. Thomson, I won't forget you or our conversation today."

Brian hoped the man was savvy enough to detect the edge in his voice. With a final look that suggested should he run into him again in a dark alley it wouldn't go well, Thomson stepped aside.

He was about to drive off when his mobile rang - unknown caller. He was about to dismiss it - he had no time to be listening to someone telling him that he was recently in an accident that wasn't his fault - when an impulse made him answer it. He recognised the woman's voice instantly, even though it was quiet and tremulous.

"Please leave me alone. I promise you I'll do nothing with the film."

It only took him a moment to recognise the voice. "Eleanor? Mrs. Thomson?"

"Did you kill Irene?"

Her question made him catch his breath so that it took him a moment to reply.

"No. Of course not."

"You hesitated - are you lying?" He was conscious of Thomson still standing at his van glowering at him. Despite the fact that there was no way he could know that Brian was talking to his ex-partner, it made him uneasy.

"I promise you I've never killed anyone in my life. Even in the line of duty when I was with the police."

"Well, someone killed her and now they're after me."

"What makes you think that?"

"They've murdered someone else we knew. You think that's a coincidence?"

Brian was so taken aback that he was convinced that the watching Thomson couldn't fail to notice his astonished expression. Fortunately, with one last baleful stare he climbed into his van and drove off. Brian's thoughts were racing so much that he was unaware of his silence 'til Eleanor said, "Hello?"

"Sorry. You just took me by surprise. Could I meet you someplace to talk about this?"

"I don't trust you."

"Fair enough but if you think you're in danger you have to go to the police."

He could hear the bitterness in her laugh. "And that would solve everything. I've had dealings with them before and it didn't go well. Besides, what am I going to tell them? Do you think I relish the idea of going to jail for extortion?"

"Better than ending up like your friend Irene." He wanted to snatch back the words as soon as he uttered them.

"Don't try to find me."

"Wait." But she had rung off.

Brian tossed the phone onto the passenger seat. He knew he should have handled the conversation better but the truth was he had been wrong-footed from the moment he heard her voice. The fact that she had contacted him so soon after he had visited her old address told him that John Edmondson had been less than honest about his ignorance of Eleanor's whereabouts and his lack of contact with her.

And what was he to make of her shocking revelation about another murder? That had to refer to the body in the churchyard that Shona was investigating, surely. Dunmalcolm was hardly the murder capital of Scotland after all. He retrieved his phone to call Shona. It went straight to voicemail so he left a message. "Hi, Shona. I realise that I'm not your favourite person at the moment and I totally understand why. But could you please give me a call when you get this. It's rather urgent."

A sudden squall threw rain against his windscreen. He sat there as the car park, the building and the grey slab of the estuary became obscured by the rivulets of water on the car's windows. After all the ground-shifting shocks of the past few weeks, it was comforting to stay there in the silence broken only by the rattle of the rain and watch the town vanish as if it had been submerged.

But he started the engine and waited as the windscreen wipers at full speed struggled to sweep away the deluge. He had to act. Because there was no mistake about one thing he had detected in Eleanor's voice. The woman was scared to death.

Chapter Twenty-Two

Archie McDonald

When he came to he found himself lying on the entrance mat just inside the door to his flat. He tried to rise but his face seemed to be stuck to the fabric. He prised it off, feeling as if he was leaving pieces of skin behind. The mat and the surrounding floor were stained with blood. He attempted to move into a sitting position but every movement was agony.

Eventually he managed to prop himself upright against his door fighting a tide of nausea and pain that threatened to drown him. He was struggling to breathe. Something inside him felt broken.

He looked down at his clothes. They were filthy with blood and mud. Tentatively he pulled up his shirt that was hanging loose from his trousers. The livid red and purple bruises that ran up his abdomen to his chest made sickness rise into his throat. He fought it down. He now knew that being beaten black and blue wasn't just a cliché.

He had no memory of how he had eventually managed to get home. He had flashbacks of stumbling down streets that were deserted, hanging on to lamp posts, frequently falling. Losing consciousness and finding himself lying in the road staring up at the streetlights. Hauling himself up and somehow shambling on. A vague recollection of a figure standing over him and saying, "You a 'right neebs?" before it staggered off into the night.

Then there were other jumbled memories of the churchyard. That man. Strong and violent. His and Moir's plan collapsing, like the house made out of straw in the story of the three little pigs as soon as the Big Bad Wolf blew on it.

Then being struck repeatedly across the back and shoulders by something long and metallic. The camera tripod? He tried to reach one hand up to feel his shoulder but he could hardly lift it to chest level. Anyway, he didn't need to touch it to know the lacerations were there. His back felt like one raw, burning mass. His shirt stuck wetly to it.

The first excruciating kick to his solar plexus. He had never experienced so much pain. It had sucked all the air from his lungs so that he felt he might never be able to catch a breath again. The repeated kicks to his body as he lay on the ground, each one opening a new blossom of agony. He could feel the ache from his kidneys. How much damage had they sustained? He should have taken to his heels as soon as he saw the minister's nose bursting open like an overripe fruit.

Moir hadn't even tried to stop the man's assault on him. Too anxious to save his own skin no doubt. The enormity of the attack insinuated itself slowly into his aching head. He might have died in that churchyard amid the rot of dead leaves, tasting earth and blood. Had his assailant's awareness of that possibility stopped him?

A memory hovered at the edge of his consciousness, just out of reach in the dark. Footsteps moving through the fallen leaves. A heavy sound like an axe striking a tree. A groan and a heavy thud that shook the ground next to where he lay. Then blackness. Coming slowly back to consciousness to find himself alone. The herculean effort to struggle upright. Then his desperation to get away from the scene forcing him to concentrate on putting one foot in front of the other.

The effort had made him oblivious to everything around him. Yet could someone else have been there? If he and Moir's theory was right and they were targeted by a group of blackmailers, perhaps more than one of them had come to the drop-off point. Covering each other's backs. His first thought was that Izzy or Angie or both of them might have been there watching, unobserved from a safe distance.

It was too much for his throbbing head to take in and dizziness threatened to overcome him once again. He reached into his jacket pocket to ascertain whether his phone was there, the movement triggering jagged bolts of pain to course through him. Thank God, it was still there and hadn't been stolen or lost during his erratic progress home. A long crack traversed its screen but it still appeared to be working.

He knew he ought to phone for an ambulance. After all, he was propped against his front door immobilised by pain, his breathing ragged and shallow. His first thought, however, was to call Moir. He needed to find out what he knew about last night. There would be time to call in the emergency services later. One thing was certain. His body might heal. Pain-killers would take away some of the physical hurt. But he could see no relief in sight for the wretchedness he felt in his heart.

Chapter Twenty-Three

Angus Moir

"Angus. Angus. Wake up." He spluttered into wakefulness at the sound of Marian's voice. It was a relief to emerge from the horrible dream he had been having. Some of its images still clung to him and made him shudder.

He had been delivering a sermon from his pulpit, the upturned faces of the congregation smiling beatifically at his words. Then their expressions had turned to looks of horror. Looking down, he realised he was naked. He rushed into the vestry clutching the bible to his body to conceal his shame and when he looked in the mirror that hung there he had the head of a goat.

Marian stood there with a cup of tea and a plate with a slice of toast and jam. "You had me worried there for a moment. I kept checking you were breathing in the night. And you were making weird noises."

He tried to muster a smile but his face ached dully and his head felt as if there was something trapped in it hammering against his skull to get out. "You'd better hurry up and get dressed. The police are coming round."

A stab of fear intensified his pain. "I told you not to call them. I said I'd go round and tell them about last night."

"I didn't. They phoned here." She seemed to be having a problem looking him in the eye.

"Marian, what is it?"

"They've found a body in the churchyard."

"What?" A wave of panic and nausea threatened to overwhelm him. He knew if he hadn't been lying down it would have knocked him off his feet.

Marian looked alarmed and fearful. "Angus, you don't know anything about this do you?"

"No. Of course not."

"It's just that you came in here last night in that state and now this."

"How would me being mugged be connected to that? Perhaps someone was taking a walk in the church grounds and had a heart attack or something. You mustn't jump to conclusions." His lies tasted like ashes in his mouth.

She looked at him uncertainly for a moment. "Better get dressed." She left him wallowing in a swamp of confusion. Images of the last few days flickered in his mind like an old film reel that had been badly edited and lit. A camera being smashed. The dark curve of Leon's penis rising out of the night, his fist coming towards him. His own face contorted in lust and pain. Him lying on the ground looking up at the sky through the boughs of the cherry tree. Floundering lurches from the churchyard his face wet with rain or blood. A boot swinging into a body with the sickening regularity of a lethal pendulum.

He was brought up short with a stark certainty that made his stomach plummet. MacDonald hadn't survived Leon's violent attack. He had been left to die among the trees outside the church. Worst of all, Angus had left him to die.

He had been so intent on escaping the scene that he had abandoned a helpless man - had hardly thought of him when he got home and became preoccupied with preventing Marian from calling the police. Perhaps if he had let her, if he had been truthful, a life might have been saved. He was lower than a fly stuck in a web of lies. He muttered under his breath, "Lord, why hath thou forsaken me?" But he knew the answer.

Inevitably the police would find evidence that he had been at the scene. They would find his blood there. It wouldn't take them long to match it to his. Perhaps they would take a sample of his DNA. He knew from the odd occasions he had watched crime shows on TV that they would prove without a doubt that he had been there. One way or another the whole sordid mess was going to come out. The police would lift up the stone and all his ugly secrets would scuttle into the light.

Wincing frequently in pain, he pulled on clean clothes. His impulse from the night before to confess and try to cleanse his soul returned. His phone rang. It took him a stunned moment to register that it was Archie MacDonald's number. He pressed accept with a shaking hand, half expecting to hear a voice from the grave denouncing him in a sepulchral voice for his cowardice and deceit.

At first there was no sound at the other end of the phone but gasping breaths.

"Hello. Is that you, Archie?"

When the caller spoke his voice was barely a whisper but Angus could make out a few mumbled words as if someone was speaking with a mouthful of cotton wool. "Say that again. I can't hear you."

"Itsh me. I ..." A trembling gasp then, "I need your help." The phone went dead. The relief he felt at hearing the other man's voice was quickly extinguished by a disquieting question - if Archie MacDonald was still alive, whose body did they discover in the church grounds?

Angus crossed to the chest of drawers where he had hidden his wallet. MacDonald's address and number were in it. He tried his phone but after a few rings it went to a voicemail message. He realised he needed to go round to see him. He owed him that much and more.

First he would have to sneak out of the house without Marian seeing him. He wasn't ready to face her - to look into her eyes and see the dread and suspicion in them. Worst of all, to see in them a concern for him that he didn't deserve. Listening carefully, he descended the stairs, conscious of every creak and groan from the wooden treads. He hoped she was in the front room and he could slip out to the back garden through the utility room. He was halfway down when the doorbell rang and she emerged from the sitting room to answer it.

He took the opportunity to scurry to the foot of the stairs and into the kitchen. He peered round the edge of the wall there, looking down the length of the hall as Marian opened the front door. He recognised the tall, well-dressed policeman who had come to the church with the female officer - Chalmers or Cameron or something. Beside him stood a rotund figure in a crumpled suit that made him look like an unmade bed.

He wanted to be confronted by the police at that moment even less than he wanted to face his wife. With a stealth born of panic he managed to unlock the utility room door and make his way into the garden. Rachel's bicycle lay discarded on the garden path as if she had just jumped off it in a hurry and simply abandoned it where it fell.

He grasped the handlebars and wheeled it to the back gate. When he reached the lane he jumped on and began pedalling as fast as he could along the lane that connected his street to the next one. He didn't want to risk the possibility that one of the police officers might happen to look out of the window and see him making off down his own road. By now they would have discovered his absence of course and it was only a matter of time before they caught up with him.

He knew that he must cut a ridiculous figure in his dark clergyman's clothes riding a girl's bike. It had no crossbar, was painted with flowers and had a basket in the front. Anyone who spotted him would no doubt register his panicked, swollen face and be able to describe him to the police.

But he couldn't worry about that now. He had to get to MacDonald to find out what he knew and to work out their next step. Dimly, he accepted that whatever that step would be it would take them both over the edge of a cliff.

He was so wrapped up in his thoughts that when the police car pulled up on the kerb in front of him, he almost lost control of the bike and sent it skidding into the back of it. The tall policeman leapt out quickly from the driver's side and more slowly and with more effort his less fit looking partner climbed out of the passenger seat.

"Reverend Moir. Hurrying down to the church for a spot of urgent prayer?"

"Nice bike," said his companion.

Angus climbed off the bicycle and propped it against a garden wall. He hung his head abjectly.

"Sergeant Cameron. We spoke before. And this is DC Buckle."

Buckle studied the bruises on his face. "Fall off your bicycle, Reverend?"

"You can tell us all about it down at the station, sir. And while you're at it you might tell us what you know about the body of a young man found outside your church."

Angus looked up, startled. "Young man?"

The policemen exchanged a curious look. "Come along, sir. You can pick up your bike later."

Chapter Twenty-Four
Shona Patterson

She was off the case. When she tried to object, Morton made it clear she was on so much thin ice that one more wrong step would plunge her into the icy waters of suspension. Her replacement was DI Agnes Barclay, who had been transferred over from traffic, for fuck's sake.

She knew she couldn't just let it go. Her in-tray was flooded with shitty cases that no-one wanted - fine dodgers, shop-lifters, minor assaults outside pubs and clubs. This wasn't what she had signed up for. She was better than this and she would prove it.

When she heard that Cameron and Buckle had brought in the Reverend Angus Moir she couldn't reign in her curiosity. She found herself once more in the room adjoining Interview Room 2 watching through the mirror as Barclay and Cameron questioned Moir. The minister was a mess. Livid bruising stood out on his face and he sat with his eyes downcast, hugging his arms around himself as if he was cold; an impression reinforced by his shivering body language.

Barclay seemed ill-at-ease too as she pointed out to Moir that he had voluntarily given blood and DNA samples. These would indicate whether or not he had been present last night in the churchyard. It would be in his own interest to co-operate and tell them what he knew.

Cameron said, "Perhaps you could start by telling us what happened to your face."

The minister's voice quivered as he said, "I think it might be better if I had a lawyer present."

Barclay leaned forward trying for a reassuring tone but not quite making it. "You're not under arrest, Reverend Moir. The body of a young man was found outside your church. We're just trying to establish whether or not you had any knowledge of him or how he got there."

"What ... what did he look like?"

"I warn you that the image we are about to show you may be rather distressing." Barclay nodded to Cameron, who took a photograph from a file that lay on the table in front of him and pushed it across to Moir. The effect of the photograph on the minister was startling. His face seemed to drain of colour so that the darkness of his bruises stood out even more vividly and his shaking became so convulsive, it looked as if he was in the grip of an ague. Shona thought that he might collapse from his chair.

His voice was a harsh whisper. "My God. My God. It's Leon."

Cameron jumped in. "Did you say Liam?"

Moir raised his head to look at him. "No, Leon. I said Leon." He suddenly began to weep. Barclay and Cameron glanced at each other with a mixture of puzzlement and anticipation. The DI waited a moment as Moir made a visible effort to get himself under control before asking,

"How do you know this man?"

Moir's voice was watery with grief as he said, "He was blackmailing me." Shona could almost feel the hairs rising on the back of her neck.

Moir's statement was delivered in a halting voice that was drenched in tears. Barclay pushed a pack of tissues towards him when he faltered.

He was often incoherent, talking one minute about a meeting in the church with a young man who had expressed an interest in church history then digressing into how, as a man of the cloth, he had to be seen to be above sin, then on to his shock at being blackmailed, when the man he had met had somehow found out that he had been on inappropriate pornography sites.

To Shona it simply didn't ring true. There were too many gaps in Moir's story and she could see from Cameron's cynical expression that he felt the same. Barclay interrupted as Moir went off into a rambling monologue about how fervently he had prayed for the Lord to give him strength to resist the temptations of the flesh.

"What happened in the churchyard?"

"It was where we were supposed to leave the money they asked for. I knew I ought to have come straight to you but my reputation ..."

"We?" Cameron interjected.

"Me and ...Oh my goodness. Archie Macdonald. You must get in touch with Archie Macdonald.

That's where I was going when you stopped me and brought me here."

"Who is Archie Macdonald and what has he got to do with this?" Barclay asked.

"He was there. He was in the churchyard. He was being blackmailed too. We were stupid - so stupid. We thought that we could persuade them to settle for less. Cut their losses with us. And here's the result - look at my face. And Leon attacked MacDonald too."

Barclay and Cameron glanced at one another. Shona felt her instincts prickling again.

"You have to help him. He was hurt. Perhaps badly. He will need medical attention."

"This Macdonald," said Cameron impatiently, "are you telling us that the man you knew as Leon was blackmailing him too?"

"Not directly. He told me he was targeted by two women but I'm sure they're all connected. You have to speak to him. This may be urgent."

The mention of the two women made Shona leap from her seat as if it had been electrified. She wanted to burst in and take over the interview but by a huge effort of will she stopped herself. Morton didn't need any more excuses to take her warrant card. She switched her phone back on. There was a voicemail from Brian.

She didn't believe in fate or planets coming into alignment or any of that bollocks. Yet it was as if something was shouting at her to trust her instincts. There were too many similarities to ignore. Brian, Moir, this man MacDonald, Dunlop, Thomson and Jeffries - she was convinced they were all linked.

In the interview room, Moir was becoming increasingly distressed so Barclay suspended the interview and asked him for McDonald's contact details. "And we would advise you most strongly to get legal representation, Mr. Moir."

Shona hurried from the building before anyone could ask where she was going. Then she returned Brian's call and arranged to meet him in the High Street near the Town Hall. When she got there she saw him standing outside the building but there was no parking space. She had to go round the one-way system again. A van pulled out in front of her on her second pass and she quickly reversed into the vacated space.

A few seconds after, Brian jumped into the passenger seat. He looked both sheepish and anxious. Shona failed to keep the cold anger from her voice as she said, "I've been taken off the case." She couldn't bring herself to be so churlish as to say, 'Thanks to you'.

"I really shouldn't be doing this, Brian. Morton's aching to find an excuse to burn my warrant card and dance round the pyre. But I'm convinced everything that's happened are pieces of the same jigsaw."

She told him about his erstwhile spiritual guide, Moir's involvement. He listened in silence as she recounted some of the latter's statement but he gave a sharp intake of breath when she mentioned blackmail and murmured, "Jesus Christ."

"Quite. It appears your minister wasn't as faithful to the main man's teachings as he should have been."

"But what on earth did they have on Angus Moir?" Brian asked incredulously.

"He claims they knew he watched porn but I'm sure he's not telling us the whole story."

"How would they even know that?" Brian's question was rhetorical, she realised as he looked distractedly at the car in front of her where a young woman was going through the convoluted process of lifting a child from a buggy into a car seat.

His attention quickly snapped back to her when she told him about Moir's revelation that there was another man called Macdonald involved and that he had been victimised by two women. He looked at her aghast. "Have they brought this other guy in?"

"They're probably in the process of doing that as we speak."

"Listen, Shona, I know I've crossed the line but remember I told you about Ali Olsen?" She regarded him with a mixture of incredulity and exasperation as he related how Ali had tracked down Eleanor Thomson's previous address and

Brian had gone round there and spoken to her former neighbour.

His reluctance and hesitation were evident in his downcast manner as he told her about his subsequent visit to Eleanor's ex and the call he had received from her. Then he seemed to steel himself as he looked into her eyes. "Shona, you have every right to be furious with me and I wouldn't blame you if you took me in right now and charged me with interfering with a police investigation. But Eleanor Thomson sounded terrified. If we don't find her soon I'm afraid she's going to suffer the same fate as Irene and the victim you found by the church."

Again she struggled to keep the outrage from her voice as she said, "If *we* don't find her?"

"How come she knew I was looking for her? It's obvious that her ex-downstairs neighbour - a guy called John Edmondson - knew more about Eleanor than he was telling me. We should pay him another visit."

"Again this *we*. I told you I'm off the case."

"I know how much that must frustrate you. I remember how tenacious you always were once you got your teeth into a case."

"You make me sound like a bulldog."

"Only much more attractive." As he blushed she felt some of her anger and trepidation dissipating.

"And if we do find out anything significant you can pass it on to whoever's running the investigation. You could do it through your Sergeant - Cameron? He seemed like the kind who would have your back."

He knew her so well, Shona thought. He knew she was burning to find her way through this morass and he knew how much she hated to be side-lined. As she sat there in an agony of indecision, he said, "And it would take just a few minutes to ask Mr. Edmondson to co-operate. That's Eleanor's old address." He pointed at a building a few yards down the street.

At least he had the decency to look uncomfortable as she gave him a piercing look. He was so taken by surprise when she sprang out of the car, that it took him a moment to follow her. She let him lead the way to a close between High Street shops. She raised a hand to her nose at the acrid aroma of piss in the close as they arrived at a blue door. There was an intercom panel but the door stood ajar.

Brian looked concerned as he made his way up the stairs to the first landing. "This is Edmondson's flat." Once again the door to the flat was wide open. He called out, "Mr. Edmondson. Are you in? Brian Lockwood. We spoke earlier remember?"

When there was no reply, Shona tried to ignore her feeling of foreboding as she pushed passed Brian and went into the flat. "Mr. Edmondson? I'm a police officer." She held out a warning hand to Brian but he shook his head and came in to stand beside her. They were in a high-ceilinged hall. Three doors led off it.

Through the first one on the right they could see a large kitchen that looked as if it still had fittings and appliances that had been installed in the eighties. Directly in front of them through the partly opened door they could make out the edge of a bed. Almost moving in synch, they both reached for the handle of the second door on the right at the same time. Shona gave Brian another warning look as she opened it.

The living room looked as if a hurricane had ripped through it. Books and CDs covered the carpet from two units that had been pulled over. Under the window that obviously looked out front onto the High Street stood an old-fashioned writing bureau. Its pull-down top gaped open, spilling papers onto the floor and all the drawers underneath had been hauled out, their contents strewn around it haphazardly.

As she took in the scene, she sensed Brian leaving the room. She found him standing at the threshold of what they had guessed was a bedroom. When he paused, she knew that, like her, his copper's nose was picking up the whiff of bad news. Using the sleeve of his coat, he pushed the door open.

More papers and books were scattered around the room but her attention was drawn to the bed on which the duvet had been untidily pulled up. There was a shape underneath it. Brian made to pull it down but she restrained him with a hand on his arm as she tugged it down. A man lay beneath it, his head on a blood-stained pillow. His face bore the marks of a recent beating. He was still wearing his glasses, one half of their broken frame and lens over one eye and the other lying askew on his cheek. Shona immediately called it in.

"It's Edmondson," Brian said, his voice hushed as if the figure on the bed might hear him. "You think this is like the others?" Brian asked. Curiosity made her pull the cover further down. He was fully clothed, his cargo shorts belted securely around his waist.

"Maybe. But I don't think so somehow. By the look of him he's taken an almighty beating but my gut tells me this is different from the other murders."

"A robbery gone wrong perhaps?"

"Could be. Someone's obviously been through his stuff. But he's an ex-neighbour of one of your blackmailers for God's sake. I believe in coincidences like that, as much as I believe if I rub this bedside lamp a genie will appear and grant me three wishes."

Brian looked stricken. "You're right and I feel responsible."

She wanted to offer him words of comfort but part of her believed he might be right. "One thing's for sure: you have to get your arse out of here."

"But I can't leave you to explain ..."

"I'll think of something. Leave now and try not to be conspicuous. I'll be in touch when we know more."

He looked at her as if he wanted to say something else but turned abruptly and left the room. She waited a few minutes, taking in the room as if it might yield up more clues.

She was waiting on the landing outside the flat when she heard the sound of sirens outside. A few moments later a male and female paramedic came rushing up the stairs. She indicated the open bedroom door. "He's in there." As soon as they had gone into the bedroom, Cameron came sprinting up the stairs. "Inspector Patterson, what the fuck?" She nodded towards the bedroom. When he had gone inside, the panting figure of Barclay appeared.

When she had got her breath back she said, "What's going on here, Inspector Patterson?"

She explained that she had found the badly beaten body of a man in his late fifties or sixties. "And you're here because?" Shona had used the short time before they got there to concoct what she thought was a plausible story about an anonymous call to the station that had reported the sounds of a violent commotion in this flat.

Barclay regarded her with such scepticism it was as if she had just told her that the queen of the fairies had visited her in a dream and told her there had been a murder in the High Street. "We'll talk further back at the station. I suggest you go back there now." She walked past Shona into the flat.

Three murders on her watch. The whole thing stank to high heaven. Shona felt she was wading through a sea of shit and the only certainty was that now she was up to her neck in it.

Chapter Twenty-Five

Brian Lockwood

He couldn't help feeling he was back in his sinking ship nightmare again, only this time he reflected it was he who had steered it onto the rocks. Had he been the one to bring death to Edmondson's door unwittingly? He thought of calling Shona to ask her to check on a certain brutish painter and decorator but he had compromised her too much already and anyway, she was bound to follow up on what he had told her or at least pass it on to colleagues.

He knew what he ought to do was to leave things alone and wait for Shona to get back to him. Her involvement with him had left her career hanging by a thin thread that he didn't want to fray any further. But the thought that he might be responsible indirectly for Edmondson's death nagged at him like an ache in his gut.

His car seemed to find its own way onto the dual carriageway to Kirkcaldy. When he arrived back at Mr. Brick Shithouse's flat there was no sign of his van. Despite his instincts telling him to back off, he climbed out of his car. As the wind blew cold drizzle in his face, he pressed the intercom. There was no response. He returned to his car and with a sense of déjà vu sat watching the rain running down the windscreen. What now? There was nothing else for it but to sit tight 'til Shona thought it was safe to call him.

His phone rang; Ali Olsen's ID flashing up. As usual there was no preamble. "Couple o' things about the Thomson bitch, ya cunt. Mind how I said she had her own wee cleanin' business for a while? Well guess who used tae be one o' her fuckin' clients? None other than that rich cunt cum acquitted rapist, Arnold Hastings. And another thing, in the process of findin' the links, I've been havin' a wee, sneaky peek into his Human Resources files."

Again a jolt of disquiet made Brian look round uneasily as if someone might be eavesdropping and he'd be implicated in Ali's illegal breaches of cyber security.

"Seems there's a bit of a pattern to the cunt's employees. Mainly female; twenties or early thirties and get this - in the last couple of years he's paid aff four of them. Moved on tae other fuckin' employment accordin' to the records but a tidy wee severance pay in each case. Considerin' the amount of time they were working for him especially. Here's my fuckin' theory. Mr. Millionaire Businessman likes to get a bit grabby when there's young fanny about the office. Disnae want done for sexual harassment or mebbe worse, given his previous. So he pays the lassies to keep their mouths shut. As bad as that film cunt in America - that Harvey Wankstain. Fae what you've told me, Thomson likes to use the flutterin' eyelashes and disnae mind gettin' her arse felt to get what she wants. Mebbe she got more than she bargained for with Hastings. Wouldnae do to get on the wrong side of that cunt."

Brian knew Ali was making some giant leaps in logic but he was galvanised by this new information. At the very least there was a connection between Eleanor Thomson and Irene Dunlop. The former's company had been employed by Hastings. Irene Dunlop had accused him of rape. Could that have been what brought the two women together? Then what? Decide to set up a campaign to punish men, particularly men who were predatory or blindly led by their libidos into taking advantage of women?

That seemed like a stretch but one thing all his years in the force had taught him was to never discount a possible scenario, however unlikely it might be. He intended to head back to Dunmalcolm and wait for Ali or Shona to contact him again but when he reached the roundabout that took him onto the dual carriageway, he found himself taking the right hand exit north instead of the left. He had no idea what he intended to achieve but he knew that Arnold Hastings had the headquarters of his double glazing business in Glenrothes. He realised that Shona would have a major seizure if he went anywhere near Hastings but he reasoned disingenuously that it would do no harm to have a look from a distance at the man's habitat.

As he approached the town he reflected on the similarities between Scotland's so-called new towns, some planned in the forties but mainly developed in the early sixties - places like here, East Kilbride, Cumbernauld and Livingstone. All of them were reached by negotiating a labyrinthine series of roundabouts like the ones he was now attempting to navigate; all were, to his eye, grey and soulless concrete spaces that had no obvious heart. Hadn't he read somewhere that Glenrothes had received a Plook on the Plinth award from an architectural magazine? As he passed through, he thought that indeed it could be seen as an unsightly pimple on the rural landscape that surrounded it.

However, an effort had clearly been made to brighten up the town's image as the centres of the roundabouts had well-maintained flower tubs and many of the public buildings had colourful hanging baskets.

Hastings' factory and showroom were in a large industrial estate around a mile from the town centre. He drove into the customers' car park and looked at the impressive conservatory style glass frontage. Through it he could discern what was obviously a reception area with a large, modern desk at the rear and a sitting area at the front with cream, leather armchairs and settees surrounding a table on which some glossy brochures and leaflets were strewn artfully.

A few people passed through: employees, by the look of their dress - formal lounge suits in the case of the men and smart blouses and skirts or fashionable dresses for the women. It struck Brian that even at this distance they all appeared to be attractive and in their twenties or thirties.

Before his sensible head could overrule him, he found himself moving towards the entrance. As he stood awkwardly uncertain of his next step, a young woman rose from behind the desk. She had long, dark hair held up by a floral Alice band that matched the pattern on her dress and her designer glasses somehow accentuated the attractiveness of her even features. She was very lovely.

"Can I help you, sir?" She smiled warmly at him in a way that suggested this was a practised greeting for potential customers but nevertheless revealed her confidence in her allure.

"I was just passing and noticed your showroom. I've been thinking it was about time I replaced some of the windows in my house."

"Please, take a seat." She gestured towards the sofa and armchairs. "As you can see these are some of our brochures." As he sat on the armchair she leaned over the table and selected some of the sales literature. Brian made a conscious effort not to look at the curve of her breasts and rear. "Why don't you have a look through them and I'll get one of our sales team to come and speak to you? May I bring you some tea or coffee?"

"I'm good, thank you."

She swept off through a door on the left leaving behind a trace of her perfume in the air, something that had both citrus and woody notes.

Brian pretended to leaf through the brochures she had given him but his mind was racing. What on earth was he hoping this would achieve?

He had just made up his mind to make a hasty exit when the receptionist returned accompanied by another very pretty, young blonde woman in a raw trim tweed suit with button detail on the jacket and skirt, the latter perhaps rather shorter than was the norm for conventional business attire. She managed to look both formal and sexy. As she sat opposite him and the receptionist returned to her post behind the desk, Brian reflected that the presence of two such glamorous women appeared to confirm Ali's speculations about the company's apparent recruitment policy.

The salesperson introduced herself as Diane Freeman, though Brian had noticed her name badge already, and asked him a few questions about what he was looking for. What kind of windows was he thinking of replacing? Did he have particular styles in mind? As he struggled to think of the windows in his house, he answered vaguely and prepared to settle down to listen to a lengthy sales pitch. This was the price he deserved to pay, he thought, for his impetuousness.

Diane had just launched into her spiel when she looked up, startled. He turned to look at the figure looming behind him. Brian hadn't heard him entering the room which was surprising given his bulk. He was wearing what looked like a designer suit but the overall impression he gave Brian was that someone had found an ape and dressed it up for a joke. The simian resemblance was emphasised by a nose flattened by too many punches, jug ears and hair that looked like coconut matting. His arms looked too long for the rest of his body and thick hair spilled from the cuffs of his shirt and covered his wrists and the backs of his hands.

"It's okay, Di, sweetheart. I'll deal with this gentleman."

The saleswoman's discomfort was evident as she rose nervously, knocking several leaflets to the floor. Flustered, she bent to retrieve them but ape-man said, "Just leave them." He seemed to realise that his tone had been abrupt as he tried to soften it with a smile that only reached the lower half of his face and more than anything reminded Brian of one of Ali's grimaces.

"Mikey Rutherglen, as I live and breathe."

"For the time being, anyway," he said, the ugly grin still plastered on his face. "Just joking, Inspector Lockwood. Long time, no see. Still bringing these naughty law-breakers to justice?"

Brian felt no inclination to disabuse Mikey of the notion that he was still a serving policeman. "Still being one of those naughty law-breakers, Mikey?"

"Who me?" He rearranged his features into what he no doubt imagined was an expression of put-upon innocence. "No way. Turned over a new leaf. Legitimately employed, me."

Brian recalled his numerous encounters with Rutherglen in the past. He was an ex-professional boxer who had lost his licence when he was found guilty of taking a hefty bribe to throw a fight. After that he had drifted into being an enforcer for an Edinburgh gang who were involved in various rackets including drug dealing, prostitution, people-trafficking and protection.

Brian was convinced that Mikey was implicated in a few gangland killings but despite the police bringing him in on numerous occasions, they couldn't make anything stick. 'Til one day, Mikey's luck ran out and his employers threw him to the wolves after he had beaten a bookie half to death. He had served a long stretch in Peterhead prison then in HMP Grampian.

"Boss wants a word."

"You mean Mr. Hastings is going to deal with my double-glazing enquiries personally? I'm honoured. How did you know I was here?"

Mikey nodded upwards to a camera in the corner of the ceiling.

Brian followed Mikey towards a door on the left. He really was light on his feet despite the thickness of his body and the image that sprang into Brian's mind of him suddenly leaning forward and dragging his knuckles on the ground. The receptionist scurried from behind her desk and followed them.

He was shown into an office. Brian expected the rich owner of the company would be ensconced in a large space with designer furniture seated behind a massive desk that reflected his power and wealth, but despite an obviously expensive leather ergonomic chair, the trappings of this office were modern but functional.

Andrew Hastings was absorbed in examining the screen of his desk top computer and didn't look up when they entered. Hastings was a well-groomed man in his early forties with a sculpted beard that looked to Brian as if it needed regular maintenance by a barber to keep its shape. Unlike his employees, he was dressed down in a navy Fred Perry polo shirt with no jacket or tie. The only indications of his wealth were the Omega Seamaster watch on his wrist and the heavy gold chain around his neck.

Mikey stayed by the door while Brian and the girl stood uncomfortably in the centre of the room as if they were awaiting an audience with a potentate. From time to time, she nervously ran her fingers through her hair and smoothed down the front of her dress. With his attention still focussed on his computer, Hastings said, "Get us some coffee, Amanda, will you? There's a good girl."

The receptionist left with an alacrity that suggested she was relieved to be out of her boss's presence. Brian was losing patience with what he presumed was the power game that was being played and was about to speak when Hastings turned his attention from the screen and said, "Take a seat, Inspector." Brian sat on a low chair that was placed to the left of the desk. It made him feel smaller than the man opposite, which was no doubt the intention.

"You've already met Mr. Rutherglen, my driver." So that was his employment description, Brian thought, as he glanced at Mikey who stood motionless and expressionless at his post by the door. "It was he who alerted me to the fact that we were having a visit from the constabulary. He saw you on the CCTV camera," Hastings went on. He was making an effort to modify his Fife accent.

Amanda reappeared with a tray on which sat a cafetiere, two cups and a sugar bowl and milk jug. As she placed it on Hastings' desk, Brian thought she angled her body awkwardly away from him as if she didn't want to get too close. When she had left, Hastings took his time pouring two coffees and gesturing Brian to help himself. He poured in some milk, aware of Hastings' scrutiny.

"Let me say first off that what was on the film that bitch gave you, embarrassing as it is, shows me doing nothing illegal. I was simply engaged in what I believe is called consensual sexual activity." Brian halted in the act of bringing his cup up to his mouth. He tried to conceal his shock and was immediately relieved that he hadn't told them that he was no longer on active duty with the police.

"Obviously, I wasn't going to give in to blackmail. I told her to do her worst so here we are." He leaned forward conspiratorially. "You're a man of the world, Inspector Lockwood. You know that some women like it a bit rough. They get off on it. That's all you'll see and hear on that film. So you can see you're wasting your time investigating it."

He leaned back casually and sipped his coffee. Brian was at a loss as to how to proceed. Hastings' revelation was like a lightning flash that momentarily illuminated the landscape before plunging it back into a deeper gloom. He struggled to wrestle with its implications. He found his tongue at last. "This woman - she was blackmailing you?"

"Oh, I won't be pressing charges. I don't need the bad publicity. I can deal with it myself quite amicably." As he said this, Brian noticed his eyes flicking to Mikey briefly. "In fact, I thought I had sorted this little misunderstanding out already. I'm surprised she came to you with this."

Brian was thinking rapidly. "Strictly speaking, she didn't. We received the film anonymously with a message that we might like to look into your affairs, Mr. Hastings. We didn't know if the sender was male or female. Perhaps you could enlighten us as to the identity of the woman you suspect."

He was improvising wildly but Hastings seemed to buy it because he looked evasive before fixing an ironic smile on his face. "As I said, Inspector, I really don't want to take this any further. This is exactly the kind of behaviour I'd expect from that sort. They're rats scrabbling about in the dirt for scraps from the tables of people like me. They want a taste of what I've got but in the end their self-preservation comes first and they go scurrying back into their holes. Now if there's nothing else, I have a business to run. Mikey will see you out." He tapped on his keyboard to reawaken his computer as a signal that Brian was dismissed. As he rose to leave, Hastings said, "If you hear from her again, you'll no doubt let me know."

As Mikey soft-shoed out ahead of him, Brian turned at the door. He caught Hastings watching him. For a moment, his casually urbane manner was gone and Brian had a glimpse of undisguised venom before he turned narrowed eyes back to his computer screen.

As they passed through the reception area the girl Hastings had addressed as Amanda looked up. She didn't smile and her eyes behind her glasses looked like those of a startled deer. At the door Mikey said, "It's been a pleasure as always, Inspector Lockwood. Don't hurry back."

Brian was on automatic pilot as he drove back from Glenrothes. Now he had impersonating a police officer to add to his list of misdemeanours but that was the least of his worries. The more deeply he waded through the undergrowth in this jungle, the more he was conscious of the dangers lurking there.

His head buzzed with questions. He knew he couldn't have asked Hastings whether it was Irene or Eleanor that he suspected without showing his hand. He was still unclear about how much their activities had led to the deaths of two men. But Irene's murder and Eleanor's terror suggested that somewhere along the path they had disturbed a rattlesnake's nest that bristled with lethal menace.

His immediate problem was how to tell Shona about his visit to Hastings and what he had found out there. No matter that he had uncovered the businessman's links to the case. He didn't think he could face her inevitable anger or any more of the look of reproach and hurt he had seen already in her eyes.

It occurred to him that he no longer cared about his own situation. The gloom that descended on him was a result of his conviction that he had held his relationship with Shona below the water line and there was nothing he could do to stop it sinking into the deep.

Chapter Twenty-Six

Shona Patterson

That night Shona slept badly. She was plagued by surreal dreams. In one of these, sinister figures pursued her through corridors that swam with a yellow stream that looked like urine. She couldn't see their faces but they were all naked from the waist down, their grotesque genitals displayed obscenely. She came to a door. As her pursuers closed in she hammered on it desperately. It was pulled open by Brian who looked horrified to see her. DCI Morton appeared behind him and drew him into an embrace before slamming the door in Shona's face. She woke in a sweat as in her dream her bleeding knuckles pummelled on the door. So vivid had the nightmare been that she checked her hands for blood.

The next day at work she struggled to focus. She sensed that her colleagues were giving her a wide berth. They were afraid of catching the virus that had afflicted her career over the past few days. Somehow she got to the end of her shift. As she was leaving she saw Cameron heading towards his car. When he saw her he quickened his pace as if he wanted to avoid her. She called to him. "Come on, Garry. You know I'm off the case so there's no need to treat me as if I've suddenly developed a personal hygiene problem." He stopped reluctantly.

"You know I shouldn't be discussing details of the case, Inspector Patterson." At least, thought Shona, he had the decency to look embarrassed.

"I don't want details. I just wondered if you had made any progress with Angus Moir." This wasn't the time to tell the sergeant that she had eavesdropped on the interview. He looked around surreptitiously before beckoning her to get into the passenger seat of his car.

"There's something very suspicious about our Reverend Moir. Uniform went round to the flat of someone whom the minister said had been in the churchyard the night of the murder. They found a guy called Archie Macdonald lying unconscious in the hall. He was in a bad way. He'd suffered a serious assault and he's in intensive care. As well as Jeffries, the murder victim, the blood in the churchyard matches that of Moir and Macdonald."

"How did Moir explain that?"

"He didn't. At least not satisfactorily. I've suggested to Barclay that we ought to pull him in again sharpish."

"Have you spoken to Macdonald?"

"We went to the hospital but it took a lot of persuading for the doctors to give us even a short time with him."

"Did you get anything?"

"He wasn't entirely coherent. Nor was Moir when we interviewed him for that matter. But one thing that both our boys mentioned was that they were being blackmailed."

"By Liam Jeffries?"

"Moir was. Something to do with Jeffries finding out that Mr. Devout Churchman was visiting some dodgy websites specialising in sins of the flesh. Macdonald, though, said that he had been targeted by two women who had been round to his flat and lured him into their web with a bit of Sapphic voyeurism, a threesome and mild S and M. He said the women put on a bit of a sexy show for him that included one of them spanking the other one." She was amused to see his eyes shift away from her in embarrassment. "And then they got him to join in. Wouldn't look good for his respectable charity job."

Shona's head swam. The certainty that she felt that all of these cases were connected was tempered by the knowledge that it didn't exactly lead to the murderer or murderers' door.

"What about John Edmondson?" she asked.

Cameron looked at her askance. "Remind me again how you came to discover his body?"

"I told you and Barclay - an anonymous tip about a disturbance in his flat." She knew she was an unconvincing liar and she prayed that Cameron was taken in by her looking him in the eye with what she hoped was an open and honest expression and that he didn't notice the blush that she felt spreading from her neck to her cheeks.

"There is a definite link - he lived in the flat below where Eleanor Thomson and her man used to stay which is a coincidence too far you might think. I could be wrong but this doesn't feel like the same killer as Dunlop and Jeffries, though. Different MO."

Shona didn't like to venture that she agreed. She'd thought the same since pulling down Edmondson's bed cover to reveal that he was still fully clothed from the waist down.

"How about her ex-partner? Do you like him for it?"

"Buckle went round to see him with WPC Dewsbury."

"Lisa Dewsbury?"

"Yes."

"Competent officer." She tried to keep her tone neutral but he still looked uncomfortable.

She knew Cameron had gone out with the tall blonde PC a few times and had tried unsuccessfully to keep their relationship under wraps to avoid the innuendo of his colleagues and the possible censure of his superiors who might have disapproved.

"Aye. Lisa ...PC Dewsbury didn't like the vibes he was giving off but he seems to have an alibi for the time of the murder. He was wallpapering a hall and stairs in a house in Park Place."

"So he was in Dunmalcolm? I'd have another look at the timeline if I were you."

"Thanks for the advice." She realised she had irked him.

"I know you will, Garry. You're thorough and this case needs someone like you investigating it. I'm not convinced that Barclay could find her backside in the dark with both hands." That seemed to placate him though she knew he was too loyal to criticise his new boss openly.

"Just one thing. I'd be grateful if you could keep me abreast of any developments." He looked as if he might be about to refuse. "I know I've come close to flushing my career down the toilet and I wouldn't want you to do anything that might land you in the shit with me. But I might be able to contribute and I promise you I won't be spending the rest of my career charging alkies who shove a couple of bottles of vodka into their knickers in Asda."

After a pause, he nodded.

"Thanks, Garry, I won't forget it."

As she moved to climb out of the car he said, "Did that really happen?"

"Supermarket security guy noticed the unsightly bulges in her jeans. I mean it was the supermarket's own brand. You'd think she'd at least half-inch some Grey Goose. And she was wearing skinny jeans. Professor Moriarty, eat your heart out." She was gratified to see that he was smiling as she left.

As she moved off through the car park her phone rang. When she saw that it was Brian she almost declined the call but despite her misgivings she couldn't bring herself to ignore him.

"Shona, do you think that we could meet up?"

"Do you think that's wise? I'd have thought you would want to steer well clear 'til things settle down."

"You know that's not how things work for me."

She did know. He reminded her of the police sniffer dogs she had encountered on a training course she had been on a few years back. Once they had been given a scent to track down they were unwavering in its pursuit. They would run through fire to find it.

"Okay. Where and when?"

She was surprised by his choice of meeting place but was positively dumbfounded when she entered the Nappy and saw Brian's drinking companion. Ali Olsen was jittering and grimacing next to Brian at a window table drinking a pint of lager, most of which he was spilling down the front of his jeans and a washed out tee-shirt from which she could just discern an impossibly pulchritudinous Amazon warrior brandishing a sword. When he noticed her standing frozen at the entrance to the pub, Brian sprang up and came over to her.

"Shona, before you get angry ..."

"Too late."

"Just let me buy you a drink and explain."

When she trusted herself enough to speak, Shona hissed as quietly as she could, given that AC/DC's 'Whole Lotta Rosie' was blasting out from the music system, "You've probably put a stake through the heart of my career already. Now what? You want to screw down the lid on the coffin and bury it at sea?" She recognised her vexation was both making her mix her metaphors and causing her cheeks to burn.

"However much you may disapprove of my involving Ali, in the short time he's been helping he's provided useful leads that the police can follow up when before, they were stumbling around in the dark."

"We'd have got there."

"Yes but remember I told you I think a woman's life could be at risk. Time is something we don't have a lot of."

For a moment she was at a loss as to how to proceed. She allowed herself to be led to the table where Ali was in the middle of a yawn so vast it made his eyes disappear in his face. He mumbled a couple of absurd obscenities as Brian went to the bar to be served by a Gothic-looking barmaid who obviously spent most of her pay on tattoos, piercings and unusual haircuts.

The pub was busy with a few uniformly unattractive regulars many of whom bore the glazed expressions of habitual drinkers. She surmised that many of them probably had been there as afternoon blurred into evening. The majority of the other clientele were dressed in work clothes sinking pints, no doubt delaying their return home after their shifts

None of the customers looked as if they had just missed out in the audition stages of 'Love Island', Shona thought, as the background music segued into Bryan Adams' 'Summer of '69'. She glanced at Ali who was staring at her tits unashamedly.

When Brian returned with a pint of Guinness for her and another lager for Ali, she was still glowing with annoyance. They all sat in an awkward silence broken only by Ali's grunts and belched-out exhortations to eat his arse or munch Axminsters.

Finally, in an attempt to relieve the tension, she said, "You certainly know the classiest places to bring a girl."

Brian's hangdog expression was lightened by a slight smile. "It's what all the fashionable set are doing - seeking out entertainment in the traditional environment of the authentic Scottish alcoholic."

They both went to speak at once, their sentences overlapping. Brian said, "Sorry. You go."

"You know what I'm going to say, Brian. This is getting so far removed from normal procedure we might as well round up a posse, swear them all in as deputies, ride out of town and head for the mesa."

"I know how you always balked at involving civilians in police business." They both glanced at Ali who still seemed preoccupied with Shona's breasts and merely continued with his complicated ritual of movements and tics. "But I honestly think that we have to try everything or we're going to have a fourth corpse on our hands." That seemed to startle Ali out of his reverie and he took a jerky gulp of his beer.

Brian looked at her expectantly and as if by fate, the music changed again to 'The Final Countdown'. His wry smile showed that the irony wasn't lost on him.

"All right. I'll probably regret this but here goes." Shona filled him in on what she had found out from Cameron about Moir and Jeffries and the badly injured Macdonald. When she had finished, Brian wore an expression of brooding animation that she recognised from their past involvement in complex cases. Shona thought it was akin to the thrill of the hunt where the pursuers had a scent of their quarry and might even glimpse it around the next corner as the undergrowth thinned out.

"Let's try to put together the pieces of this puzzle. What we seem to have is a team of blackmailers who are organised and have done their homework on their victims. They knew their weak spots."

Shona interrupted, "But how do they do that? They seem to know they have sexual predilections that they're ashamed of. Ashamed enough to pay up to keep them quiet. We won't know what the Reverend Moir was really into until we impound his laptop. He's obviously not telling us his darkest fantasies but the involvement of a rent boy who turned tricks with male customers might give us a clue. Whatever he was into, his blackmailers knew what it was."

Ali perked up at this information, licking his lips before opening his mouth so widely they had an unpleasant view of his rather yellow tongue and back teeth that were full of fillings, before muttering, "The fucking minister's a secret shirt-lifter?" Brian held up an exasperated hand as if to stop him. Shona suspected he knew that she was having second thoughts about letting Ali be a party to information about the players in this drama.

Nevertheless, she pressed on, "And it appears that Macdonald liked girl-on-girl action and spanking." As Ali muttered, "Dirty cunt," Brian said,

"For fuck's sake, man." Ali appeared unapologetic.

In an obvious attempt to move the discussion along, Brian said, "It sounds as if they had access to the men's computers somehow. How easy would that be, Ali?"

"A competent hacker with a few of my fuckin' skills - no' as brilliant obviously - could do it. Cunts that like to watch a lot of naughty movies think they can just erase their browsin' history at the end of a wankin' session and it all disappears. But it disnae and it wouldnae take much to get a look at their hard drives." He seemed to find this amusing. His laughter was like the braying of an asthmatic donkey. "Ken whit I mean."

He subsided and took another gulp of his lager. "Wan possibility was that some fucker got their hands on their computers somehow."

Shona and Brian digested this for a moment. Tentatively she ventured, "But how does Brian fit into this?"

"You into necrophilia fantasies, ya cunt?"

Brian looked thunderous for a moment. Ali must have sensed the change in atmosphere because he lapsed into a series of frenetic tappings and gestures accompanied by alarming facial contortions. Shona wished that she had never asked the question.

Brian was evidently finding it an effort to keep his voice steady as he said, "It's as I said earlier: they know the victims' weak spots. They knew that I was still grieving for my wife and hadn't had any - dealings - with the opposite sex since her death." He cast a look at Shona clearly trying to gauge her reaction. Shona composed her features into what she thought was a sympathetic expression.

"So they come up with a plausible scenario to suck me in. A fellow sufferer. Someone who's recently been bereaved and deprived of human contact for a while. She's even dressed in dark clothes and she's pretending to sleep so that in her mind she can stay faithful to the memory of her late husband."

319

"Say what you like but these women were smart. They knew which buttons to press. They knew you might go along with it because you're driven by compassion as much as desire."

"That's good of you to say that, Shona, but there's no way of sugar-coating this. I behaved really badly."

Ali chipped in, "So what you've got in common with these other cunts is you were all outwardly upstandin' respectable members of the community who were led around by their dicks."

As Brian lapsed into a shame-faced silence, Shona leapt in. "There's more to it than that. I think that the whole thing was driven by the two women. I'm not sure how they got together in the first place but when they did, they found they were kindred spirits. One of them was probably a victim of rape and the other suffered abuse at the hands of a man. I think they wanted revenge against the male sex in general and more specifically, men who in their eyes were hypocrites, covering up their - baser desires - with a cloak of respectability. I think they would find it easy to recruit someone like Liam Jeffries - an addict who fed his habit by being abused by others."

Ali rattled his empty glass to get Brian's attention. He rose and pointed at her glass which was still three quarters full. She shook her head and he went to the bar to get Ali another pint.

When he was gone, Ali said, "We still have no fuckin' idea how they pick their victims and get the gen on them."

"I think you're right about the IT connection," said Shona, trying to ignore the fact that Ali's eyes never lifted above her chest level. When Brian returned, Ali said,

"What kind of porn do you get off on, Mr. Lockwood?" Brian's hand shook as he was setting Ali's glass down, slopping some of it onto the table. "It's just that the inspector here thinks that the good old inter jerk is how they choose their fuckin' marks."

Brian attempted to recover his composure before responding, "Nothing unusual. Nothing involving having sex with women while they're

321

sleeping if that's what you're getting at." He gave a mortified glance at Shona. A thought seemed to strike him. "I did recently have a look at a few online dating sites."

Shona tried to suppress a stab of jealousy and resentment. So he would rather hook up with strangers than call her.

Ali's features never relaxed enough to indicate that he was thinking but she thought that the fact that his eyes left her breasts and looked towards the window might suggest that he was mulling this over.

"You get that piece of crap that you use serviced by me, do you no'?"

"Yes, but I got so sick of your snide comments I traded that piece of crap in recently for a reconditioned model."

Shona and Ali said together, "Where?"

"Place in Croft Street that sells stuff like that - you know, second-hand laptops, tablets, phones, computer games and so on. The thing is a couple of months after I got it I had to take it back to the shop. They fixed whatever glitch was making it malfunction and I've had no bother since."

"Might be worth checkin'," Ali said.

Brian looked anxious. "But the clock is ticking and we haven't exactly got a large list of suspects. I have a hunch that the blackmailers pissed off someone powerful and dangerous. Two of them are now dead and the other one may be next on the list."

"Don't forget John Edmondson. He's connected to all this too," said Shona. Ali looked puzzled or at least that was the closest approximation she could give to the expression that rippled like sand across his face. He might have been grappling with trapped wind.

"Speaking of someone powerful and dangerous, after I had tried to get Ben Thomson in, I went to see Arnold Hastings."

"You did what?" Shona listened open-mouthed as Brian related his encounter with Hastings - his and Ali's suspicions about his relationship with his female employees and the revelation that someone had attempted to blackmail him.

"This is fucking unbelievable, Brian, even for you. You go back to visit someone who might be a suspect in a murder enquiry; someone with a history of violence. Then you follow that up by questioning a local businessman who may or may not be a serial groper of women and worse, but on paper is as clean as freshly laundered sheets."

"Bet he's got plenty of fuckin' filthy linen in his closet, but," offered Ali.

Shona ignored him.

Brian said, "I know it's wrong to assume mud sticks, there's no smoke without fire and all these other clichés but Hastings has some laundry that's at least a bit stained if you take into account his trial for rape."

"You seem to forget that he was acquitted so legally he's clean. Brian, you also need reminding that you're not a copper anymore." Brian winced. Shona didn't want to hurt him but she was both furious with him and worried about his safety. "These people are dangerous – from what we know they're potentially killers. Leave it to the police to investigate them for God's sake."

"You're right, of course." Brian downed the remains of his soft drink and seemed on the point of leaving. Shona was torn – on the one hand, she wanted him to follow her advice to protect himself and if it took his hurt pride to make him stop so be it; on the other, she was vexed by the thought that he would go off under a dark cloud and their relationship would never recover from the coming storm.

In a welter of confused emotions she rose from the table. Brian rose with her as if he wanted to prevent her from going and for a moment there was a naked appeal in his eyes. Shona's pulse quickened with the recognition that he might be as fearful of untying the insecure knot between them as she was.

They both stood in silence for a moment. Ali writhed and fidgeted in his chair as if he was caught up in the electrical current that passed between them. Finally, Brian composed himself and said, "I mean it, Shona. You're right and I'm an idiot. You were also right when you talked about dangerous people. Arnold Hastings has Mikey Rutherglen working for him."

"That thug is employed by Hastings?"

"Says he's his driver but we both know Mikey's CV suggests he wasn't employed for his chauffeuring skills."

Shona paused. "We can presume that Hastings was fronted up by Eleanor Thomson. After all, he knew Irene Dunlop so it's unlikely she would approach him directly. You think Hastings's Rottweiler has been set on them and that's why Thomson sounded so frightened?"

"Told you that cunt had friends in low places," Ali interjected.

"I don't know, but it's another stream of sewage flowing into this foetid swamp. If she's going to be saved we have to get to the bottom of this, quickly."

He looked at her apprehensively before adding, "*You* have to get to the bottom of this."

"I'm off the case, remember." He regarded her knowingly and she gave him a wry smile.

Ali broke in with, "Fuck's sake. Get a room." Shona hoped her face hadn't reddened as much as Brian's.

"Look, Brian, I know I shouldn't be doing this but I'll let you know if there are any developments in the case as soon as I find out about them myself. In the meantime, try not to get into any more trouble."

"Thanks, Shona, I appreciate that." His warm look of gratitude ignited a spark of intense feeling in her. The moment was interrupted by Ali reaching for her three-quarters full glass of Guinness and asking, "Are you leavin' that?" Without waiting for a reply he took a large gulp of her beer. Brian continued to stand. She could feel his eyes on her back as she left.

Chapter Twenty-Seven
Brian Lockwood

For a long moment after Shona had left the bar, Brian continued to stand and stare at the door as if he expected her to reappear. Ali reached into the inside pocket of his long, black, faux leather coat that he had slung on the back of his chair. Brian thought that he might have fondly imagined that he resembled the hero in 'The Matrix' even though that fashion must be over twenty years old. Ali laid some pages on the table.

"Didnae want to show you these 'til she left cos she's still an active member of the pigs and that and I didnae want to take the chance she might dob me in."

Brian sat down. " Shona wouldn't do that and will you stop with the pigs stuff?"

"Sorry. Nae offence - a serving officer wi' the intrepid boys and girls in blue."

Brian ignored the sarcasm and leafed through the papers Ali had produced. They contained the files of three women. "These are some of the ex-employees of Mr. Hastings I was tellin' you about that I've managed to track down. The wans that left under a fuckin' cloud as you might say but nae doubt wi' a large manila shoved in the back pockets of their designer jeans to ease their dissatisfaction wi' their employer."

A head and shoulders photograph of the women was attached and despite the graininess of the print copies, Brian could tell they were all young and attractive. "You might want to give them a knock - see if any of them want to talk about their fuckin' short careers in double glazing sales."

Shona's condemnations of his actions were ringing in his ears still and part of him felt he should heed her warnings, not least because she was motivated by her concern for him rather than simply watching her own back. Yet he knew he couldn't just walk away. A couple of lines of enquiry had opened up to him. One was to find out how much Hastings might be involved and the other was to follow the IT link.

He knew Shona would drop a word in the right ears and the police would pursue it but they weren't going to be driven by the urgency he felt to find Eleanor Thomson. Besides, Hastings had proven bullet-proof in the past when the police had tried to bring him down. He turned back to his - what? - partner in crime? Ali was draining Shona's beer. "Thanks for this, Ali. I'll follow it up. Meanwhile, do me a favour and find out what you can about that computer shop."

"Couldnae refuse a request from you, Mr. Lockwood, especially when you're kindly payin' my fuckin' bills at the moment."

That evening Brian tried to contact the young women on the list Ali had given him without success. None of them answered their phones and because he wanted his enquiries to remain clandestine he didn't leave messages. The next morning he tried again. This time he had more luck. When they answered he maintained his subterfuge about his current status with the police, ignoring the pangs of guilt.

Of the first two who answered, one immediately cut him off as soon as he identified himself and mentioned that he wanted to ask her about her employment with Arnold Hastings. After an initial protracted silence, the other - a Madeline Leopold - asked why the police were interested. She sounded prickly and suspicious but he detected an undercurrent of alarm in her voice.

When he tried to reassure her that he was making routine enquiries about the business, she was silent once more before saying in a rush, "I don't think I have anything useful to tell you. I've moved on to another job and I feel disloyalty to my former employer wouldn't go down well with my current one." The formality of her words only served to emphasise her anxiety. It was as if she was trying to spray perfume ineffectually to conceal an insistent stench.

Brian said, "I'm really not asking you to be disloyal, Miss Leopold. I merely want to find out ..."

But she interrupted with, "You haven't told me the exact nature of your enquiries but I'm sure there's very little useful information I could give you." And she was gone. The women's reluctance to talk made him itch with curiosity.

With diminishing hope that he would find out anything at all, he dialled the last woman on the list again. Sarah Fairbanks answered just as he thought the call was going to go to voicemail once more. Her voice had that familiar edge he had detected in the other women's replies. As soon as he mentioned Arnold Hastings in his preamble she cut in with, "Can I ask what this is about?"

Unexpectedly, his routine enquiries line was met with a laugh that managed to sound bitter, sceptical and forced and her next words made him jerk to attention. "Has that shit been at it again?" Before Brian could compose himself enough to formulate a reply, she went on, "Look - I'll talk to you but not over the phone and I'm not coming into the station. I quite like the way my face looks at the moment and I don't fancy the idea of it being spoiled."

Brian blurted out, "I promise you can speak to me in confidence. Would you be prepared to meet with me somewhere public and neutral?" She hesitated for so long that Brian thought he had blown it.

Eventually, she said, "Two o' clock. Where?" The first place that came into his head was Giamatti's. When he suggested there she rang off without confirming the rendezvous.

Brian got to the cafe fifteen minutes early for the meeting. Donna Dolan greeted him once more like a long lost friend as she took his order. She was wearing a new-looking maternity dress under her apron which flattered her growing figure. Her hair looked as if it had been professionally highlighted and she had taken greater care with her makeup than he remembered from his last couple of visits. "You're blooming, Donna. "

"Thanks, inspector. Sorry, *Mr.* Lockwood. Fruit scones are guid the day."

"Just a flat white, please, Donna. You and your partner must be getting excited about the impending arrival."

Her smile seemed muted all of a sudden and he detected a flicker of sadness in her eyes. "He's no' around any mair unfortunately."

"Sorry to hear that, Donna." Brian was embarrassed by his presumption and quickly changed the subject. "How's your brother doing?"

"He's daen' great. Two days a week at the college noo. I still worry aboot him like. We help each other oot, ye know. We're close." As she left to get his coffee, he felt saddened by the young girl's situation. Like so many young women who had been born into her social circumstances, her future seemed to be about to take a prescribed pattern.

Abandoned by the father of her child, she was going to become a single mum, probably on benefits since the minimum wage she was earning from her waitressing job would be insufficient for her and her baby to live on. He couldn't help admiring her resilience. It would have been unsurprising for someone in her position to succumb to despair at her lot and get sucked down into the sewer of drugs, alcohol and worse. Here she was - ineffably polite and smiling and keeping her head above the shit that flowed around her. She returned with his coffee; her warm smile restored.

Her optimism humbled him. For a moment he was bowed down by a feeling of hopelessness. Donna's partner no doubt dumped her as soon as she told him she was pregnant. Yet another example of a man stained by ignominy. It occurred to him that all of the men he had encountered in the last few days - Coulter, Thomson, Hastings and Rutherglen were lower than snakes crawling on their bellies in the dirt. And wasn't he down there in the muck with them? From what Shona had told him, Moir and Macdonald were hardly paragons of male virtue either.

Yet Shona still felt she could see some good in him and Donna's brother was reportedly engaged in cracking the mould that life had shaped around him. Maybe there was some hope for his sex. It suddenly occurred to him that Jamie Dolan was employed in the same shop that he had asked Ali to take a look at. The town of Dunmalcolm was a small world indeed.

He glanced at his watch. Sarah Fairbanks was late. Perhaps she had decided not to meet him after all. He sat there as the minutes ticked by, his coffee left untouched and growing cold. Just when he was about to give up, he spotted a young woman outside the cafe. It was her. He recognised her from the photograph in her file.

She passed by the window apparently trying to appear nonchalant, though her eyes scanned the customers as she disappeared from sight. Brian was about to leap up to follow her when she reappeared, once again carefully checking the interior of the cafe. He caught her eye and nodded cautiously.

She hesitated at the entrance. Then she appeared to have made a decision and entered, looking to right and left as she approached his table. "Are you Inspector Lockwood?"

"Yes. Miss Fairbanks?" He rose and motioned for her to sit.

She was skittish. Her eyes continued to move restlessly round the cafe. As her photograph had suggested, she was very pretty, though it was as if she had made an effort to play down her attractiveness. Her long, brown hair was scraped back from her face and she wore no trace of makeup. She was dressed in a light green rain jacket and a baggy sweater in a lighter shade of green and she wore a pair of fashionably ripped Levis, through which the pale flesh of her legs was visible.

When Donna came over she asked for sparkling water and Brian ordered another coffee to replace the one he had hardly touched. The waitress gave his companion a curious look and Brian realised that she must be wondering how every time he had been in here recently he had been accompanied by a series of attractive women.

He decided not to breach the silence that followed as they waited for their drinks. Sarah resembled a startled colt that might bolt at the slightest noise. "Sure I cannae tempt you tae a scone?" Donna asked when she returned.

"No thanks. This is fine." He was relieved that she hadn't addressed him as Mr. Lockwood as he had so often urged her to. He needed to cling to his bogus police status for a while longer to have any chance that the tense young woman sitting opposite him would tell him anything.

Sarah waited 'til the waitress was out of earshot before leaning towards him and saying in a voice that was barely audible, "It took a lot for me to come here. I nearly didn't." She sipped her water and licked her lips nervously. "Only I've read a lot recently about how if one person comes forward it often gives others the courage to do the same."

Her words fired him with anticipation but he knew he had to tread carefully. One wrong word could make her flee back out into the damp afternoon. "Thank you for this, Sarah. May I call you Sarah?" She nodded. "You're doing the right thing. Why did you leave your employment with Arnold Hastings?"

She suddenly looked stricken and her body language showed she was torn between the impulse to talk to him and her flight response. With her head bowed and in a voice so low he strained to hear her she said at last, "That evil bastard assaulted me."

"Hastings?" She nodded. She began to tremble.

Brian tried to make his voice gently reassuring. "I know how difficult this is for you, Sarah. Take your time."

She took several rapid sips of water as if she was suddenly parched. "I'm not proud of how I handled it. I did threaten to report him for sexual harassment at first but then I was - persuaded - it would be in my best interests to leave the company with a generous pay-off rather than opening up a can of worms. I've regretted it ever since. He made me feel dirty." She looked up at him. Tears stood out in her eyes.

"Whatever happened, it's certainly not your fault."

"I know that - logically - but I just ..." She struggled to find the words as her eyes brimmed over. Brian handed her a tissue as some of the customers began to regard them curiously. His frank stare made them avert their gaze. "The thing is I know I'm not the only one. I'm almost certain he's been doing this to other women in the company and getting away with it."

"These kind of men always do. It takes someone with your bravery to challenge them."

"Oh, I'm not brave. Every time I relive it I want to tell someone but the truth is I'm shit scared."

"Can you bring yourself to tell me what happened?"

She wiped her eyes and straightened up as if she had come to a decision.

"I enjoyed working there at first. Everyone was nice to me and Hastings himself was charm itself. One of the other girls warned me that he could be a bit inappropriate and one actually advised me to avoid being alone with him. But generally he was professional with me.

"He did put a hand on my shoulder or back occasionally so I thought that was probably what the other girls were referring to in these politically correct times. Looking back now, I realise I should have paid more attention to the little warning signs - the back of his hand brushing against my breast when he took paperwork from me, complimenting me on my hair or dress, that sort of thing. And sometimes I caught him - looking at me in a certain way."

She stopped to wipe her eyes and take a sip of her water.

"Then one night he asked me if I wouldn't mind staying on a bit later so we could review my contacts and sales." A perceptible shudder went through her and she faltered and fell silent. Part of Brian wanted to stop her - to spare her from revealing any more. He sensed the bleak inevitability about what she was going to tell him that gave him a sick feeling in his stomach.

After a visible effort to compose herself, she continued in a dead, emotionless voice that was somehow more disturbing than her tears. "When we were in his office he went out to take a call that he obviously didn't want me to hear. When he came back I was leaning over his desk looking at some files.

"I sensed him coming up behind me. He put a hand on the back of my neck. I was about to object when he ran it down my back and onto my bottom. I know I should have stopped him, shouted at him, but I just froze.

"The next few minutes were like a bad dream. He pushed one hand onto the small of my back to bend me further over the desk and he - he pulled up my dress at the back with his other hand. Then I felt him pulling down ..." She stopped and took a juddering breath.

"He pulled down my tights and pants and put his hand between my legs from behind. The feel of his fingers there made me turn around and push him off. When he was a bit off balance I dodged around him. It was hard to move away because my - my underwear was still around my thighs but I made it to the door. He said - he said - 'Calm down love, you know the score'. That's what he said – 'you know the score'."

She shook her head in disbelief and perhaps, Brian thought, as if she might erase the memory. "I was numb with shock at first and then I couldn't stop crying. I knew I could never go back there.

"I spent the next few days just holed up in my flat. I couldn't face anybody. I didn't answer my phone even - God knows what my mother was thinking. I knew I should report it to someone but I thought it was just my word against his. I mean you read about how hard it is for women to prove these things.

"Then I had a visit from that tame gorilla that drove Hastings around - Rutherglen his name is. He handed me a letter that said something along the lines of the company were not extending my trial period of employment with them. It was news to me that I had been serving a trial period. It said I would be provided with satisfactory references and included details of a severance payment that was to be paid into my account. It was quite a lot of money."

When she looked up at Brian he could see the fear in her eyes. "I was so angry. I said I was going to report him. I wanted to tear the letter up and throw it in the guy's face but then he said, 'Mr. Hastings trusts that this will be the end of the matter.' I mean he was using this formal tone but it was really threatening underneath. Then just as he was leaving he said, 'I don't suppose you've seen what acid can do to a person's face. It's really not pretty.'

"I just sat down on the floor in the hall. I couldn't stop shaking and I was shivering as if I had a fever." She stopped abruptly as if the effort of telling her story had sapped her of energy.

"Listen, Sarah, this wasn't just sexual harassment, though that's bad enough. This was sexual assault."

"I know and I felt violated. I thought I could write it off to experience - a very bad experience - and move on but ...I can't seem to shake it off. I can't concentrate on anything and I'm constantly looking over my shoulder."

"It's no wonder. You've suffered a traumatic experience." He took out the small notebook he always carried - old habits die hard - wrote down Shona's details, tore the page out and handed it to her. "I want you to contact my colleague."

"But aren't you going to ..."

"I just feel that this would be better if a female officer handled this. She's highly experienced in cases of this nature. Not only will she follow this up but she can put you in touch with a support network of counsellors and so on."

Sarah's voice rose. "But I've told you about how that man threatened me."

"If necessary we can arrange protection for you." Her fear and vulnerability almost made Brian tell her the truth about his part in the investigation. He felt a stab of self-recrimination for having to dissemble but he had climbed out on a shaky limb that could come crashing down at any moment.

"I have to go." She edged quickly from her seat.

"Promise me you'll speak to Inspector Patterson."

"'ll have to think about it."

"Sarah, we can't let scum like Hastings get away with this. You need to do this for yourself but we both know this wasn't a one-off incident. Several other young women have left his employment under similar circumstances to yours."

She gave him an agonised look before heading blindly out of the café, just avoiding colliding with Donna who was collecting cups and dishes onto a tray. Brian watched her hurrying down the street with his emotions in turmoil. He swallowed back a rising feeling of panic that his interference Might have put someone else in danger, though in his heart he knew that the frightened, young woman who had just left would never find peace if she didn't heed his advice.

A cold rage sat in his gut like a stone. Rage at the arrogance and presumption of men like

Hastings who assumed his position and privilege would grant him immunity from the consequences of any action he wanted to perpetrate against women like Sarah.

Other thoughts gnawed at him. Was Hastings behind Irene's death? Was the dread he saw so nakedly displayed on Sarah's face what had driven Eleanor to call him? She might have easily felt as intimidated by Hastings and his hired muscle. He was pulled back from his turbulent thoughts by the reappearance of Donna.

"Finished inspect - Mr Lockwood?"

"Yes thank you, Donna."

When she had lifted the cup and glass onto her tray she hesitated.

"It's nane o' my business, but that lassie that was with you looked as if she was shittin' hersel'. She in trouble?"

"You could say that, Donna. But we'll get it sorted out."

"Sure you will, Mr. Lockwood. You're wan o' the good guys."

Brian was touched by her comment but as she went back to the counter he brooded. He wasn't convinced she was right.

Chapter Twenty-Eight

Archie Macdonald

Archie lay on his back in the hospital bed in his own bubble of pain. The morphine they had given him earlier was wearing off and his head throbbed rhythmically. His whole body ached. An army of devils walked up and down his spine in heavy boots of fire and one of them was plunging a spear again and again into his side. So this was what hell was like.

As if on cue, a dark figure appeared at the foot of his bed as he reached for his buzzer to summon a nurse. Archie peered through the gauze that covered his left eye. The Reverend Moir was a sorry-looking sight. His face was covered in bruises that were turning some interesting colours and he looked as if he had shed weight from his already skinny frame.

Even with his vision restricted, Archie could discern the haunted look in the minister's eyes and his posture suggested he was finding it an effort to will his legs to hold him up. He looked broken.

In a voice that sounded hoarse with emotion and perhaps disuse, Moir said, "How are you?" Archie indicated the chair next to his bed with a tilt of his head that caused daggers of pain to plunge into his neck and head. Moir slumped into it. At first Archie could only croak,

"You see it all," before his visitor poured some water into the plastic cup on the bedside unit, stooped over the bed and held the straw to his lips with a shaking hand.

Archie sucked on the straw greedily, feeling the lukewarm liquid running over the stitches in his mouth. He held up a bandaged hand to signal that he had drunk enough and Moir subsided back into the chair. The minister broke the tense silence with, "What are the doctors saying?"

"I'll survive apparently. They had to remove my spleen and there's some trauma to my kidneys that they're monitoring closely." He noticed the minister's eyes drifting to the bloody catheter bag by the bed. Archie thought he looked nauseous.

"There's no permanent damage to my eye they say and I ought to get normal vision back. Looks worse than it is. Sounds stupid but I've probably been lucky." He attempted to smile but his dry, cracked lips made it uncomfortable.

"Have you had ... " His voice broke, making him start again. "Have you had visitors?"

"Derek and Sally came from work - they left me that basket of fruit from the team. Help yourself." Moir showed no inclination to do so. He still looked green around the gills. "And I got a call from New Zealand. Spoke to my wife and daughter. That cheered me up."

After another lengthy silence, Moir said, "Look at what we've become."

"Forgive me, Mr. Moir, but you look in better shape than me." He thought to himself, but that's not saying much. He had to look away as Moir began to weep openly. He made a visible effort to pull himself together before saying in stuttering breaths,

"I'm so, so sorry. May I?" Without waiting for a reply, he took a bunch of tissues from the box at Archie's bedside and blew his nose loudly.

"I have a bit of a weakness for Western movies which I have to indulge in private because my wife - my wife can't stand them. The character I think I resemble most from those films is the one that shies away from the gunfire. The yellow-bellied storekeeper who refuses to stand up to help the sheriff against the bad men."

"Mr. Moir, you're a minister, not Clint Eastwood."

"I realise that but I should never have deserted you that night by the church. I'm like Peter on the eve of Our Lord's crucifixion. The memory of it makes me burn with shame. But no more. I hope you won't think even more badly of me than you do already but I've decided to tell them everything. For some time now I've been struggling with feelings of a homosexual nature."

Archie tried to conceal his surprise.

"Oh, I know that we live in a so-called more enlightened age and that there are even ministers who are being ordained who are - that way inclined. But I can't help feeling that it's wrong. There are plenty of admonitions in the scriptures to abjure such feelings after all. Perhaps I'm old-fashioned; out of step with the times. But that hasn't stopped me being tortured by my conscience."

There was a long pause before he said, "I had relations with the man who beat you so grievously." Archie must have failed to conceal his reaction because Moir went on, " I realise you're shocked but I feel that the only way out of this wilderness is to tell the truth in all its naked ugliness. So I've told my wife - and the police. I'm not sure where that leaves Marian and me. She's very upset. Somewhat surprisingly my daughter, Monica, was quite forgiving. I think she has Social Studies classes at school where they take a liberal view of what I believe are called LGBT issues."

The minister looked wrung out. "The thing is the police will want to pursue this with you so I thought I'd better warn you. As well as apologising for my stupidity and for my craven behaviour."

Archie said, "Maybe telling the truth is the way forward. Look at the dirty, crooked path that guilt and shame about sex has led us down after all."

"Yes. Yes. I believe that too. But I pray this won't compromise your job. And then there's the money you've lost. We've both lost. The police didn't find the bag in the churchyard. Another deserved punishment perhaps."

"Did we really deserve punishment, Mr. Moir? Maybe what we did wasn't so very wrong. We were so afraid of how people would judge us when who knows what sordid little secrets those same people are hiding themselves." His voice was fading to a thin rasp. Moir held the straw to his lips once more.

"I shall have to resign of course. I don't know what I'll do. I envisioned devoting my whole life to my calling. I'm not equipped for anything else. Then there's the damage I've done to my family, financially as well as emotionally. We won't be able to live in the manse anymore." He looked on the verge of tears again but he shook his head, stood and placed the plastic cup firmly on the unit.

"Listen to me - wallowing in self-pity when you're lying there in pain. As you've discovered I'm a weak man, Mr, Macdonald."

"We've both been weak. I hope you find a way through this, minister. I think we both will. We'll learn the lesson and move on. Despite everything that's happened we still have things to offer. We're not bad men and you surely have to believe that there's still forgiveness and compassion out there."

Moir moved to shake his hand before remembering Archie's bandages. He gripped his shoulder briefly instead, smiled thinly and hurried away.

Archie realised his whole body had been clenched during the minister's visit and he lay back, exhausted. But before retreating into the dark cave of his physical pain once more, he reflected that he hadn't been offering Moir merely tired aphorisms to make him feel a little better. Part of him, at least, believed what he had said.

They may have felt they were both stranded at the bottom of a well with no hope of rescue but if they looked up they could see blue sky and hear reassuring voices approaching. He pressed his buzzer to summon a nurse.

Chapter Twenty-Nine
Shona Patterson

The next morning Shona worked her way through an in-tray of minor cases that were as riveting as would have been the details of Hercule Poirot waxing his moustache or Miss Marple watering her garden. Her mind was preoccupied by the murders and she often found her thoughts drifting back to Brian and the last look he had given her in that shoddy pub.

Despite the fact that he had jeopardised her job, she understood what drove him because in her heart, she was like him. She felt connected to him by an invisible bridge built from shared instincts, a clear awareness of good and evil and a burning desire to confront the latter.

She wished that he would sit on his hands for a while 'til the police investigation caught up, as it surely would, but she knew that was like wishing her fairy godmother would appear and transform her into one of those beautiful detectives who inhabited the fantasy world of American TV crime fiction.

It was no real surprise, then, when she received a call from a young woman who informed her that Inspector Lockwood had advised her to contact her. Shona's first thought was - Inspector Lockwood; what the fuck was Brian playing at? But when she learned that the woman was an ex-employee of Arnold Hastings who was calling about a possible sexual assault, she was quick to assure her that she had done the right thing and offered to go round to see her. After a lengthy silence, the woman gave her name and contact details.

For the rest of the morning Shona's mundane case load was forgotten as she pulled the file about Hastings and his trial.

At lunch time she spotted Cameron sitting alone in the canteen and after collecting her food, she made for his table. "Mind if I join you?" She sat down without waiting for his reply. She felt as welcome as a eunuch at a sperm donation clinic. She ignored his truculence with the same determination with which she ignored the fact that he was picking his way through a salad while she was about to tuck into sausages, beans and a generous portion of chips. Maureen, the canteen woman, liked her.

She decided to bite the bullet and tell Cameron about her call from Sarah Fairbanks and her suspicions about Arnold Hastings. Cameron looked annoyed and puzzled. "Why did she get in touch with you?"

"I'm not sure. Someone whom I've dealt with in the past perhaps?" Shona lied.

"You can't go round and see her. This is connected to a case you're no longer on remember!"

"If this is a sexual assault case and she contacted me in confidence, how do you think she's going to react if a couple of other officers show up at her door? You know how carefully we have to tread with the potential victims in these cases."

Cameron looked nonplussed. He abandoned his salad and put down his knife and fork. "I don't like this one little bit."

"We could treat it as an initial routine enquiry that happened to come across my desk." Cameron continued to look fretful so Shona decided to shift the subject along. "How's the investigation of John Edmondson's death going? Have you had another look at Ben Thomson?"

"We spoke to the couple whose house Thomson was decorating. He was there on the day of the murder all right but he went out late morning, early afternoon. He said he was going to the paint shop to get more gloss but that gave him a time frame in which he might have paid Edmondson a visit. The problem is, there's no forensic evidence to show he was in Edmondson's flat and he does have a receipt for the paint but it still makes his alibi as shaky as my six year old niece's front tooth."

"I didn't know you had a six year old niece. You've never mentioned her."

"My sister's kid - bright as a rocket and twice as explosive and unpredictable." He smiled fondly before quickly shifting back to professional mode. "Again I probably shouldn't be telling you this but there's another thing that casts a wee bit of doubt on Thomson's involvement. Edmondson's post-mortem showed he had been attacked by more than one person and it wasn't the beating that killed him. His heart gave out."

He rose, leaving Shona to puzzle over this information. His parting shot was, "When you go to see this woman, I don't need to tell you to do it by the book and keep us informed every step of the way."

"Of course, Garry. What do you take me for?" His raised eyebrows and ironic half-smile were answer enough. She watched him as he encountered WPC Lisa Dewsbury on her way in. They chatted briefly but the awkwardness of their body language suggested that neither of them was enjoying a cosy, social catch up. Shona felt rather sorry for him. She'd bet he wished he had brought a packed lunch and eaten it at his desk.

She left her own lunch half-eaten partly because of a spasm of guilt at its calorific content but mainly because she was anxious to speak to Sarah Fairbanks.

She went directly from the canteen to the car park to avoid any difficult questions from her team or potentially distracting cases of petty theft or break-ins that might have landed on her desk. The girl's flat was in a modern development that had gone up at the bottom of the town on the grounds of the long demolished Western Hospital.

She pressed the flat's intercom button and waited. There was no reply. When she tried twice more with no success she had a sudden vision of the young woman lying lifeless among the debris of her possessions. She tried to calm down, telling herself the reason her imagination was leading her down such a dark path was because she had seen far too many corpses recently.

A middle-aged woman in a nurse's uniform came out of the building and eyed her suspiciously. Shona was conscious that she had been muttering to herself. Before the woman could close the entrance door, Shona moved forward, holding up her warrant card. "Excuse me. I'm from the police. I'm here to see a Miss Fairbanks?"

The woman examined the card carefully before replying in a broad Geordie accent, "Sarah? Yes she's on the same floor as me. But you're out of luck, I'm afraid. She's gone away for a few days. She said she needed a break. Left me her key so I could water her plants."

Shona stared at her, uncomprehending. Why would she do that when she had finally found the nerve to approach the police for help? Her first suspicion was that someone must have got to her. That was all she needed - another frightened woman gone into hiding.

"She's not in any trouble is she?"

Shona attempted a reassuring smile. "No. Nothing like that. Can I ask you how she seemed when you spoke to her?"

The woman looked around as if she was worried about being overheard. "To be honest, she hasn't been herself for the last wee while. She was always such a confident, vivacious lass but since she left her last job she's been - I don't know - a bit miserable looking and not nearly as outgoing and chatty. To be honest, she had a kind of startled rabbit-in-the-headlights look every time you met her."

"I don't suppose she told you where she was planning to go on this break?"

"No, sorry. You're sure Sarah's not in bother?"

Shona thought that Sarah might be in a whole world of bother but said, "Don't worry, Ms.?"

"Barr - Deirdre Barr. I'm a staff nurse at the Vic. "Which you probably got with you being a detective and that." Her smile as she looked down at her uniform showed she had meant the remark to be humorous rather than caustic. "And I'd better get to work now."

She took the card Shona proffered and assured her she would phone her when Sarah got back.

After she left, Shona stood outside the building paralysed by indecision and a creeping feeling of dread. She looked up to the slate grey sky as if she might find an answer to the question of what to do now written there. A steady drizzle began to fall.

Chapter Thirty

Brian Lockwood

After he had told Shona about Sarah Fairbanks, she had been silent for so long that he thought she had rung off. When she eventually replied with a curt "I'll look into it," Brian could sense her seething anger. He thought his meddling had already been burying their relationship and now he was shovelling another layer of earth onto it.

But she had continued, "I am mad at you, Brian, but at the moment I'm even more angry with that bastard Hastings and his like. If he's involved in these murders I promise you I'll nail his balls to the wall."

He had determined to let things settle for a few days and let Shona run with it but the next day, he received a call from Ali. "Been takin' a wee look at the computer shop as fuckin' requested, Herr Commandant. The Electronic Exchange it's called. Load of reconditioned phones and tablets in the windae. Some no' bad stuff at reasonable prices. Place was busy. Decent selection of Play Stations, X boxes and Nintendo and that. Actually bought a game wi' the wages o' my present fuckin' employment. The new 'Last of Us' game."

As far as Brian was concerned, Ali might have been talking in a different language. "Asked a few discreet questions like." Brian could imagine Ali's idea of discretion. No doubt, he might as well have brought out a loud hailer in the shop and asked everyone if they knew anything about three murders.

"Now, here's the interestin' fuckin' thing - the proprietor of said emporium is wan Crawford Welles." Brian was searching his brain for the significance of this when Ali went on, "Welles. Get it? Where have you heard that name afore?" Then Brian had it.

"Welles was Eleanor Thomson's maiden name."

"Got it in wan. Thought you were a bit slow on the uptake there, chief. Memory no' as sharp as it used to be? Maybe a relation to your woman? Big fuckin' coincidence if he's no'."

"Thanks, Ali. Good work. I'll follow it up."

"You can demonstrate your gratitude in the usual fuckin' way. Any luck wi' they lassies that were gettin' their fannies felt up by that sticky pawed cunt, Hastings?"

Ignoring Ali's crass take on sexual assault, Brian said, "Inspector Patterson's looking into it as we speak."

"Hope she manages to get somethin' on that slimy bag of broon stuff."

"She's a good officer."

"You tryin' to get into her police regulation knickers, Inspector?"

"Bye, Ali."

So it was that despite his resolution to take a back seat, Brian found himself outside the Electronic Exchange in Croft Street. It was nearly five o' clock and he thought the shop might be closing soon but, as Ali had indicated, it seemed to be enjoying a brisk trade. The clientele were somewhat mixed - a couple of middle-aged men were looking at tablets and an exasperated woman was arguing with her young daughter about iPhones, the gist of which seemed to be that the girl wanted a more top-of-the-range model that her mother was insisting was outside their price range. But teenage youths predominated.

A group of boys in school uniform was examining racks of computer games on the right hand side of the shop. Brian was ignorant about the world of gaming consoles by and large, but he knew that the violence and sexual content of some games meant they carried an 18 rating and he wondered idly how strict the staff were in checking IDs.

Two of the boys from the school group made a selection and headed for the counter that was at the left centre of the shop, while their companions drifted to the door and hung around there waiting for their friends. Brian went over to examine the games. He was shocked at some of the prices displayed. The cheapest games appeared to be around £25 and some that he looked at were almost £50. When he was the age of these lads his pocket money just about covered a visit to the sweet shop and the pictures.

He was startled by a voice behind him. "I can recommend the new Red Dead Redemption, Inspector Lockwood." He turned to find Jamie Dolan with an armful of empty games cases that he was about to replace in the racks. Brian had a flashback to the times he had interviewed the slight, wiry youth at the station. He had let his hair grow since Brian had seen him last - it had been shaved to the bone then but he now sported a neat short back and sides. He was dressed more smartly then in those days, too. Now he wore light coloured chinos and a blue sweater that bore the shop's logo.

At that time, he had tried unsuccessfully to conceal his fear under a facade of bravado and Brian thought that now he still seemed ill at ease beneath his nervous smile.

"Hi, Jamie. Your sister told me you were working here."

"Aye. Donna telt me you'd been speakin' to her in the café."

"She says you're doing well now."

"No' bad. I like it here and I'm goin' to the college. Mr. Welles, the boss, has helped me and that. He really kens his stuff."

"Glad to hear it, Jamie."

"Anythin' special you were lookin' for?"

"I have to confess to being a bit unfamiliar with all of this." Brian swept his arm round to indicate the games on display.

"Aye. You dinnae strike me as the Grand Theft Auto type. Maybe you shouldnae start. It's easy to get addicted to the games. I wance played Call of Duty for three days straight." He looked embarrassed as he began to restock the display units with the cases he was carrying. "So what can I help you with?"

"Is your boss around?"

Jamie dropped a few of the cases. Brian bent to help him retrieve them. "It's a' right. Inspector. I'll get them. Mr. Welles is no' in. Can I gie him a message?" Brian noticed his eyes drifting to the back of the shop.

"It's not important. I'll call back later. Keep up the good work, Jamie."

"Aye, thanks."

Brian moved to the door. When he glanced behind him, he saw Jamie hurrying to the counter where he deposited the cases and moved deeper into the shop towards a closed door at the back. Brian waited a moment before following him.

When he eased the door open he found himself in a workshop area. There were several large tables and work benches upon which were strewn electronic components and phones and laptops in various stages of repair. Jamie was standing at one of the tables talking urgently to a stocky looking man who was peering through his glasses at what looked like the shell of a mobile phone with its internal parts arranged neatly beside it.

They both looked up, startled, at his entrance. They wore the guilty, fearful looks of thieves caught red-handed in the middle of a robbery.

"Sorry to barge in, Jamie, but there was something I forgot to ask you. Is this one of your colleagues?"

Jamie looked as if he might speak if only he could remember any words. The man took off his glasses. "It's okay, Jamie. Get back to the shop. I'll deal with this." Jamie hesitated a moment before brushing past Brian, giving him a strange look that combined contrition and defiance.

"I'm Welles. I own this place. Sorry about our little subterfuge. Jamie's a good lad really. I ask him to tell people I'm not in so I won't be disturbed at my work. Doesn't do to get side-tracked when you're dealing with the internal workings of some of this stuff. What can I do for you?"

"I'm trying to find Eleanor, Mr. Welles."

"Eleanor?" Welles was trying for nonchalance but Brian had caught his initial unguarded expression. Shock? Fear? If he was related to Eleanor it wasn't reflected in any physical resemblance. Whereas she was striking, Welles was at best nondescript-looking with his unkempt, greying hair and a threadbare jumper that didn't conceal his paunch.

He paused before going on. "You're no relation then?" He could almost see the wheels going round as Welles worked out how to respond. Eventually he must have thought that there was nothing to be gained by lying.

"She's my sister. Why? What's she done?"

"When did you see her last?"

Welles looked as if he was trying to remember but Brian reflected he wasn't going to win any acting awards.

"Haven't seen her for a while. Sometimes I don't hear from her for months at a time. She likes to keep a low profile. Mainly because she doesn't want that psycho arsehole she was married to knowing where she is."

Brian regarded him in silence for a moment. His eyes slid down to the phone he was working on to break eye contact, then moved across to an adjacent table apparently to retrieve a small screwdriver. Brian thought it was so he wouldn't see him squirm.

"Well if you do hear from her, could you ask her to get in touch with me? Lockwood's my name. She has my number. It's important."

"Will do. But I wouldn't hold your breath. As I said, we're not in regular contact." It was clear that Welles was itching for Brian to leave.

Once outside, Brian went to fetch his car. He parked on the opposite side of the street from the Electronic Exchange, outside a sewing shop that was closed for the day, where he could watch the entrance unobserved. Half an hour went by as a trickle of customers came and went.

Eventually Jamie came out and pulled the metal shutters down over the shop's windows, shortly followed by Welles who was carrying a laptop bag and a tool case. The shop owner secured the shutters over the door. The two nodded briefly to each other and Jamie left.

Welles glanced around and then headed in the opposite direction. Brian watched his progress along the street before edging out and following slowly. Welles turned down a side street on the left and Brian slowed as he passed it. He glimpsed Welles opening the back doors of a white van that was parked a few yards down the street and placing the bag and case inside it.

A hundred yards down the street Brian swung round at the entrance to a car park and drove back, just in time to see the white van coming out of the side street and heading towards him. Brian cursed quietly to himself as he tried to find a suitable place to turn again to follow him. By the time he had done so the white van was out of sight.

He was just reflecting that this didn't happen in the seamless world of TV crime dramas where police trying to pursue suspects didn't tend to lose them in the first few minutes, when he spotted the van a few cars down stopped at traffic lights.

When the traffic began to move, Brian managed to remain a few cars behind the van which appeared to be heading west out of town. As he drove he was troubled by self-doubt. What if Welles was simply going home? Should he be doing this at all given Shona's warnings? Besides, his relationship with her was fractured already because of his continued interference. Did he really want to risk breaking it off completely?

The traffic became lighter as they drove west out of the town. Brian managed to keep at least one car behind Welles's van. They passed through what used to be mining villages in the distant past but were now so built up with new housing developments that they no longer merited the title of villages.

The white van appeared to be heading towards the Kincardine Road. Brian hoped that Welles wasn't going to go across the bridge there towards the motorways to Glasgow, Edinburgh and Stirling, but the van turned off the bypass onto a narrow country lane that passed a small graveyard and fields that contained bales of recently harvested hay. Dusk had fallen so Brian was conscious that his headlights could be seen by Welles when he looked in his mirror since theirs were the only two vehicles on the road. He attempted to hang well back.

The road narrowed as they approached a cluster of cottages and he could see the flash of brake lights as the van slowed and then drove up to one of them. Brian pulled his car over onto the grass verge and approached cautiously on foot. The cottage outside which the white van was parked looked to have been renovated recently. The rough cast on the walls looked fresh and he could just discern what looked like new tiles on the roof. After making sure that Welles was not in his van, he edged up to a window from which light spilled onto a small, overgrown garden area.

He ducked under the window. He could hear nothing except the light wind rustling through some nearby poplars and the isolated calls of birds settling for the night. Carefully, he raised his head and peered over the sill. He was looking into a modern-looking kitchen whose units and worktops had been designed clearly to give a rustic effect. He could see that the room was empty but he quickly ducked back down as Welles entered, followed by the unmistakeable figure of Eleanor Thomson.

He squatted there in a stunned mixture of disbelief and excitement before risking another look into the kitchen. Welles and his sister were standing at either side of a central breakfast bar. He was talking animatedly but Brian could not make out the words courtesy of the efficient triple glazing that had no doubt been part of the cottage's renovations. Eleanor looked as if she had just been told a live grenade was about to be hurled into the room.

When Welles finished speaking, she looked at him with such an expression of helplessness and despair that Brian felt an unexpected wave of pity for her. She looked as if someone had struck her and all she could do was wait for the next blow. Welles took a bulky looking envelope from his coat and handed it to her before tentatively patting her shoulder and leaving the room.

Brian scuttled round to the other side of the house. From there, he watched Welles coming out, getting into his van, reversing and driving off in the direction he had come. After waiting for a moment to ensure he wasn't returning, Brian returned furtively to the kitchen window. Eleanor hadn't moved. Her stillness and wide-eyed stare made it look as though she had been frozen by a camera flash.

Brian tapped lightly on the window. Eleanor couldn't have looked more startled and fearful if a gunshot had gone off. She dropped the envelope she was still clutching onto the breakfast bar and her hand flew up to her throat. After a quick glance at the window, she moved to a row of knives that were secured to the wall next to the sink on a magnetic panel. She selected a large carving knife and turned, holding it in front of her with both hands. Her eyes flickered anxiously towards the door and she rushed out of the kitchen.

Brian deduced that she was moving to check if the front door was locked after her brother's departure so he ran to the front of the cottage. He saw the handle turn and heard the rattle of a security chain. He knocked on the door and called, "Eleanor, it's Brian Lockwood. I know you're afraid but I promise you I don't mean you any harm. I think you're in danger and ..."

"You think I don't know that." Her voice sounded as if she was standing just beside the door. "Just go away. You can't help me."

"Let me at least try. Someone's killing your friends and I think they might be looking for you. If I can find you, then they can too."

"How do I know it's not you? After what Irene and I ..." He detected a catch in her voice.

"I promise you can trust me. I'm not looking for revenge or whatever. I know something of what you and your friend suffered. I'm not like those men and I get why you did what you did. I can't condone it but I understand it and in many ways I don't blame you. Can we talk face-to-face without this door between us?"

There was a long silence. Brian was about to plead with her again when he heard the security chain being withdrawn and a key in the lock. When he tried the door, the handle turned. She was standing in the narrow hallway still holding the knife in front of her. Without taking her eyes off him she backed into the kitchen. Brian followed, careful to keep his distance from her so she wouldn't feel threatened and strike out at him in fear.

As they stood regarding one another warily, he experienced a strong sense of déjà vu. He had once stood in another kitchen confronted by another frightened woman clutching a knife.

"There's no need for the knife, Eleanor." Her whole body was taut as a wire. Gradually, the wire seemed to break strand by strand and she turned from him and draped herself loosely over the sink. Brian waited 'til she eventually straightened up, threw the knife into the sink and faced him. Tears stood out in her eyes.

She was undoubtedly good looking but she now looked more gaunt and thinner than the voluptuous woman he had first encountered in the Coulters' bedroom. There were some grey roots showing in her red hair and her face looked as if something had leeched any spirit or animation from it.

"I was going to try to get out. Leave the country." She glanced at the envelope. "Leave all this mess."

"That wouldn't have solved anything. You don't want to be looking over your shoulder constantly." She nodded dejectedly. "Eleanor, who do you think did this to Irene and ..." He couldn't recall the name of the man who had been found in the churchyard.

"Liam. Poor guy. He was just like me and Irene, you know. Another victim."

"And who's victimising you now?"

She laughed without humour. "Take your pick. We made a lot of enemies. Including you." She looked at him directly for the first time.

"I'm not your enemy. Did you know that your old neighbour, John Nicholson, has been murdered too?"

Her eyes flickered fearfully from the window to the door as if she might see the killer standing there. She swallowed nervously but it was as if she had come to a reluctant decision.

"I first met Irene, ironically enough, at a victims' support group. We got on straight away. When I told her about Crawford's business she was more than intrigued and she came up with the idea of gathering information from people's devices and using it to ..."

"So that's how you selected your ..." He didn't want to use the word 'victims' in case she retreated behind her defensive shell once more. "Targets."

She hesitated and for a moment he thought he had lost her. After all, in her eyes he was still a policeman and she had committed a crime. But she sighed resignedly and went on. "Yes; the shop. My brother could get loads of information on people from the devices they put in for repair. That's how we knew about you going on dating sites."

Her look was wry and almost apologetic.

"That's how we knew about the minister's - tastes - and what that charity shop guy liked. Men are all a bit pathetic really aren't they? I didn't want to involve you, but Irene thought you were fair game. She had been treated so badly by the police and the courts after her - assault."

"So was this all about revenge?"

She slumped onto a stool by the breakfast bar and began to spin the envelope around distractedly. "Partly, yes but frankly we needed the money. I wanted enough to get right away from my ex. He was all Mr. Charm with our friends - good old Ben: salt of the earth. But behind closed doors he could turn into a violent brute at the least thing. Though I learned to avoid provoking him. That's why I went to ground so to speak."

"I get that. I've met him."

Her expression had softened when she looked up at him. "And Irene was broke after the trial. As well as broken." She smiled bitterly. "I would say Irene was always more - driven. It was as if she thought by punishing men she could exorcise some of her own demons."

"How did Liam come to be part of all of this?"

"I guess you could say Irene sort of recruited him. She and I would meet up in local pubs initially but when we were - discussing plans - we usually went outside somewhere we couldn't be overheard. We were in the park one night and he was there, sitting shivering on a bench – from the cold or withdrawal or both. Irene offered him a cigarette and they started this intense conversation. Turns out he was there to pick up tricks. Irene persuaded him he deserved better but I suspect she could see how potentially useful he could be to her scheme. The rest, as they say, is history. The three of us started meeting at the same spot in the park."

"What about Hastings? I can't imagine he's the type that would have called on Crawford's services."

"That was a massive mistake but looking back I think Irene always had him in her sights. She was desperate to make him pay for what he had done to her. Liam set it up. He knew from his contacts in the - trade - that Hastings was in the habit of frequenting some low-rent girls who were so desperate for their next fix they would do pretty much anything."

"I can guess that Hastings made them earn their money."

"I couldn't even watch the phone footage Liam shot of this poor girl being brutalised by that beast. The things he made her do." A visible shudder ran through her. "It went smoothly at first. When I contacted him with the film, he paid up. The cash was nothing to him. We thought that was that but we should have known better with a man like Hastings."

"You think he was responsible for your friends' deaths?"

"I think he's more than capable, don't you?"

Brian was silent as he mulled over everything she had told him. He knew she was right about their folly in poking a stick at a dangerous animal like Hastings - one that would turn on them savagely in an instant. But there were still some aspects of it all that sat uneasily with him.

"What about the night Irene was murdered? Weren't you in the Wallace with her that night?"

"Yes but I left her there. She said she wanted to have a quick ciggie. There were a couple of police officers patrolling the High Street so she didn't want to linger in the smoking area there. That was the last time I saw her. I can only assume she spotted the yard as she passed it and decided to have a quick smoke there. She was always talking about quitting but couldn't seem to summon up the willpower." Her smile was bitter.

"What about the churchyard? What was all that about?"

"That was Liam's idea. He wanted to access the cash more quickly rather than wait for the money transfers. I told him it was too risky."

Brian leaned towards her and said quietly, "You realise that your only hope is to come in and face the music."

She looked at him fearfully. "But they'll put me in jail. And what about Crawford?"

Brian knew that the maximum sentence for extortion was fourteen years but he thought that in the circumstances she was unlikely to face more than six and probably less. "There are factors in these cases that would make a jury sympathetic to you. You didn't demand money with menaces and your brother was only guilty of providing you with illegally accessed information. You know what the alternative could be."

She hung her head for a moment. Her eyes swam when she looked back up at him but she nodded.

"I suggest I take you back to my house and I'll phone a colleague of mine, Inspector Shona Patterson, from there. She'll understand your motives for all this if anyone can and I can assure you she'll be very interested in gathering evidence against Arnold Hastings. You can tell her what you told me and then you can arrange for a good legal representative to meet you at the station with her."

As she rose from the stool, she swayed for a moment and Brian thought she might faint. He moved to her but she held up her hands. "I'm all right. I'll get my coat."

"You'd better put that somewhere safe, too." He indicated the envelope. She picked it up and exited to the hall. When she didn't return after a few minutes, he began to worry she might have changed her mind and sneaked out. He glanced out of the window. There were one or two cars parked outside but he couldn't be certain which of them, if any, was hers.

He went out into the hallway and was about to call her name when he saw that the front door was ajar. He moved to it quickly and looked out into the night. There were no streetlamps and he could make out little in the lights that shone from the other cottages. The floorboard behind him creaked but before he could turn, pain exploded from the back of his skull and darkness descended completely.

Chapter Thirty-One
Shona Patterson

After wading her way in a desultory fashion through a few of the files on her desk that would never have featured in the casebook of Sherlock Holmes - a punch-up at a Chinese takeaway; a spate of vandalism to cars in the Chapel View Estate - Shona went home.

She perused the scant contents of her fridge before selecting a piece of cheese that had been in there for God knew how long. After cutting off the hard edges, she made herself an unappetising looking sandwich. As she rummaged in the cupboard for a packet of cheese and onion crisps, her eyes lit on the bottle of cabernet there. Maybe just one glass to take the edge off a frustrating day?

As she poured herself a glass, her mind ricocheted like a pinball from her concerns over Sarah Fairbanks, to her bemusement over Garry's information that John Nicholson had been attacked by more than one person. On an impulse she decided to give the sergeant a call.

"I'm off duty, Inspector. Can't this wait 'til tomorrow?" She could hear music and raised voices in the background.

"Sorry to bother you when you're in the pub, Garry, but I was just thinking about what you said about John Edmondson's murder."

"Hold on a minute." When he came back on the line it was obvious he had moved outside. "Listen, we pulled Ben Thomson in today since his alibi didn't hold up. Barclay gently suggested we might have evidence that he had been in Edmondson's flat on the day of the murder."

"Garry, you know that's ..."

"I know. I know. If his brief had been present he would have torn her up for arse paper. The thing is, when we mentioned the word murder, all his hard Mr. Macho aggression turned to jelly. He looked as if he was going to wet his pants. Anyway, in the end he held his hand up to visiting Edmondson but insisted all he'd done was to give him a bit of a slap when he wouldn't cough up his ex's contact details. He was adamant that when he left to go back to his decorating job in the town, Edmondson was still alive and nursing a sore face."

"Did you believe him?"

"If he was lying he deserves an Oscar. You had to be there in the interview room to see how the man crumbled to dust like Dracula in the sunshine. Obviously we've held him for further questioning so we'll see how it goes tomorrow."

"Thanks, Garry. I'll let you get back to your date."

"How did you know ..." She rang off before he could finish, more perplexed than she had been before the call. Was it really possible that Edmondson had been visited by someone else after Thomson? Someone who'd done more than just slap him around.

She downed the rest of her wine and poured herself another glass. There were too many things that they weren't getting in all of this. She switched the TV on to distract her from her confused deliberations and after channel hopping, she settled on an American detective programme in which an impossibly glamorous female cop was chasing down a suspect. She brought him down and handcuffed him in one swift movement. She had a few carefully arranged hairs out of place but no perspiration had smudged her beautifully made-up face. "Just like real life, " Shona muttered to herself.

She realised she must have dozed off when she woke with a start as her phone went off. She groaned at the stiffness in her neck and wiped some drool from her chin as she answered. It was Brian but his voice sounded distant and muffled. "Brian? I can hardly hear you."

"I've been attacked and Eleanor's gone. Can you come?"

"Eleanor. What the hell is ..."

"I'll fill you in when you get here. Have you got something to take down the address?" She knocked over her wine glass as she rummaged on her coffee table for paper and pen but left it to drip onto her rug in her haste to get to Brian. She switched off her television, which had moved onto some programme in which a man was being encouraged by a jolly, female presenter to look at the exposed vaginas of several women in cabinets lit by differently coloured lights and hurried to her car.

She punched the address Brian had given her into her satnav. Her wheels screeched as she took off and for a surreal moment she imagined herself as a less glamorous version of the character in the detective programme she had been watching earlier. She paid little attention to the countryside that flashed passed, only focussed on the dulcet instructions of the voice of her satnav as she edged up to eighty. She only slowed when her satnav voice told her to turn right and directed her down a narrower country road. Further down it, she recognised Brian's car pulled up on the grass verge.

When she was informed confidently that she had reached her destination she pulled up outside a cottage. Its door was wide open and she entered cautiously, calling Brian's name. She found him in a brightly lit kitchen sitting on a stool holding a blood-soaked dish towel to the back of his head. She had to resist her first instinct to rush to him and hold him. "My God, Brian, let me take a look at that."

Gingerly she took the towel, in which he had placed some ice cubes, away from his scalp. He winced as she examined the wound. Blood had run down from his scalp and soaked the collar of his shirt. "We have to get you to a hospital to get this looked at."

He grabbed her hand. "There's no time for that, Shona. They've got Eleanor."

"Who's they?"

"I was going to take her to my house and then phone you from there. She was only out of my sight for a couple of minutes. Someone sneaked up behind me and hit me on the head. When I came round I looked all over the cottage but there was no sign of her."

Haltingly, he filled her in on the events of that evening and what Eleanor had told him. In his urgency he stumbled over his words and occasionally moved his head from side to side as if to clear it. Shona realised that not only had she been listening to him open-mouthed, she was also still clutching his hand.

"I have to call this in, Brian, and bring Barclay and Cameron up to speed and we have to get you to Accident and Emergency. You may have concussion."

"Don't you see? That'll be too late. You know how long it takes for the police to grind into gear. They'll alert patrols to be on the look-out for her but I don't even know what car they took her away in. By the time they interview Crawford Welles and follow up on the other links it'll be too late. You heard what Eleanor said about Arnold Hastings. I'm almost certain that he's behind this and the police have nothing on him. They have no evidence to pull him in or search his properties. Mikey Rutherglen would have no more compunction about getting rid of Eleanor than he would for squashing a troublesome fly."

"So what do you propose we do?"

"Right now, we should check out Hastings's showroom."

"Will you listen to yourself, Brian? Even if we did that there's no guarantee they'd take her there. In fact, that might be the last place they'd go if Hastings wants to keep his lily-white hands clean."

"We have to try. I asked her to trust me. Implied I'd protect her."

"This isn't your fault and you're in no state to do anything." He looked so desperate that she wavered. "If we do go on this wild goose chase, promise me you'll back off then and leave it to the police."

He looked up at her gratefully and nodded. His legs wobbled as he tried to stand and she thought he might fall. She clutched him under his arms and they stood for a moment, uncertainly clinging to each other like shipwreck survivors as he steadied himself.

"I'm all right. Thanks, Shona."

"Brian, this is really idiotic."

When she looked up into his face he was smiling weakly. "Somehow I didn't imagine it would be like this the first time I held you."

She was almost overwhelmed by her conflicting emotions; the warmth of her feelings towards him was at odds with her doubts and fears. She was suddenly self-conscious but as she moved away from him he reached for her hand again. She realised she didn't care if it was a gesture of affection or if he didn't trust himself to walk unaided. She liked the intimacy of it too much.

As they left the cottage she recalled DCI Morton's words, 'Batman and fucking Wonder Woman'.

Chapter Thirty-Two

Brian Lockwood

As Shona drove along the road to Glenrothes, Brian's head felt as if someone with a large hammer was trying to smash their way out of his skull. The oncoming headlights made his headache worse and he felt sick. He didn't want to close his eyes since that might signal his pain to Shona but he knew if he threw up it would be worse. She would pull the plug on what even he believed was a futile mission and drive him straight to A and E.

He remained still and silent hoping that the nausea would pass. He had listened to Shona relaying a version of the night's events to her colleague, Cameron, and giving him the address of the cottage. No doubt a team was already on its way there but it was evident from Shona's expression and body language as she listened to the sergeant that he was giving her a hard time on the phone. She had signed off abruptly, telling him she was on her way in. Her thin-lipped frown had made him think she was going to be sensible and do just that but here they were on the dual carriageway.

He thought she was driving too fast but knew better than to say anything. It was as if she was anxious to get there and get this over with so she could get back to following the normal procedures. Brian was touched both by her willingness to trust his instincts and her courage in plunging with him into unpredictable, dark waters.

He also felt vaguely ashamed that he might be exploiting an aspect of her nature he had noticed many times in the past in their working lives together. She had a propensity to throw caution to the wind if lives were at stake. If there was the slimmest chance that their actions tonight might save Eleanor, he knew she would take it.

The silence in the car crackled with the electricity of his unspoken fears for her and her own doubts. He caught her glancing at him anxiously from time to time. He had a sudden impulse to tell her to turn back and leave it to her colleagues after all but she spoke as they reached the slip road towards Glenrothes.

"How do you think we ought to play this when we get there?"

"I think we should just have a quick recce of the area around Hastings' showroom. If there's nothing we head back. There's no way I'm going to jeopardise your career and worse by stupid heroics. Anyway, as you can tell I'm in no shape to face down the bad guys."

"You should be getting that head seen to. And I need mine examining as well for letting you talk me into this."

When they arrived at the industrial estate, Shona drove slowly passed the showroom, turned and then cruised passed once more.

"See anything?" she asked.

Brian could see from the illumination coming from the well-lit interior that the car park was deserted.

"Nothing."

"It's all locked down for the night obviously; I think we've wasted our time."

"Pull over here. I'm going back on foot to have a nose around."

For a moment he thought she was going to ignore him and drive on but she brought the car to an abrupt halt.

"Just wait here. I'll be back in a minute." He tried to sound reassuring.

"Kiss my arse." Brian bit back a retort that actually he'd rather like to. Clearly she was in no mood for ribald banter. She undid her seat belt and climbed out. When he went to follow her he was overcome with dizziness for a moment but shook it off. He couldn't afford to show weakness.

They strolled towards the front of the building as if they were about to go window shopping though there was nothing on display in the conservatory. Security lights blazed on as they neared the entrance.

"Shit. They've probably got CCTV as well and someone patrolling the estate at night to deter potential thieves or vandals. This is a really bad idea."

Brian didn't reply but moved passed the entrance and began to edge up the left hand side of the building. He could hear Shona's exasperated sigh but after a moment she followed him. He briefly reflected that it hadn't ended well earlier that evening when he had gone sneaking around outside buildings but quashed the thought as he heard Shona shuffling along behind him. At the rear of the premises there was what looked like a private parking area and Brian came to an abrupt stop that almost made Shona collide with him. She whispered urgently, "What?"

They were plunged into darkness suddenly as the security lights at the front of the building cut out. Shona was breathing rapidly behind him as he indicated the rear of the building with a nod of his head. She came up beside him and he silently pointed out the car that could just be discerned by an overhead light that shone from above a back door entrance to the showroom.

Even from this limited view, Brian thought it looked like a red top-of-the-range Mercedes, probably an S Class.

"What now?" Shona said, sotto voce.

Keeping his voice low too, Brian said, "I think someone's here. They would hardly be likely to park a car like that at the back of the building overnight."

"So - what? We just saunter up, knock on the door and explain that we couldn't sleep for thinking about double glazing and wondered if there was anyone around who could help us at this time of night?"

To Brian her acerbic wit demonstrated that at least she still retained her sense of humour. Her face was close to his and he caught the faint whiff of alcohol and cheese and onion on her breath. It was pleasantly reassuring and intimate somehow and he looked at her fondly.

She regarded him curiously. "What?"

Before he could answer, the back door swung open and a figure emerged holding a small suitcase. It was Mikey Rutherglen. He paused to double lock the door and crossed to the Merc. By the car's interior light, they could see him tossing the case into the back seat, getting behind the wheel and starting the engine. The sudden beam of the headlights galvanised Brian into rushing from the cover of the building. He heard Shona calling furiously, "Brian, wait!" but his only impulse was to stop Rutherglen from driving away. He placed himself in front of the car.

Not for the first time that night, Brian questioned the wisdom of his actions as for a moment it looked as if the driver might just step on the accelerator. A sardonic thought crossed his mind that it was hardly a dignified way to end up - a crumpled heap at the back of a double glazing show room. Shona appeared at his side.

"What was that you were saying about stupid heroics again?" she hissed at him. There was a tense hiatus during which Brian was overwhelmed with his fear for her safety. He was about to grab her and pull her from the path of the car when Mikey climbed out.

"Sorry, Inspector, we're all closed up for the night. Bit late for a visit isn't it?"

"What's happening here, Mikey? Boss happy about you using his motor?"

"I'm off-duty and he doesn't need the car. I expect he's sitting at home in his comfy jammies sipping a Horlicks and listening to Book at Bedtime on the radio. Who's your girlfriend?"

Shona stepped forward, raising her warrant card. "Inspector Patterson, don't you remember me, Mikey? I sat in on some of your more colourful interviews."

"This light's not good and I don't like to dwell on the past but you do look a bit familiar. Gone up a bit in the world?"

"Can I ask what you're doing here at this time of night?"

"Just dropped by the show room to pick up a couple of things. I was thinking of going on a little trip."

"Where were you earlier tonight?"

"Dropped Mr. Hastings at home after a meeting. It went on quite late. Then I went home to make some arrangements for my trip. What's this about?"

"You weren't paying Eleanor Thomson a visit then?" Brian interjected.

"Eleanor who? Don't believe I know the name. If you'll excuse me officers I have to get on. I assure you I haven't been drinking but I'm happy for you to breathalyse me and let me go on my way."

"We're not from traffic, Mr. Rutherglen. Could we take a quick look in your car?"

"You got a warrant?"

"You have to get up to speed with the current Police Stop and Search regulations, Mikey. We have the power to stop and search you and the vehicle you're travelling in if we have reasonable grounds."

"And what grounds would they be?"

"Reasonable suspicion that you have committed, are committing or about to commit a crime, or that you're carrying an illegal item."

"But I'm not doing any of these things."

"Then you won't mind if we search the car."

"But I do mind. Two police officers show up on private property late at night and want to search a car parked in a private parking space. Technically you haven't stopped me because I was simply exiting my legitimate place of employment."

"Let's not stand here quibbling about legal niceties, Mr. Rutherglen," Shona sighed.

"Just wait." He took out a phone. "Mr. Hastings. Got a problem at the showroom - being harassed for no good reason by Lockwood and another police inspector. They want to search your car. Could you get Stenhouse pronto? Need some legal back-up." He rang off. "Now I'm going to leave and we can take this up later with my lawyers."

Shona stepped forward. "Mr. Rutherglen, I am detaining you on ..."

But Mikey interrupted, "You're detaining no-one, sweetheart."

Brian said with more confidence than he felt, "Come on, Mikey. You're just delaying the inevitable. Let us take a quick look and you can be on your way."

Rutherglen squared up to him. "Let's all just calm down shall we? No need for any unpleasantness." He pointed to Brian's blood-stained collar. "You look as if you've had a nasty knock. It's obviously clouded your judgement. And I'd think again if you're contemplating any police brutality here."

Brian knew he was taunting them. Neither he nor Shona would fare well against a seasoned hard case like Rutherglen if he decided to resist arrest which he undoubtedly would. He was playing the odds. Whatever he was hiding he didn't want it discovered. Brian reasoned that it must be because it would have greater consequences than if he were charged with resisting arrest or, he reflected chillingly, assaulting two police officers.

They all stood tightly coiled and frozen in the car headlights 'til Rutherglen said with apparent sang-froid, "Well if you'll excuse me," and moved to get back in the car.

Shona shouted, "Wait!" She would have moved to him but Brian restrained her. She gave him a furious look. As she started to object, Brian became aware of a faint thump and muffled sounds coming from the direction of the rear of the car.

They stole an uncertain glance at one another. The noises began again. They were coming from the boot. Before they could react, Brian heard the engine of the Mercedes revving up and it accelerated towards them. He felt as if he was moving through treacle as he threw himself instinctively at Shona. He had a moment to feel the rush of air as the car narrowly missed them before he landed heavily with Shona, face down beneath him, on a gravelled area surrounding the parking space.

He had his arms around Shona's front so they took most of the impact and he could feel the sting from the backs of his hands where they had scraped along the gravel. Shona turned her head to look at him. She looked shocked and winded. The absurd thought flitted through his mind that if anyone could see them they would look like lovers caught in a clumsy embrace. Then he heard the car skidding to a halt.

Brian knew they had to move but his body didn't seem to be receiving the urgent messages from his brain. He turned his head slowly. The rear of the car was skewed at an angle. His head was ringing so that he could only just hear its engine ticking over quietly.

The driver's door opened and Mikey stepped out and began to stroll towards them as if he was taking in the night air and hadn't just attempted to run them down. Behind him, the noises from the boot had grown more frantic and insistent. Brian reflected that you hardly needed forensic detective skills to deduce that someone was shut up in there and he had a pretty good idea who it might be.

Mikey reached them and loomed over them, his anthropoidal shape momentarily concealing the car. He looked down at them disdainfully as if they were a minor obstruction he had come across in the road.

"Tut. Tut. Look at you two. You really ought to have just let me go on my way." Brian barely listened to him. His attention was fixed on the gun he held in his left hand. His fear seemed to sharpen his memory for detail. He had forgotten that when Rutherglen boxed for a living he was a south paw.

He focussed on the gun. Later on in his career he had done some firearms training and for a surreal moment he found himself identifying the gun as being different from the standard police issue Glock 17. It looked more like a Sig Sauer - perhaps a P226. He knew it was issued to some forces down south. A bit more heavy-duty than the Glock and, at this range, horribly deadly.

He felt Shona's sharp intake of breath as she lay still half underneath him. He turned his head to face their attacker. He was familiar with the metaphor 'staring down the barrel of a gun' but never expected it to be quite so literal as it was at that moment.

"Come on, Mikey. You don't want to do that. It's obvious you're in deep shit but now it's just up to your waist. If you shoot two police officers you'll sink so far down it'll close over your head." He felt Shona trying to move beneath him but he tried to hold her still.

"I like the way you talk, Lockwood. Eloquent like. I'm sure that'll come in handy when you're arguing your case with St. Peter. Surely you can appreciate you've boxed me into a corner here, see, so I've no choice. No hard feelings eh?" He flicked off the safety catch and Brian threw his body across Shona's. Even as he did so he was assailed by a moment of despair at the futility of his attempt to save her.

As he braced himself for the impact of the shots, the parking area was illuminated by another set of headlights. Brian forced himself to glance round. Mikey's attention had been drawn to the new arrival. He resembled an animal scenting the air for danger.

The car that had stopped sported a taxi sign on its roof and after an unbearable moment during which Mikey's attention flitted between the car and his cowering victims on the ground,

Arnold Hastings stepped out of the cab. It instantly accelerated off into the night. Hastings called after it, "You fucker," before marching over to them.

"I told that bastard to wait but the minute he saw that fucking gun he took off as if someone had set fire to his arse. Mikey, would you like to tell me, what the fuck is going on here?" The last words were shouted but Mikey didn't flinch.

"Just taking care of some business, Mr. Hastings." Brian thought his apparently respectful address to his employer had an edge of contempt.

"Have you taken complete leave of your senses? You're not seriously thinking of shooting cops? They'll send you down forever."

"We all know this has nothing to do with you, Arnold, so why don't you get back to your cocoa and the crossword and leave me to sort out this mess?" Again, there was an ironic note in his voice.

There was a suspicious tremor in Hastings' voice. "I can't pretend to know what's going on here, Mikey, but I do know this isn't in anyone's interest; least of all yours." It was as if he was putting on a deliberate act for the benefit of the listening pair on the ground.

To Brian's ear, there was a scarcely concealed subtext to the men's conversation and their eyes appeared to signal to one another. He rose painfully and tentatively and pulled Shona to her feet beside him, his attention never wavering from the gun that Mikey continued to point at them. He was conscious that Shona was trying to suppress the shivering that threatened to convulse her, but her voice seemed confident when she spoke. "Better listen to him, Mikey. This could all end very badly for you."

"Who asked you, bitch?" Mikey said with menacing softness.

Hastings said urgently, "Come on. Mikey. Just take off. I've phoned Mr. Stenhouse. He's waiting for my call. Once I get a bit of legal advice we'll see how the land lies. I'll sort this out and get in touch."

For a moment Mikey wavered. His eyes narrowed and a frown creased his forehead making him resemble an ape even more. Brian thought he could almost detect the cogs going round in his brain as he considered his options. He felt the ice in his spine as he reflected that one of these options was pulling the trigger.

Mikey appeared to come to a reluctant decision. Still pointing the gun at them, he backed towards the car.

Shona's voice rang out, "Hold on. You might like to let your passenger out."

"Passenger? But there's no-one else in the car." Hastings looked alarmed.

"They appear to be travelling in the boot." Brian couldn't help but admire the air of authority she had managed to summon from somewhere, despite the obvious weakness of their position.

"What are you talking about?" If Hastings was putting on an act for their benefit it was fairly convincing. Again, Rutherglen appeared to hesitate as his hand reached for the driver's door. Then he pressed the key in his hand. The boot flipped open and he went to it and using one arm, effortlessly hoisted a bundled-up body from it and dumped it unceremoniously on the ground.

Hastings called out, "Mikey," but his erstwhile chauffer ignored him, climbed back into the car and sped away. Brian and Shona reacted simultaneously as they rushed to the supine figure. It lay facing away from them but Brian could tell from the shock of red hair that it was Eleanor Thomson. They knelt beside her and she raised her head gingerly. Her hands and feet were tied with what looked like washing line and a paisley patterned scarf was tied around her mouth. As Shona worked at the knot on the scarf, Brian set to work on the ties on her hands and feet.

"Are you all right?" he asked her, as she sucked in air as the gag was removed. She nodded weakly. Her tear-stained face wore an expression of dazed disorientation. A bruise was forming on her forehead and Brian deduced she must have been banging it against the inside of the boot to attract attention.

Shona said, "Take a moment. When you think you feel able to stand we'll get you to hospital to get checked over." She took out her phone and began to speak rapidly into it, issuing instructions to alert police patrols to be on the look-out for a red Mercedes S Class. She gave them the registration number. Brian thought again what a formidable woman she was. Even as they had lain there, face down in the dirt and staring into oblivion, she had managed to get the vehicle's registration.

Hastings appeared at their side. "I trust you don't think that I had anything to do with this, Inspector. I hadn't a clue what my driver was up to. I'm as shocked as you are." He affected an air of bemused innocence. Brian thought it was as convincing as the denials of a five year old caught with his hands in the sweet jar, surrounded by wrappers. Eleanor looked up at him. Brian had never seen an expression of such naked hatred.

"You can explain all that round at the station, Mr. Hastings."

"You're taking me in?"

Eleanor signalled that she was ready to attempt to get up. Brian and Shona took an arm each and helped her. They held on to her as she struggled on shaking legs. "We'll get round to you, Mr. Hastings, don't worry. In the meantime, I suggest you report to the station with your lawyer. If you refuse to do so you can be assured we will hunt you down."

"I have nothing to hide."

"We'll see. Wait here with her, Brian. I'll bring the car round." She moved off up the side of the building in a stiff run. Eleanor seemed steadier on her feet but Brian still held her arm. In the awkward silence she continued to glare intensely at Hastings who moved away, apparently preoccupied with his phone.

When Shona drove up at last, Brian helped Eleanor into the back of the car. As he climbed in himself, Hastings reappeared. "Look, Inspector, I've just tried to get a cab but they're refusing to come out. I think their driver must have reported the - unfortunate incident - with the gun earlier. You couldn't drop me ..."

Brian interrupted him. "Sorry, Mr. Hastings, but Ms. Thomson gets carsick easily. Especially if she smells strong, unpleasant odours." A petty dig, he thought but satisfying nevertheless and he detected a faint smile on Shona's face.

Hastings glared at them with a murderous expression. Despite the fact that he ached from head to toe, Brian managed to give him a pleasant smile and a cheery wave as they drove off.

Chapter Thirty-Three
Shona Patterson

She took Brian and Eleanor to A and E. While they sat in the waiting room Shona phoned Garry Cameron to bring him and Inspector Barclay up to date. The sergeant listened to her mainly in silence - probably too stunned and furious with her to trust himself to speak. He informed her brusquely to wait for them at the hospital.

The waiting area wasn't busy - a young mother holding a begrutten and feverish looking toddler on her lap; a middle-aged man who grimaced in pain as he clutched his right arm to his chest; an old woman dozing in a wheelchair accompanied by a younger woman who watched her anxiously.

When Shona occasionally caught their eyes as they glanced over at the three newcomers, they quickly averted their gaze. She reflected on what a curious picture the three of them must present: Eleanor sitting slumped and glassy eyed; Brian with blood matted into hair and soaked into his shirt. The backs of his hands were lacerated and there was mud all over his coat. She was conscious of the graze on the side of her face that had happened as he had thrown her to the ground and the knee that poked through a large rent in her trousers looking red and angry.

The man and the mother and toddler were taken away. Shona offered to get coffee from the vending machine. Eleanor only shook her head but Brian accepted gratefully. She had gone to the machine before she realised she had no cash on her. When she returned embarrassedly to ask Brian for money, he was insisting to a nurse that she should see to Eleanor first as he was afraid she might be suffering from shock.

After she was led away, Brain rummaged in his pockets for change but smiled ruefully when he came up empty-handed. She sat back down beside him. Without looking at him she said quietly, "Thank you, Brian."

He said cynically, "What for? Trying to wreck your career and nearly getting you killed?"

"For trying to save me back there."

"If I'd been wearing a bullet-proof vest I might have stood a chance. That was just daft."

"But you tried." She reached out for his hands but she had forgotten the deep gouges in them and pulled her own hand away when he winced. "Sorry. I forgot."

At last they looked at one another. He said, "Does that hurt?" For a moment she wondered what he was referring to 'til he indicated the scrape on her face.

"Not too much." Warmth suffused her as she realised that he was moving his face towards her to kiss her.

"Mr. Lockwood?" A nurse stood over them. They sprang apart. Shona felt her face redden but Brian looked at her tenderly as he followed the nurse out.

They had no sooner disappeared than Barclay and Cameron entered with two uniformed police officers at their heels. Shona was mildly amused to see that one of them was WPC Dewsbury but was immediately chastened by the filthy look DI Barclay gave her. Just for a moment, Shona thought she might be better off taking her chances with Mikey Rutherglen.

Barclay said nothing but approached the reception desk, pulling out her warrant card. The uniforms followed her but Cameron sat on the edge of the chair next to her. Despite the lateness of the hour he still managed to look as if he had stepped out of a tailor's shop window. His appearance was marred only by the dark circles under his eyes and a scattering of stubble on his face. He made her aware of her own sorry appearance and she tugged self-consciously at the patch of cloth hanging from the knee of her trousers.

With his usual foresight he said, "You look a mess."

"You, on the other hand, look your usual lovely self so don't sit next to me in case people compare us unfavourably."

Cameron shook his head and looked round at the two women who were left in the waiting room. The old woman in the wheelchair continued to doze while the sudden police activity clearly had piqued the curiosity of her younger companion. Barclay returned. "We're going through to see Thomson."

Shona began to stand up but the DI said brusquely to her, "You wait here."

When they left, a nurse called her name. Dewsbury followed her as she was ushered into a curtained cubicle but was asked to wait outside. After having her blood pressure and temperature taken and answering a series of routine questions about medication, diabetes, etc. she was left alone for what must have been only fifteen minutes but felt interminable, as she worried over what was happening with Eleanor and Brian.

A short, slim, young, Asian woman appeared. Her dark hair was tied back in a ponytail and she was wearing a colourful blouse and light brown slacks. She introduced herself as Dr Choudhury and Shona couldn't help thinking she looked like a first year undergraduate.

She shone a light into her eyes, examined the graze on her face and asked her to remove her trousers so she could look at her knee. Shona was embarrassed at revealing her faded, pink knickers whose waist band had begun to detach itself at one side but reasoned that the doctor must see much worse on a daily basis.

After the nurse had returned to clean up her cuts and grazes and put a dressing on her knee, Shona asked the waiting Dewsbury if she could check on how Brian was doing. The young officer looked uncomfortable - no doubt conflicted about following the orders she had been given and having to deny the request of a senior officer. She felt sorry for the young woman and decided not to push it. Fortunately, as they passed a series of curtained booths they came across one that was open. In it, Brian was sitting on the side of the bed.

His face lit up when he saw her. "Hey, you okay?" he said.

"Just a bit bruised and battered - nothing serious. You?"

"They want to keep me in overnight for observation. Because of this." He indicated the back of his head, where a patch of hair had been cut away so that they could get at the wound there. "I expect your lot will want to interview me."

"I expect so. Anything you need?"

He shook his head. It wasn't just the presence of the young policewoman that made Shona feel suddenly shy and awkward with him.

"Well, hang in there. Catch up later?" He smiled and nodded.

Back in the waiting area they sat once more. Shona felt bone tired and, for reasons she couldn't articulate, quite weepy. Eventually, Cameron reappeared. "Lisa, could you go and join PC Langford. They're going to admit Thomson to a ward and we need to keep an eye on her. I'll make sure you're relieved at the end of your shift." They exchanged bashful glances before Dewsbury left.

He turned to her. "We're not going to get much out of Thomson tonight. Barclay and I are going to have a word with Lockwood. You'd best get off. We can pick this up in the morning. I'll arrange for a car to take you home."

Your Sin

"There's no need. I'm okay."

"You're not driving yourself."

The next morning Shona woke with a start when the faceless figure that loomed out of the darkness pointing a pistol at her in her dream pulled the trigger. She was gasping and sweaty. It had been the early hours when she had eventually got to bed and she had tossed and turned before falling into a troubled sleep.

She glanced in the bathroom mirror at her grazed face before taking an awkward shower, as she tried to keep the dressing on her knee dry by holding a shower cap over it. Her body ached. She had bruises on both legs and her left breast and arm. As she was drinking a strong coffee and applying makeup to attempt to conceal the damage to her face, her doorbell rang.

Cameron looked a little more rumpled than usual.

"Have you managed to get to bed at all?" she asked him.

"I got a couple of hours. Thought I'd swing round for you seeing how your car's still at the hospital."

"That was thoughtful, Garry."

He cast his eyes down and shuffled his feet embarrassedly. "A patrol picked up Hastings's Mercedes on the Edinburgh road early this morning and apprehended Mikey Rutherglen. He's due to be interviewed later at the station once his lawyer gets there."

"Stenhouse?"

"Nothing but the best. Paid for no doubt by Hastings - who's also coming in to make a statement incidentally. Let's get your car."

"I'd like to be in on the interview with Rutherglen."

"You know that's not possible. You're too involved in this."

She nodded her head resignedly. "You'll let me know how it goes then?"

When Cameron had dropped her at the hospital she went in to enquire about Brian but discovered he had been discharged earlier. She determined to visit him at home when she had made her own statement and knew more about the direction the case was going in.

It didn't take her long to discover that direction was badly. She gave her account of the night's events to DC Buckle who could scarcely conceal his disbelief. Shona thought uncharitably that if he was ever at the wrong end of a gun he would be an unmissable target. After she had managed, finally, to buttonhole Cameron, it was late in the afternoon and she immediately drove to Brian's house.

She saw his elderly next door neighbour watching her from her window when she arrived and gave her a wave and a smile that probably looked more like a grimace. Brian led her into his neat living-room. She declined his offer of tea or coffee. There was a distinct awkwardness between them as they sat at opposite sides of the room.

"How are you feeling?" she asked.

"Still a bit spaced-out to be honest and my head feels as if I've got the mother of all hangovers. You?"

"I've been swallowing paracetamols but my legs and face are still sore and my left boob aches." Too much information, Shona.

"Did they get him?"

"This morning. But Sergeant Cameron told me that Rutherglen and his expensive brief no commented them at first. After they'd had a confab the lawyer came back with the claim that his client had nothing to do with the murders of Irene Dunlop and Liam Jeffries. He offered to plead guilty to abduction, assault and possession of an illegal firearm if we dropped the murder and attempted murder charges."

"But surely they have him bang to rights on attempted murder after what happened to us last night. And what about John Nicholson?"

"Apparently, after more consultation, Stenhouse came back with a statement from his client that he had assaulted Mr. Nicholson but certainly had not killed him. Frankly, I don't think

Mikey would have confessed to any of the other stuff if Hastings hadn't been in the background pulling the strings. Mikey's street-wise. Normally, he'd have stayed quiet and taken his chances. You and I both know that Hastings put him up to the attack on Nicholson and Thomson. He's no doubt offered his pet heavy a substantial nest egg if he does the time just to keep his name out of it."

"So the slippery bastard wriggles off the hook." Brian looked so crestfallen that she had to restrain herself from going to him. "Shona, do you think Rutherglen was responsible for all of these murders?"

"I'm damn sure he was instrumental in Nicholson's death. That he administered the second beating that caused his fatal heart attack when he was trying to get information about Eleanor Thomson's whereabouts on his boss's behalf. The same reason why Eleanor's ex assaulted him, only Mikey was prepared to be a bit more - persuasive. I've no doubt we'll be able to get forensic evidence that puts him in

433

Nicholson's flat. Whether that'll be enough to get a conviction I'm not so certain. Especially with a lawyer like Stenhouse in his corner. At the very least he'll be able to plead it down to manslaughter."

"What about Irene Dunlop and Liam Jeffries?"

As if her doubts and anxieties jolted her from her seat, Shona rose and hobbled on her injured knee to stand uncomfortably at Brian's fireplace. "I don't buy it. It's possible that Mikey might have got rid of Irene on Hastings' orders. He could have been watching her and seen her with Eleanor. But that's a stretch. And I just can't figure out why he would have killed Jeffries."

"If you're right then the murderer is still out there."

"And if, as expected, Eleanor Thomson gets out on bail, she could be in danger still." She turned and stared into the fireplace. Brian had kept a coal fire as a feature of the room and she looked at the neatly knotted paper, and the carefully arranged sticks and coal that were set ready to be lit. She thought it showed his usual meticulous organisation.

He rose to stand beside her. They both were looking into the unlit fire as if they might see answers written there. She was conscious of his proximity but was too nervous to look at him closely in case he detected her naked longing for him to put his arms around her.

"Another thing that ..."

"There's also the unexplained ..."

They spoke simultaneously and she risked an apologetic glance at him.

"You go," he said.

"I was going to say there's nothing to explain how Irene and Liam were found. Why would Mikey Rutherglen want to expose them in that way? It just doesn't make sense. And Nicholson was fully clothed. I checked."

"You read my mind. It's as if someone was punishing them with that final indignity. Someone who felt they had suffered something similar because of their blackmail."

"Or had a grudge against blackmailers in general."

She was unreasonably disappointed when he moved back to his chair and sat pensively. The silence stretched between them until she felt her knee stiffening and she had to sit once more.

Eventually Brian said, "If you're right, then why was Eleanor's brother not a target? After all, from what we know Crawford Welles was the one who got the information about potential victims by using his IT skills."

"Maybe he's still a target. In which case, we have two potential victims to worry about. Anyway, I expect he'll be pulled in once Eleanor's told them what she told you."

"Poor Jamie."

"Who?"

"Jamie Dolan. Young lad who works for Welles. And from what his sister told me, Welles was sponsoring him through college too. Families like that rarely seem to get the opportunity to get on their feet and when they do the rug gets pulled out from under them. You met his sister in Giamatti's - the waitress who was pregnant."

There it was. The core of compassion and sympathy she recognised in him that made her - what - love him? Suddenly she was overtaken by a desire for him to take her by the hand and lead her to his bedroom. They could lose themselves in each other for a while. Remind one another that sex could have a lovely face beneath the veil of ugliness it was forced to wear by those who would exploit it for money or power or vengeance.

"Shona, I don't suppose you'd like to ..."

"Yes. Of course."

"But you don't know what I was going to ask."

She found that she was halfway out of her chair, so wrapped up was she in her fantasy. God knew what her expression and body language were communicating to him. Desperation, desire, determination? He looked puzzled. She gave herself a mental shake and reigned in the wild horse that was galloping towards the sunset with the two of them astride it.

"Yes. Sorry, What?"

"I wondered if you might want to go with me to talk to Jamie's sister tomorrow. I just feel the bad news about the shop might be better coming from me. Then we might grab a drink if you fancied it and go over everything that's happened again. See if we could get to the bottom of this swamp."

"Could do. Pick me up after work?" She knew that her erratic breathing and red face belied the casual tone and manner she affected. "Just use your loo before I go?"

"Just out there and turn right."

Great. Now he thought her flustered demeanour was caused by an urgent need to get to the toilet. Could she have appeared any less romantic and desirable? Way to go, Shona, she chided herself. Nevertheless, she was careful to pee against the front of the pan in case he might hear the splashing of her urine in the bowl.

Chapter Thirty-Four
Brian Lockwood

After Shona left, Brian sat gazing into space. He thought he might be suffering still from the after-effects of the blow to the head but part of him knew he was being disingenuous. The sexual tension between him and Shona had been palpable. He knew he couldn't have imagined it. Yet he hadn't had the guts to do anything about it.

Perhaps it was just as well. He had complicated her life enough already. He began to have second thoughts about having asked her to accompany him to see Donna Dolan the next day. Several times in the course of that evening he reached for his phone, intending to tell her he'd changed his mind but only got as far as staring at her name in his contacts list.

He persuaded himself it would be better for Donna to have an official there - and a woman at that - when they were imparting the bad news about the implications of the case for her brother's future. But he knew he wanted her with him for more selfish reasons. He craved her presence.

When he picked her up the next evening, she looked better. She had obviously showered after work - her hair was damp and sleek. He thought she was limping less and the graze on her face wasn't so prominent. She had concealed it more effectively with foundation. He tried to avoid it as he moved to kiss her cheek in greeting and only succeeded in planting his lips clumsily under her right eye and on the side of her nose.

When he asked if there had been any developments she told him that they were still holding Mikey Rutherglen. She thought the chances were they would refer the case to the Procurator Fiscal but she was pessimistic about the coming horse-trading. When he brought the car to a halt in a parking space in the town centre, he notice the dispirited expression on her face.

"Shona, whatever happens Mikey is going down."

"But for how long? I'm sure that Eleanor Thomson will get bail but knowing our luck they'll probably throw the book at her and Rutherglen will get a much lighter sentence than he deserves. And Mr. Teflon Hastings will walk away unscathed. DCI Morton cut me dead when I met her in the corridor today so you don't have to be clairvoyant to know what she thinks. Clearly I'm not her favourite person at the moment."

As they walked to the cafe, Brian thought he would be wasting his time trying to talk her out of her disconsolate mood, particularly as he suspected that some of her despondent predictions might be right.

He knew that Giamatti's opened later on a couple of nights a week but when they got there the cafe's closed sign was over the door. He peered through the misted glass and spotted Donna wiping tables down. He tapped on the door and she turned round looking startled. When she recognised him, she raised a hand and came to unlock the door.

"Sorry Mr. Lockwood. We're no long shut."

"That's okay, Donna. It was you we wanted a quick word with. You remember Inspector Patterson?"

"Aye. I mind you. You were in before. Just come in. It's only me here. The boss has left me to lock up."

When she took off her apron and invited them to sit at the table she had cleaned, Brian noticed she was wearing another good quality maternity dress and her hair looked as if she had been to the hairdresser's recently.

Shona pointed to the locket that the young waitress was wearing around her neck and said, "I love that, Donna. Really delicate."

"Thanks. It's real gold. Hallmarked and everything. Jamie bought it for me. What's up?"

Brian decided there was no way to soften the blow so he plunged straight in. "We think The Electronic Exchange might go out of business soon. It's been linked to an ongoing investigation and ..."

Donna looked as if he had reached across the table and struck her, "Oh no. What aboot Jamie?"

"That's why I wanted to speak to you myself, Donna. I hate to be the bearer of bad news but I thought it was better you heard it from someone you knew."

The girl's face crumpled and she put a hand up to her eyes to try to stem the tears that were beginning to flow. Brian took a bundle of tissues from his pocket and handed them to her. When she had recovered some composure she looked at them glumly.

"It's aye the same wi' us. Just when you think things are maybe lookin' up a bit somethin' kicks you in the teeth again."

"I know this is the last thing you need, Donna, after everything else that's happened to you."

"Aye. Ewan's death hit me hard but I was just beginnin' to look forward to the wee one bein' born and that."

"Ewan?"

"My partner."

Brian kicked himself mentally for jumping to conclusions on their last meeting.

"I'm really sorry, Donna. I hadn't realised. When you told me he was no longer around I assumed ..."

"Aye I keep wonderin' how I'll tell my bairn when she's old enough that her dad killed himself?"

The shock that ran through him made him think this must be how it feels to be tasered. He sensed Shona stiffening beside him. Before he could recover, she asked, "How did it happen?"

"Hung hissel'. In the park."

Brian wondered why he was so stunned. He knew all about the worrying statistics about young men who took their own lives. Yet something about the death of Donna's partner had aroused an intuitive presentiment that travelled up his spine before his conscious brain could process the information.

Shona reached over and put her hand on Donna's. "I'm sorry."

"It was wan o' his favourite places, the park."

Brian found his voice at last. "Do you have any idea why he might have done it?"

"He was that happy - he was lookin' forward to bein' a dad and that. But then a couple of weeks before he - died - he started actin' a bit funny. No' himself. I asked him what was wrong but he just said there was nothin' the matter and clammed up. It was afterwards when Jamie's boss was lookin' at Ewan's laptop he found this - stuff." She stopped to wipe her eyes and blow her nose.

"I know this is painful for you, Donna. If you don't want to tell us any more we'll understand." Brian looked at Shona who was smiling at the young girl sympathetically but he sensed that, like him, she was hoping that she would tell them more. The silence was fraught with tension - an elastic band that might snap and break at any moment.

"He had been chattin' wi' a lassie online. A' innocent like at first. Then there were photies of this braw lookin' Asian girl. In the later ones she wasnae wearin' much. Her texts asked Ewan if he would show her his - body. Then there were these selfies he'd taken o' himself. You know - revealin' ones. No' soon after that, the messages changed

- became really threatenin'. Sayin' they would post his pictures online if he didn't send them money."

Shona said, "And Crawford Welles showed you all this?"

"No. He told Jamie all about it and Jamie told me. Mr. Welles knew how upset Jamie was. Him and Ewan were best pals. I expect he thought if we could understand why Jamie might have done it we'd at least be able to make some sense of it."

Brian's thoughts were racing but one word kept flashing like a neon sign in his head - blackmail. He could tell by the stricken look Shona gave him that she was aware of how significant Donna's revelations might be. If only he'd been a bit more curious before - asked her more questions about why she was single and pregnant. His own assumptions and unconscious prejudices had clouded his judgement.

Donna went on, "I mean, I thought I was enough for him."

"None of this is your fault, Donna." Shona gripped the girl's hand more tightly.

"The thing is I'd have forgiven him. He must have felt that ashamed but he didnae need to. Our wee girl's future was more important than a' this - this."

She was failing to put into words her ex-partner's behaviour and Brian could sympathise. He knew he had to try to be delicate with the fragile girl in front of him but he also had to know if the suspicions that were breaking over him like waves had any substance.

"How did Jamie react to all this, Donna?"

"He became really broody. He was never one to show his feelin's. Even when Ewan died he seemed to bottle everythin' up. I mean it must have been terrible for him when he found him in the park that mornin'."

Brian and Shona exchanged a look. He wondered if she sensed the dread that was beginning to envelop him in a chilling embrace. "Jamie found Ewan's body?"

"Aye. I was up early that day. Couldnae sleep - I've been a martyr to indigestion since - " She indicated her bump. "There was nae sign o' Ewan.

I was worried. He never usually went out that early. I went and woke Jamie and asked him if he had seen him. He thought maybe he'd just went for a walk. He'd taken to doin' a lot of walking lately. Usually in the park. Him and Jamie knew that park like the back of their hands ever since they had played there as kids. That was the first place Jamie thought of lookin'. He knew Ewan's favourite spots there. That was how he found him - at the - the tree."

Tears began to run freely down her face once more. Shona spoke to her softly, "We're sorry for making you go over this again, Donna. It must be really painful for you."

"Aye."

Brian knew Shona shared his compassion for the girl but he had to risk one more question, however insensitive it might appear.

"I couldn't help noticing the last couple of times I've seen you, Donna, that you've been getting your hair done regularly, buying new outfits. And then your new jewellery." He ignored Shona's reproachful look.

Donna brightened a little. "Aye. Jamie's been really generous. Says Mr. Welles has been that pleased with his work he's gave him a bonus."

Shona's brows were knitted as she looked at him and he did his best to conceal his scepticism. "You're just knocking off for the night obviously and you're upset. How about if Inspector Patterson and I give you a lift back to your flat?"

"Ta, Mr. Lockwood. That's good of you. I'll just finish up here and get my coat."

When the girl moved to the tables to the rear, out of earshot, Shona said, "I think I know where your mind's going with this, Brian."

Lowering his voice, he said, "Donna's partner kills himself. Why? He was being blackmailed. I don't know about you but that set off alarm bells for me."

Shona nodded. "And her brother discovered the body. Are you thinking that might have triggered ...?"

"He was never one of the suspects I'd have gathered into the drawing room before the denouement and the last thing I want is to find out Jamie's involved. But another coincidence? And Jamie knew something about how Welles operated. Another thing - where's he been getting the cash to give to his sister? I don't believe Welles dishes out generous bonuses to his staff."

"Maybe when we take Donna home we can have a quiet word with Jamie."

As if on cue, Donna returned, buttoning up what looked to Brian like a new coat.

Chapter Thirty-Five
Shona Patterson

As Brian drove them to the Chapel View estate, Shona sat in the back of the car with Donna. She wanted to signal to the still distraught girl that she was there to support her rather than bring more trouble to her door.

Brian parked outside an ugly, grey building surrounded by similar ugly, grey buildings. She noticed that he looked around warily when he got out as if he suspected that this wasn't the safest place to leave his car unattended. The flats were on three levels, two flats facing each other on each level. Donna's was at the top and there was no lift.

They let the pregnant girl lead the way. She climbed the stairs laboriously. Shona, behind her, could see the dark blue tracks on her calves that signalled the beginning of varicose veins.

One or two of the flats they passed had scuffed looking paintwork on their doors. There was a child's buggy outside one that they had to navigate around and the distinctive sickly smell of weed emanated from another. Nevertheless, the stairwell looked reasonably clean and well-kept and there was an absence of the graffiti that Shona had encountered before in other blocks of flats on the estate.

At the top, Donna unlocked the door to the flat on the left. They found themselves in a hallway so narrow they had to remain in single file as they went along it. The air freshener or potpourri that Shona smelled failed to disguise an underlying odour of bleach. Five doors led off the corridor. Donna called, "Jamie? Are you in?" before leading them to a neatly furnished living room at the rear.

The first thing that caught the eye was what looked like a 55 inch wall-mounted television. The furniture was utilitarian but it looked well cared for and there were some colourfully embroidered cushions on the small settee.

Shona felt a pang of sadness mingled with respect for this girl who, despite everything the world threw at her, clearly tried to keep her own small sanctum clean and ordered.

"Have a seat. Would you like tea or coffee?"

She and Brian declined. "Looks like Jamie's oot but I'll just check his room. Sometimes when he gets his heid stuck into one o' his computer games you could put a bomb under him and he wouldnae budge."

When she left, Brian went over to the television set. "This looks new. These things cost around one and a half grand." Donna returned.

"Sorry nae sign o' him. Mebbe held up at the shop. Sometimes he helps Mr. Welles wi' cashin' up and that. No' that he'll be daein' that much longer." She looked bereft once more.

"Donna, do you think we could take a quick look at Jamie's room?" Shona asked gently.

"What for?" She eyed them suspiciously but as Shona was trying to think up a plausible reason she said resignedly, "Aye, I suppose so. But I warn you he's no' the tidiest." She took them back along the narrow corridor to the first room they had passed when they came in. On the door was a sign that said 'Toxic Waste. Keep Out'. "See what I mean?" She opened the door and stood aside so that they could look in.

The curtains were drawn but they could see in the gloom that, in contrast to the neat living-room, Jamie's bedroom was chaotic. The bed was unmade and clothes were strewn around the floor with what looked like a pile of dirty pants and socks lying in one corner. Toxic indeed, thought Shona but at least the lad had a sense of humour. Donna opened the curtains and, bending with difficulty, began to pick up some of the discarded clothes. "Sorry about this."

Shona shrugged and smiled at her as Brian moved to a desk unit that was under the window and started examining some of the boxes that lay open around a computer with a decent sized screen and a gaming console. The games that lay randomly around the desk indicated that Jamie was less than conscientious about returning them to their correct cases. "I recognise some of these titles from the shop," said Brian.

"You've been to the shop?" Donna looked anxious.

Brian ignored the question and said, "You think he might still be there, Donna?"

"Mebbe. Do yous want to wait for a wee while. He might no' be long."

"That's okay, Donna. We'll catch him later." Shona wished immediately that she'd chosen a less ambiguous phrase but the girl didn't seem to pick up on it. Shona looked at Brian and indicated with a slight nod that they should go. He got the message and headed for the door.

"Thanks, Donna. We'll be in touch."

As Shona was about to follow them, she took a last look around the room. Her eyes lighted on a handle that just protruded from under the unkempt bed. She could hear Brian and Donna chatting in the hall as she knelt quickly and pulled out a new looking sports bag. She glanced nervously at the door, fearful that Donna might return, as she pulled the zip across. With a shock of realisation she saw the two bundles of bank notes that lay at the bottom of the bag.

Just in time, she kicked the bag back under the bed without bothering to zip it back up as

Donna put her head around the door. "Everythin' a' right?" Shona gave the girl what she hoped was a reassuring smile, praying the girl couldn't detect her consternation at her discovery.

Back in the narrow hall, Brian looked at her questioningly but she avoided his eyes as she attempted to inject a cheeriness she didn't feel into her farewell to Donna.

Outside as they made their way to his car Brian said, "What?"

"We have to find Jamie Dolan urgently."

Chapter Thirty-Six

Brian Lockwood

Brian's heart sank when Shona told him of her discovery in the bedroom as they drove back to the High Street. Not only because he had been hoping that their suspicions were unfounded but also because of the likelihood that the presence of the sports bag and its contents placed Jamie at the churchyard on the night of that young man's murder - he seemed to have a mental block about his name.

When they reached The Electronic Exchange, the shutters were pulled down over the windows but the ones above the door were only halfway down. Brian winced at the noise they made as he pushed them up. When he tried the door he found it was unlocked. Shona put a restraining hand on his arm and said, "Maybe it would be better if I went in first."

He thanked her but said, "I know Jamie, Shona. If he's here he might listen to me." She nodded reluctantly and they made their way cautiously through the shop to the workshop at the rear. Brian listened at the door. He thought he heard voices inside. One of them seemed to be distressed so he abandoned his tentative approach and burst in.

The place looked as if a tornado had torn through it. The work benches were covered with the smashed remains of computer screens and mobile phones and the floor was littered with glass and bits of equipment that were impossible to identify from their crumpled metal and the wires that protruded from them.

In a corner at the back, Crawford Welles was cowering almost as if he were trying to squeeze himself under the bench. Jamie stood over him holding a baseball bat. When he saw that the intruders were him and Shona, Jamie raised the bat higher and said, "Dinnae come nae closer, Mr. Lockwood."

Welles made a strangled sound and covered his head with his hands.

Shona spoke. "Come on, Jamie. Don't make this worse for yourself."

Jamie laughed bitterly. "Worse? How could it get ony worse for me? Ye ken this man's a piece of blackmailin' scum just like the rest of them. I thought your lot would have him in the jail after I heard you'd picked up his sister. I caught him takin' all the money oot the till and grabbin what he could in here. He was obviously goin' to make a run for it.' "

Brian tried to look relaxed. He put his hands into his coat pockets and leaned against one of the benches. He spoke quietly. "We know what happened to Ewan, Jamie. We know how much that must have hurt."

Jamie suddenly looked like the frightened boy Brian remembered from his early encounters with the would-be delinquent. His grip on the bat seemed to loosen but just then Welles made a move to rise and he brandished it once more. "Dinnae move or I swear I'll smash your fuckin' heid in." Welles froze with his hands still over his head.

"Jamie, it must have been horrible finding your best friend like that but this isn't the answer."

"Fuckin' horrible? You dinnae ken the half o' it." Tears stood out in his eyes as they stared into the darkness of the past. "He was hangin' there. From the tree. His tongue was stickin' out and his face looked kind of black. The worst thing - the very worst thing - he'd been wearin' these low rise jeans and they'd fallen down around his ankles. Mebbe when the - the rope jerked. I mean it wasnae dignified. Anyone could have seen him hangin' exposed there in shit-stained underpants. I wanted tae cut him doon. Cover him up. But I knew I couldnae so I phoned. When the emergency services arrived I couldnae bear them seein' Ewan like that."

"Jamie, did you kill Irene Dunlop and ..."

"Liam Jeffries," Shona interjected. Why the hell couldn't he remember the guy's name, Brian chided himself.

"I knew what him," he gave Welles a look of loathing, "and his sister and her pal were up to. I mean they had nae idea the torture they were puttin' folk through. They were just as bad as the bastards that got to Ewan. I started followin' the two women. Saw them meetin' up wi' that big guy. They used to meet up in the park. They never saw me watchin' them. I ken that park inside out like. A' the time it was buildin' up inside me. When I saw the two lassies comin' out of the Wallace that night I thought to myself - you've been plottin' to ruin some other poor bastard's life; I followed the blonde one. Saw her lightin' up in the yard at the back and it was like a red mist came ower me. She never even heard me. I grabbed a brick and hit her - just the once but I knew when I saw the blood she was ...I smashed her phone and chucked the brick. Then when I looked at her lyin' there I thought back to Ewan. I yanked the skirt she was wearin' above her waist."

There was an appeal in his eyes as he regarded them.

"I mean, I wasnae interferin' wi' her or nothin' like that. It was just I wanted her to be found like Ewan. Christ, I sound as if I'm aff my heid."

Shona asked, "What about Liam Jeffries?" She had her hand in her coat pocket and Brian suspected she had set her phone to record the conversation.

"One of the nights I followed them from the park I saw them goin' into the church. I saw the big guy buggerin' this guy against the wall. He was wearin' a dog collar so I assumed ..."

Brian heard Shona give out an involuntary gasp.

"Mrs. Thomson was filmin' it so I knew he was goin' to be wan of their marks. Then after I done - what I done - I knew it was dangerous for me to be near them but I couldnae help myself. I kept watchin' the two of them when they met in the park.

"One night after they'd split up I followed the guy to the church. I saw him deckin' the minister and then settin' about this other guy that had been hidin' wi' a camera. I mean I thought he was goin' to kill him. I had this wi' me." He indicated the baseball bat," So I ...At first I thought I was just stopping him fae beatin' the man to death but then I saw him as one of the scum that made

Ewan do what he did and I started really layin' into him.

"Then I thought I'd leave him like the blonde woman. I pulled doon his kecks. I saw he wasnae wearin' pants but I thought, serves you right. I checked the guy he had been hammerin' was still breathin'. The minister had run - so much for doin' the Christian thing, eh? I noticed the bag wi' the money so I - I took it."

"Now what, Jamie? You planning to kill someone else? This isn't you. Even when you were getting into trouble in the past I could always see that underneath the tough exterior there was a decent young man." Jamie looked uncertain for a moment. There was a lost look in his eyes. Brian stood up carefully and took a couple of steps towards him, holding out his hand.

"Stay back, Mr. Lockwood. I'm warnin' you." There was no conviction in the threat.

"Jamie, come on, just give it up. You know I'll do my best for you. Remember I did it before." For a moment they all stood motionless. Brian could sense Shona tensing beside him. Welles was hardly breathing, staring up at Jamie wide-eyed as if anticipating the smashing impact of the bat swinging into his upturned face.

At last, Jamie seemed to relax his hold on his weapon but as Brian took another tentative step, he suddenly threw it at him and raced for a door at the back of the workshop. Brian was caught off-guard by the sudden pain in the elbow and forearm he had held up instinctively to protect his head. When he had recovered, he made to follow Jamie but Shona gripped his unimpaired arm and said, "Wait, Brian." She had her phone out. Before she could use it, Brian said to Welles, "Where does that door lead to?"

"There's an alley that goes to the High Street." His voice was a hoarse croak. "But he took my keys. The keys to my van."

"Wait here," he said to Shona as he raced towards the door, though he was unsurprised to find her hard at his heels. "Okay. Let's get to my car. I know where Welles parks his van." They ran along the alley and jumped into his car, both of them awkwardly fastening their seat belts as he accelerated along the High Street. Sure enough, Brian recognised the white van as it careened recklessly with its headlights off from the street where Welles had parked before.

Horns blared angrily as the van swerved in front of a Volkswagen Golf, barely missing it as it took the southbound exit from the roundabout. Shona was on her phone to the police. She told them that they were in pursuit of a possible murder suspect in a white van - she gave them the vehicle's registration and current location - and issued instructions that patrols should attempt to intercept it.

Jamie was driving so recklessly that Brian struggled to keep the van in sight. He barely braked at road ends and cut up other vehicles ruthlessly, some of them screeching to a halt to avoid collision. Brian recalled Jamie's petty crimes in the past had included joy-riding. None of the gang he ran with at the time had so much as a provisional licence between them. He wondered if Jamie had even sat his driving test in the interim.

They raced south through smaller villages whose tentacles reached out to Dunmalcolm, as commercial and residential housing developments proliferated. Brian gripped the steering wheel 'til his knuckles whitened, as his imagination painted the scene ahead red. He envisioned Jamie losing control and smashing into oncoming traffic; in his mind's eye he saw the bloodied and broken bodies of unsuspecting pedestrians or cyclists.

He was aware of Shona beside him with her hands on the dashboard, her foot pushing into the floor in involuntary spasms of phantom braking. Her voice trembled as she said, "Brian, I think he's heading for the Road Bridge."

The Firth of Forth was traversed by three bridges. It always filled Brian with a sense of awe when he saw these magnificent testaments to the ingenuity of men. The original Forth Bridge was a miracle of Victorian engineering that carried rail traffic to and from Fife. Its sister bridges were no less impressive. The newest bridge, the Queensferry Crossing, had been opened just a few years before to cater for the relentless increase of road traffic. The older road bridge, opened in the sixties, now was used only by public transport, motorbikes, cyclists and pedestrians.

Brian thought that Shona was right - it was to the latter bridge that Jamie was heading. He was struck suddenly by a sense of horrible foreboding as the white van accelerated towards its northern entrance. Traffic was light so he pushed his foot to the floor. He saw that he was gaining on the van and he could hear sirens in the distance. He was still a few hundred yards behind as both vehicles sped onto the bridge.

In a confusion of tortured brakes and smoking tyres the van came to a halt, slewed diagonally across the carriageway. The driver's door was thrown open and they watched as Jamie emerged running and vaulted the barrier onto the pedestrian walkway. They pulled up a few yards behind the van and he and Shona leapt out and hurried in pursuit.

Brian thought his worst fears were about to be realised when Jamie climbed onto the outer rail that ran the length of the bridge. For a moment he perched there precariously. He was looking up towards the St. Andrew's cross bracing of the upper part of the bridge, rather than down at the dark mass of the Forth and this only served to increase Brian's sense of unease. Perhaps the young man was steeling himself to jump and couldn't bring himself to look down. A stiff wind blew across the bridge and they could see Jamie swaying as he clung to his perch.

He followed Shona's lead as she slowed down a few yards from him, aware that she was fearful of getting too close and possibly precipitating an impulsive reaction from Jamie.

"Wait, Jamie."

"That's far enough, Mr. Lockwood."

"Think, Jamie. This isn't the answer."

"There's nae answer, Mr. Lockwood. I'm finished."

"I promise I'll help you in any way I can."

"What can you dae? Mind, when you took us to see they long term cons in Saughton. I admit they put the fear of god intae us about finishing up behind bars. I couldnae face that."

"Jamie. I'll get you the best legal help I can. There are mitigating circumstances. You might not have to do much jail time." He could feel Shona's doubtful gaze on him but he knew she was sensitive enough to realise he was trying to solve the immediate problem of talking the young man down. They could deal with the rest afterwards.

"Who do you think you're kiddin'? I killed two folk. I'll get done for murder."

"Come on - you're young. You can still have a life after all of this." As he spoke, he was taking slow tentative steps towards the rail. "Think, Jamie. Think of how you felt when you found Ewan. Think what it did to Donna - is still doing to her. How is she going to cope with another suicide? She needs you, Jamie."

Their eyes met, Jamie's full of doubt and torment.

"What good will I be to her in prison? What's she goin' to do - bring the bairn wi' her on monthly visits?"

"At least you'll be here. She won't be left to mourn her brother as well as her partner. What do you think this is going to do to her?"

For a moment he seemed to be wavering - Brian took the opportunity to close the gap between them. He had been aware vaguely of the approaching sirens but now a police car sped onto the bridge. Shona, showing more athleticism than he would have expected, ran back towards it and leapt the pedestrian barrier back onto the carriageway, holding her warrant card in the air and flagging them down.

Jamie looked at the car and then for the first time leaned out and looked at the iron waters far below. Directly across from them the Queensferry Crossing sailed above the darkness like the rigging of a beautiful and intricate schooner. Brian was so close to him now that he could see his grip slackening on the rail and the tears that stood out in his eyes, caused partly by fear and desperation and partly by the wind that had picked up considerably during their impasse.

"Please Jamie. Think of Donna."

Brian was now within touching distance of the fearful, disturbed boy - and that's all he is, he thought. After another brief glance at the drop below him, Jamie turned back to Brian with such a look of misery and resignation that it pierced his heart. There was a moment of relief as he realised that Jamie had decided he couldn't go through with it, but it was short-lived as there was a sudden fierce gust of wind and Jamie appeared to overbalance.

Brian had a momentary impression of a white, shocked face as Jamie began to fall. He made a despairing lunge towards the rail, hitting it with an impact that winded him and only just succeeded in gripping the sleeve of the boy's jacket as he fell. For a moment, he feared that the momentum of the fall might wrench the shiny material of the jacket out of his grasp but he managed to swing his other arm across and get a hold of Jamie's forearm.

He gritted his teeth and looked down at the terrified youth suspended above the grey waters of the river hundreds of metres below. He felt the sweat dripping from his brow and more worryingly felt its treacherous slipperiness on his hands.

Jamie hissed, "Mr. Lockwood, please dinnae ..."

The muscles in arms that already had taken some punishment in the past few hours screamed at him, as he tried to maintain his grip. He was conscious that he was being forced further over the rail in an effort to pull the boy up. As the wind whipped at his coat, he realised that if he didn't let go there was a real danger that at any moment they could both plummet to their deaths.

Just as he thought his muscles couldn't take the strain any longer he felt two arms grabbing him from behind and attempting to pull him back. He caught Shona's voice, muffled by the wind and the roaring in his ears. "Hold on, Brian."

He was about to tell her to back off - that their efforts were futile - when he became aware of two yellow high vis jackets at his side. In his peripheral vision he could see the taller of the two uniformed policemen leaning over the rail precariously, anchored by the shorter burlier figure of his partner who clutched his lower legs furiously to his chest.

Policeman one managed to grab the bottom of Jamie's jacket and pull vigorously. Brian felt the strain in his arms lessening as his helper got hold of the belt on Jamie's jeans and began to haul him up. Reinvigorated by hope, Brian redoubled his own efforts. He caught a glimpse of the policeman's hat sailing off on the currents of the wind to the waiting waters below before he, Jamie and Shona collapsed in an ungainly heap onto the pedestrian walkway.

They lay there for a moment, Brian drained and panting for breath, close enough to Jamie to feel the shivers that wracked his body. Shona was first to recover and made her way over to the two officers who looked shaken as they leaned on the rail. The tall one continuing to gaze down at the river as if he was reflecting that he might have suffered the same fate as his hat.

There was a brief exchange of words. Brian rose on jelly legs and drew the shuddering, unresisting Jamie to his feet as the officers made their way over to them. The shorter of the two reached for his handcuffs but Shona stopped him with a hand on his arm and a shake of her head. The sirens that Brian had dimly registered during the struggle on the bridge were those of an ambulance that pulled up beside the police car.

Two female paramedics ushered Jamie into the back of the ambulance, accompanied by the shorter policeman. Shona said, "You okay?" Her concern made his eyes prick with absurd tears which he hoped weren't visible in the intermittent pulsing blue lights.

He managed to murmur, "Yes."

"I'll drive though, eh? Just give me a minute."

She went over to the tall cop who continued to stand bare-headed in the biting wind. Somewhere in his own wind-blown thoughts Brian tried to tell himself that at the very least they had managed to avert a death and all its heavy consequences to those who remained but he could find little comfort. To distract himself from the chill that seemed to seep into his core, he looked up at the towering structure above him. He felt diminished and insignificant.

Chapter Thirty-Seven
Shona Patterson

She could see Brian through the window of the cafe. It was the first time she had seen him in weeks, though they had talked on the phone frequently as she kept him abreast of the case. They were conversations that left her feeling restless and dissatisfied as if there was so much they weren't saying to one another. So often she had been tempted to suggest that they might meet up but her courage always failed her.

His head was bowed low over his cup and his shoulders were slumped as if he had weights attached to them. She was overwhelmed by a sudden wave of affection for him. When she entered she was surprised to see Donna taking an order over to a couple at one of the tables.

When the young woman spotted Shona, she came over to her and embraced her in a fierce hug that both touched and embarrassed her. "Thanks for everythin' you done for oor Jamie, Inspector. I dinnae think I could have coped if he'd ..." Shona suddenly felt compelled to return the affectionate greeting with equal force that made her conscious of the tight drum of the girl's belly between them.

When they broke apart she said, "I'm surprised you're back working, Donna, so soon after everything."

"Nae choice. I need the money, though Mr. Lockwood's been brilliant. And anyway I couldnae stand sittin' in the flat on my own."

Shona glanced over at Brian. Like most of the customers, he had noticed the two women's exchange though they averted their curious gaze quickly and he continued to stare at them, half-standing as if he was uncertain whether to come over to them.

Donna looked from her to Brian and back again as she said, "You're lucky. You've got a good man there."

"Oh he's not ...I mean we're not ..." She felt the flush that suffused her cheeks. Awkwardly, she said, "Just a cappuccino, please, Donna," and made her way over to Brian.

"I went to your house. Thought I'd find you in here."

"You know me so well." He looked uneasy as if she might read too much into his light-hearted remark and he added hurriedly, "I thought I might look in on Donna."

"She says you've been helping her out."

"A bit, yes." He looked sheepish.

"No need to be coy about it, Brian. It's good of you."

He seemed to relax as if her approval had reassured him and he looked her in the eye for the first time since she had come in. "I figure she needs a bit of support. Frankly, I marvel that she hasn't crumbled after everything she's had to endure. There's a core of steel in that girl and let's face it, she's going to need it. Actually, she reminds me of someone else I know."

The frank admiration in his eyes made her look away for a moment and she was relieved when Donna arrived with her coffee. "On the hoose, Inspector." As Shona began to protest, Donna said. "Standin' you to a coffee's the least I can do."

When she went to serve another customer, they sat together quietly for a moment, sipping their drinks. She knew Brian was probably itching to hear of developments but she was enjoying this moment of silent connection. At last he broke the silence. "So, any bad news for me?" His smile failed to reach his eyes and she knew he had been fretting about the case.

"Some. It looks as if Mikey Rutherglen's going to plead guilty to the manslaughter of John Edmondson, abduction and possession of an illegal firearm."

"As we thought - probably getting off lightly." His expression was grim.

"He's still going to do significant time, Brian. Eleanor and her brother are out on bail. She's been charged with extortion and he's been charged under the Computer Misuse Act."

Brian laughed humourlessly. "There but for the grace of God goes Ali Olsen."

"On the bright side, that advocate you know that's in Jamie's corner is hot stuff. Looks as if she'll be aiming for getting him a lighter sentence by emphasising his disturbed state of mind during the offences - diminished responsibility and all that."

"Sandra Chong's pretty formidable. If anyone can get Jamie a lighter sentence she can." He didn't seem cheered by this and Shona caught his worried look over to the coffee machine where Donna was busily engaged.

"Here's something that will cheer you up - Sarah Fairbanks has come forward, claiming Arnold Hastings sexually assaulted her. She'd gone back to lie low at her parents' house because she got cold feet but she read about the arrests and that and the simmering resentment she felt about Hastings made her decide to step up."

"That's good news - though I hope it doesn't go pear-shaped for her. These things are notoriously difficult to prove and Hastings will take cover behind some heavyweight legal defences. Look at what happened to Irene Dunlop."

"Ah but something else - another of Hastings' female ex-employees has also made accusations of sexual impropriety against him - a girl called Madeline Leopold."

Brian leaned forward looking animated for the first time since Shona had met him in the cafe. "I spoke to her on the phone."

"You know how these things work, Brian. It often just takes a couple of women to have the guts to confront their attackers and it paves the way for others to follow. Who knows how many other victims might poke their heads above the battlements?"

"If that bastard gets just a little of what he deserves some good will have come out of all this sad, sordid business." Shona felt emboldened to give him a smile of encouragement, hoping that at least some of the dark clouds that hovered over him were dissipating.

He gave her an apologetic smile in return. "Sorry, Shona, I've been so wrapped up in this that I haven't even asked how you are."

"I'm pretty much back on the team. Oh, Morton ripped me a new one but at the end of the day she could see we'd got a result."

"I'm glad. You finished your drink?" As she preceded him towards the door, he stopped for a moment and said to Donna, "I'll look in later to see if you need anything."

"Thanks again - to both of you." For a moment Shona was afraid she was going to envelop them in another tearful hug but she simply smiled sadly and began clearing tables.

They hesitated together outside the cafe. Shona thought they were more like a couple of awkward teenagers than two people whose relationship with each other had been forged in the fire of their shared experiences. Just when she thought they were simply going to exchange meaningless pleasantries and depart, he took her hand.

"Shona, when the dust settles on all of this I'd really like it if ...what I mean is, it would be great if I could see a bit more of you."

"I'd like that, Brian."

He squeezed her hand and smiled shyly before walking away. Shona stood for a moment in the late autumn sun that suddenly peered through a break in the clouds.

Epilogue

A new day is dawning. There might be some autumn sun today. Do you really want not to be there to see it? You aren't the first to feel ashamed and you won't be the last. Is what you did so bad?

There must be people you pass in the street every day who are harbouring worse secrets about themselves than you and they're not climbing trees with ropes at the crack of dawn. An absurd image springs into your head of all the trees around you with desperate people perched on their branches, queuing up to hurl themselves off.

Again a faintly hysterical giggle bubbles up inside you. Isn't this a reminder of how fragile you are emotionally? Won't it be better to go away from here and wait 'til you're more clear-headed? You can confess to everything and if the fall-out is as bad as you anticipate you always have a way out later.

Or is this just fear talking? If you step back from this now, perhaps you'll never summon up enough courage to do it. You'll have to go through life a disappointment to the people who love you; shunned, whispered about and pointed at behind your back.

You hear a rustle in the branches and a grey squirrel scampers onto the branch. Discovering you here doesn't seem to disconcert it and it merely sits there watching you. In the past you've brought bags of nuts to feed the squirrel population of the park. So many walkers do this that they're bold in their approach to people. Presumably deciding there's no food to be had here, it turns and with a flash of its tail begins its agile descent of the tree. It scurries off through the fallen leaves without a backward glance.

Is it a sign? After all, it shows the life that will go on around the park and around the town when you're gone and its indifference is a reminder of your comparative insignificance in the scheme of things. Not many people will care one way or the other about your shameful behaviour and those who do surely will get over it.

This is a mistake. Give it up and go home. But as you turn to reach up and remove the noose, your body slips on the frosty branch and darkness claims you.

About the Author

Bruce Adam lectured for many years in Drama, English and Communication Studies. He has written mainly for the theatre and continues to act, direct and adjudicate drama festivals. He lives in Fife.

About the Publisher

L.R. Price Publications is dedicated to publishing books by unknown authors. We use a mixture of traditional and modern publishing methods to bring our authors' words to the wider world.

We print, publish, distribute and market books in a variety of formats including paper and hard back, electronic books (e-books), digital audio books and online.

If you are an author interested in getting your book published; or a book retailer interested in selling our books, please contact us:

www.lrpricepublications.com

L.R. Price Publications Ltd,

27 Old Gloucester Street,

London, WC1N 3AX.

(0203) 051 9572 publishing@lrprice.com

Printed in Great Britain
by Amazon

84102811R00280